MARCH INTO HELL

M.P. McDonald

MARCH INTO HELL

BOOK TWO IN THE MARK TAYLOR SERIES

M.P. MCDONALD

ISBN: -10: 1481226215
ISBN-13: 9781481226219

For my husband, Robert and my three children, Brian, Tim and Maggie.

e

CHAPTER ONE

Mark Taylor clenched his jaw in an attempt to bite back the anger and hurt. He turned his back, unable to watch as she packed her bags. Already the apartment seemed emptier, as though all the energy had been sucked out. He wandered to the dresser and picked up the photo of the two of them in front of the Ferris Wheel at Navy Pier. What a great day that had been, his first carefree day in almost two years.

He faced her. "Why? Can you give me that much, Jess?"

She paused as she zipped the suitcase, her blond hair forming a curtain that hid her face from his view, but he heard the catch in her voice. "I just need some time to clear my head."

After closing the suitcase, she tossed her hair over her shoulder. The tears swimming in her eyes tore at him, and if he could take away her pain, he'd do it in a flash.

"It's not you, Mark." She bit her lip, her expression wavering as she spread her arms. "It's everything. The camera, your CIA job, the dreams...I thought I could handle it, but I was wrong."

"It's not really a job, I only pass along info that might be important, and the other stuff...you knew about all that. Hell, you're the one who urged me to start using the camera again."

"I wish you hadn't listened to me."

She hauled the biggest bag off the bed, and out of habit, he moved to help her, but halted. If she wanted to move out, he couldn't stop her, but damned if he was going to help.

"I'll pay my part of the rent for the next couple of months; by then you should be able to find a roommate or someone to sub-let the loft."

"I don't want to move and I sure as hell don't want a roommate." Mark flung the picture onto the bed, but the soft thump of the frame hitting the pillow lacked the power to assuage his anger and hurt, and he immediately regretted his show of anger when she flinched.

He approached her and caressed her cheek, looping her hair over one ear like she did so often. "I *have* a roommate." Mark pulled her forward and kissed her forehead, closing his eyes as he drank in the light floral scent of her skin and hair. "I'll wait."

Tears tracked down her cheeks as she pulled away. "I'm sorry, Mark. You don't deserve this...but I feel like I'm trapped in a spy novel or something. Clandestine meetings, coded phone calls...and don't get me started on your future photos."

It always came back to the camera. Everything that went wrong in his life the last four years stemmed from his use of the damn future-capturing camera, and yet, he'd tried to put it aside--tried to ignore it. He couldn't. It was like an addiction. If he went more than a few days without using the camera, he was plagued with confusing nightmares of people dying. Surreal mixed up nightmares that left him in a cold sweat. During the day, he was jumpy and irritable--like a crack addict in withdrawal. Jessie knew that.

"What do you expect of me, Jess? You're a detective, your work isn't so much different. Would you just ignore clues and let a murderer go free just because doing your job might interfere with your personal life?"

"Of course not; but that's different." She tapped her chest. "That's my job."

"Well, dealing with the future photos," he thumped his own chest, "is *my* job."

They glared at each other in a standoff. The battle had been brewing for the last few months, beginning when Mark developed a photo that showed a shootout at a high school. In trying to prevent it, there had been a skirmish, and he'd been slightly injured. That was only four months after the Wrigley Field incident, and now she was skittish whenever he developed a future picture.

She shook her head, her arms dropping to her sides. "I give up. Yours isn't the same as my job, but you won't see that. I have backup." She began ticking off on her fingers as she continued, "I have regulations, training, procedures--procedures that have been tested. At the high school thing, you decided that police weren't doing enough and took out the shooter yourself. Instead of just breaking your arm, you could have been killed. You...you just rush in all by yourself, like you're back in the Wild West."

Mark recoiled as the sarcasm in her voice speared through him. Is that how she saw him: as a maverick cowboy? He held his hands up and stepped back. "You're wrong, but I guess you've already made up your mind."

Turning, he stalked out to the living room and stared

out the window. He was losing her...again, only he couldn't blame the government this time. This time, they weren't torn apart by outside forces. Now, it was personal.

* * *

It didn't make sense. Mark tossed the collapsible light reflector into the back of his van where it bounced off his other camera equipment. He slammed the tailgate down and strode to the driver's door and climbed in. With a squeal of tires, he backed out of his parking spot. A passer-by jumped back as Mark roared past, and chagrined, Mark tapped the brakes, feeling foolish for driving like a reckless idiot. At the first red light, he closed his eyes and took a deep breath, allowing the air to ease out. In the month since Jessie had left, he'd felt off balance, adrift. She'd been his anchor, his safe harbor.

He opened his eyes and watched the cross traffic whiz past him. As difficult as it was, he had to quit thinking about her. Yeah. Right. Might as well think about not breathing while he was at it.

He fished in his pocket for his cell phone and called the studio as he accelerated on the green light. Voice-mail answered, and he left a message, "Hey, Lil, I have one more thing to do, then I'll be back to close up."

Lily Martin had been an acquaintance before his time in prison. She'd worked some of the same jobs he did when big events called for multiple photographers. He'd always gotten along well with her, and one day she'd come into the camera shop where he'd worked. After some brief catching up, where he'd skimmed over the prison issue, she'd asked him if he was still shooting. After that, she began calling him with jobs she couldn't take on. For the last four months, they'd been partners in a studio. It worked out beautifully and to top it off, there was a vacant loft above the studio where he and Jessie had moved.

Everything had been going great, which left him even more confused about why Jessie had left. No sooner had he put his phone back in his pocket and contemplated grabbing some Chinese food for dinner, when his phone rang. He checked the number that flashed on the screen.

Lily. His shoulders slumped. After a month of no calls, he should be over expecting that every time his phone rang it would be Jessie, and it wasn't like he didn't like Lily. She just wasn't Jessie.

"Hello?"

"Hey, Mark. I just got back to the studio and there are at least a half dozen messages from some reporter named Denise Jeffries."

A reporter? Had someone finally decided to print a story about how his name was cleared in the enemy combatant thing? Part of him wished for some public acknowledgment, but the rational part wanted the whole thing to go away forever--to be forgotten by everyone on Earth, including him. "What does she want?"

Lily sounded puzzled. "She didn't really say on the messages. Just said it was important and for you to call her back as soon as possible."

"Okay, I'll call her when I get back to the studio. I was just going to pick up some Chinese food for dinner, and then head back to develop my film."

"If you pick up enough for two, I'll keep you company while you eat, and I'll even help you develop the pictures."

She sounded innocent, but Mark wasn't fooled. He laughed. "You're just curious to know what the reporter wants. Admit it."

He heard the smile in her voice as she answered, "You better believe it, and if I can get a free meal and satisfy my curiosity at the same time..."

"Sure. I'll even get some of those stinky egg rolls you love so much."

"I think I love you," she said, her tone light and teasing

Mark smiled. "Yeah, right. See you in a bit."

He brightened at the prospect of not having to eat alone. If the timing had been right, he might have seen Lily in a romantic light. Her bright red hair that she wore in tousled spikes gave her a fun look matched by the sparkle in her green eyes. He had met her years ago though, and at the time, she had a steady boyfriend. Later, when they had partnered up in business, he'd had Jessie. Neither had anyone at the moment, but it was too late; they'd grown into a comfortable friendship.

Twenty minutes later, he plopped the bag of food onto his desk in the office of the studio. Lily was at her own desk retouching photos on the computer. Mark found that aspect of the job tedious and was thankful that she loved doing it. She wasn't crazy about photographing kids and babies, so he took most of those shoots. It worked out well.

Lily glanced up. "I have the trays set up in the dark room. You want to do your special photos now or after we eat?"

"After. Not much point in rushing to develop them since I won't know details until I go to sleep anyway."

It was the other thing he loved about Lily. She accepted that his first priority lay with changing the photos and the dreams. Before he agreed to go into business with her, he'd told her about the camera. After not telling anyone the first few years he'd had it, and then getting locked up as an enemy combatant, he'd learned his lesson. He shared the information with a few people now. It lightened the burden.

She thought it was wild that he dreamed about the photos and had asked him all kinds of questions at first. Questions like how did he remember the dreams? How did he know they weren't just regular dreams? Did he have to do anything specific when he looked at the photos, like meditate or pray or anything? She had offered to try and meditate on a few, hoping to have the dreams too, but it hadn't worked.

The first few times he'd used the camera or changed an outcome when she was with him, she'd been in awe. Now, it was old hat.

"Sounds good. I'm starved." She stretched her arms above her head. "Oh, wait. Don't forget to call that reporter chick." After a bit of rifling through papers and proofs, she dug the paper out from under her coffee cup and thrust it towards him.

"Reporter chick?" Mark chuckled as he took the paper, wiping it on his jeans to get rid of the ring left by the cup. "Is that who I should ask for?" He sat at his desk and pulled the phone close, opting not to use his personal cell phone.

"Smart ass. Her name is right there." The twinkle in her eyes belied the false toughness in her words.

Mark nodded and winked before dialing the number.

It was answered after just one ring.

"Hello?"

Surprised at the quick answer he stuttered, "Ah--uh, yeah. This is Mark Taylor. I had a message from a Ms. Jeffries?"

"Yes, this is Denise Jeffries. I'm a reporter with the Tribune. I have a few questions, if you don't mind." She didn't wait to find out if Mark minded or not. "I found some very interesting tidbits about you while researching a Good Samaritan."

The hairs on the back of Mark's neck swept up in a chill. "Tidbits?"

"Yes. For instance, you're the same Mark Taylor who was held as an enemy combatant."

It was a statement, not a question, so Mark kept silent.

"Hello?" Jeffries sounded as if she expected some kind of confirmation of the information.

Mark shot a look at Lily, who made no pretense about not listening. She'd pulled her chair right up to the desk and had her chin in her hand, her eyes glued to him.

Uncomfortable under the scrutiny, he glanced away. "I'm still here."

"Well?"

"Well what? You didn't ask me a question."

"Ah, I see. Can you confirm that you are the same man who was held as an American enemy combatant?"

"Yes. That's true." Mark felt Lily watching him, but he kept his eyes averted. She knew about his time spent in prison, but he rarely spoke of it.

"And...? Why did they let you out?"

He clamped his lips into a hard line as he felt anger build. "No comment."

"No comment? But according to the records, you were held for fifteen months, and from what I've learned about enemy combatants, it couldn't have been an easy time."

His release had been secured, but he'd had to sign a statement that he wouldn't go public about his experience. Since he'd been eager to forget it anyway, the silence contract had been easy to keep. "Sorry. No comment. Now, if that's all--"

"No! Wait, I have some other things I'd like to ask you."

Mark waited.

Taking his silence for a go ahead, Jeffries launched into an avalanche of questions. "You were injured when you interfered with an undercover officer making an arrest back in early 2001. Is that true?"

"Yes."

She sounded exasperated when she said, "I have a whole string of similar incidents that I've found. The incidents are spread over the city, and it seems I'm the only one who connected them back to you."

"Incidents?"

"You must know what I'm referring to. You swoop in and save the day. You saved a baby with CPR, a child from being hit by a car, a teen from getting shot by an off-duty officer." She paused and when he didn't fill the silence, she continued, "I could go on and on. I cross checked your name in the paper archives with a source with the police filled me in on some that never made the news. How do you explain the string of incidents?"

"I don't understand why an explanation is necessary. Why are you asking?"

"Are you a religious man, Mark?"

Taken aback, he darted another glance at Lily. She was the religious one. In spite of her tendency to dress as a free spirit, she practiced her religion with a quiet devotion Mark admired, even if he didn't understand it. "What business is it of yours?"

"Do I hear defensiveness in your tone?"

"I have no idea what the hell you hear. I have dinner getting cold, so if you don't have something else you needed, I'd like to eat it."

"Do you work other miracles?"

"Listen, I have no idea what you're talking about."

"In the report on the baby who almost drowned, it says that there had been no heartbeat and you had to do CPR. Within a few minutes, the baby was crying and in fact, suffered no lasting damages."

"Yes. So?"

"Do you realize that nearly all children who require CPR end up dying or are left with severe neurological damages?"

"No."

"It's true, but the little girl you saved, Christy, is just fine. I spoke to her mother this morning."

He had never learned the outcome of that save, but hoped she'd recovered. The infant had appeared okay when he'd last seen her just before his arrest, but he knew that sometimes there were complications. "That's great."

"It is, and I have several more incidents that you were involved with that could be considered miracles."

Mark leaned forward, his elbows on the desk as he held the phone to his ear. "What are you implying?"

"Mark, do you feel like you have a connection to God?"

His mouth dropped open and saw Lily's eyes shoot up in question. He looked away. "Ms. Jeffries, I think you need to find another story, and I need to eat before my meal is ice cold." Ignoring her protests, he clicked the phone off. Scrubbing his hands down his face, he sighed and bent his head, massaging the muscles at the back of his neck. What a nut.

"You okay?"

Mark let out a sharp chuckle. "Yeah, that reporter had some crazy notion that I worked miracles."

Lily stood and began pulling the cartons of food out of the paper bag. She shrugged. "What's so crazy about that? Isn't that pretty much what you do with your camera?"

"Okay, I admit the camera is probably something miraculous, but I can't tell her about that, and I'm just a regular guy, so yeah, it is a crazy notion."

Lily opened a carton and pulled out an egg roll, pointing it at him. "You don't give yourself enough credit." She bit into the roll with a grin. After chewing a few seconds, she said, "I believe in miracles, and I believe that some people are special."

Mark waved his hand in front of his face as the scent filled the room. "Yeah, well, that reporter was just looking for a story. The last thing I want is to be someone's story." He leaned over and grabbed a carton, opened it and snagged a chunk of chicken. The rich sauce flowed over his tongue and his stomach growled in response.

Lily chatted while they ate, never seeming to mind that he wasn't much at making small talk. After finishing his fried rice and cashew chicken, he headed to the dark room so she could eat her second smelly egg roll without gagging him.

She called after him, "You don't need my help?"

Mark turned and walking backwards, smiled. "No, but if you want to hang out and see what develops, that's fine." He'd welcome some company tonight and hoped he didn't sound as lonely as he felt. He didn't wait to hear her answer. If she was here when he came out, great. If not, well, he'd be fine.

He swallowed his disappointment when he came out with the photos in hand only to find a note from Lily saying she'd forgotten about her church choir rehearsal. The photos were some of the worst he'd developed after September 11th and the Wrigley Field incident, and he'd hoped to have her insight. Not that he could tell her much until tomorrow anyway.

Tossing the photos on the desk, he flipped the page on the appointment book. Would she be in early? She had a couple coming in for engagement photos at ten, followed by a location shoot at one. He had an actor coming in for new head-shots at one, and later, was holding a go-see for some models for an upcoming job for a national ad for a major retailer.

He picked up his special photos. There were three of them, but all were darker than he would have desired. Most of the people in them were hidden by robes. They had a surreal quality, as if taken on a movie set.

In the center of one was a tall cross, and he thought the photos were of a church, but there were none of the other things, just the cross, the hooded people, and in the last photo, a pale young woman crouched on the floor. She looked tiny, terrified, and nude.

He hoped it was a movie set. That would explain the

robes as costumes. There was a studio out in Cicero. He'd been there before, taking stills during filming of some television shows. Peering closely at the photos, he couldn't determine if the background matched the studio. Of course, if it was a new set, he wouldn't be able to tell from the photos anyway.

* * *

Mark paced the office. He had rushed down from his loft over an hour ago, only to realize that it was still only eight-thirty a.m. and Lily wouldn't be arriving until a little later. While trying to pass the time, he caught up on some overdue book work but now he was finished, and getting impatient.

The dream last night had left him shaken and he needed advice. Lily was good at interpreting clues in his dreams. She was creative and tended to have a unique perspective.

It was his nature to look at the photos as literally black and white, but she had pointed out that some of the saves he did had repercussions he wouldn't have thought about. Like the time he saved a man from stepping in front of a city bus when the guy hadn't been paying attention, too busy caught up in his cell phone conversation to notice that the walk light had changed. The man was a heart surgeon, and the call had been about a patient. Lily pointed out that by saving him, Mark had potentially saved the dozens of patients that doctor would go on to save in his career. It was mind boggling and he wasn't sure he wanted all that pressure. Other times, he could save someone and down the road, that could cause someone else to die.

Lily called it the ripple effect. Trying to keep all the angles straight made his head spin and it was too complicated to handle alone.

There came a clank and rattle from the front of the building and Mark strode out of the office to the studio area. Lily had her back turned as she re-locked the front door.

"Hey, Lil." He hoped his impatience didn't come through in his tone. She would pick up on that right away. Needing to do something, he began setting up the backdrop she'd mentioned she wanted to use for the first shoot.

"Morning, Mark." She turned towards him, her expression puzzled. "Is something wrong?"

"No, not really." He tightened the handle on the side of the backdrop frame. "I just...I wanted to talk to you about this one." He gave the handle one last turn then motioned towards the office. "I have the photos on the desk, if you want to see."

She went ahead of him, but looked over her shoulder, her brow furrowed. "You sound scared. What was the dream about?"

"Scared doesn't begin to cover it." Mark sprawled in the swivel chair behind his desk, waiting until Lily had taken her seat before sliding the photos he'd developed last evening across to her side.

He recounted the details of the dream, suppressing a shudder at the vision. It was so clear in his mind. He leaned across the desk when he finished sharing the nightmare. "A...a ritual murder, Lily! How can I stop something like this? I didn't even get a good look at where it takes place. Just a quick glimpse of a street sign and the interior of what looked like a warehouse. And a damn cult--can't forget that."

He lowered his head, elbows propped, and ran his hands through his hair. "I don't have enough details! What the hell does it want me to do?" He slapped a hand down on the photos in frustration and leaned back.

"I don't know." Lily's brow furrowed in concern. "Maybe you can call Jessie? She might know something about cults. At the very least, she might know which warehouses on West Ohio are abandoned and give you a location to start."

Mark sighed and said, "Yeah, I guess. Doing that opens a whole new can of worms, but I need information, and she might have it. Thanks." Lily was right. While he hated involving the police and specifically, Jessie, it didn't seem like he had much choice. If he was going to stop this, he needed some help.

Lily reached for his hand, squeezing it lightly. "Promise me, whatever you do, you'll be careful, Mark."

* * *

"Come on, Jess, just hear me out," Mark pleaded, his eyes skimming the photo, ever hopeful that some new clue would turn up. He held the phone with his shoulder as he flipped through the three pictures. Over the years he had found that often clues showed up in one photo and not the others. It was like the camera recorded different points of view. Nothing caught his eye this time. Of course he wouldn't get that lucky. He sat forward in his desk chair and held the phone to his ear, drumming his fingers on the desk. "I just need--"

"Listen, Mark. You know I'd help you if I could, but this isn't my investigation. I could get into a lot of trouble for leaking information. Plus, I'm up to my eyeballs in paperwork on another case."

"I...I know you're busy and I wouldn't ask if it wasn't important." He fidgeted with a pencil, then lowered his voice, almost pleading, "Come on...for old time's sake?"

There was a long pause before she sighed and grudgingly gave him the little bit of information she had. He jotted down the details about several empty warehouses that she knew off the top of her head. Her knowledge of the religious sects was a bit sketchier.

"We're investigating one cult that we suspect has been running drugs and a money laundering operation. They don't seem too interested in the religious aspect; they seem to use that as front to recruit members."

Mark shook his head even though she couldn't see him. "What I saw was more than a show. These guys were serious about what they did. Or rather, what they are going to do." The whole time frame perspective always confused him when he spoke about it. None of the events depicted had taken place yet, except in his dreams. "Anyway, thanks for your help. I appreciate it."

There was silence on the other end, and Mark wondered if she was as reluctant to hang up as he was. When Lily had mentioned calling Jessie, he couldn't help the thrill of anticipation that shot through him. He'd have a reason to call her...to hear her voice again.

Jessie sighed, her breath loud in his ear. "I wish I could help you more, but as long as your gift has to remain a secret, there's nothing more I can do. Can you call Jim with this? Would he be able to help?"

Mark tossed the pencil onto the desk. "I thought about calling him, but this isn't exactly a national crisis. I'm pretty sure it would fall under the jurisdiction of local law enforcement--and you know my history with Chicago P.D."

"But he's still heading up the FBI office, right?"

"Yes, that's true."

"Just because he's CIA doesn't mean he can't act in the capacity of FBI. Give him a call. It couldn't hurt."

"I don't know."

"Listen Mark, I know you still don't like talking to the guy. I *get* that. But you agreed to keep him informed if you see anything that could be a threat."

"Yes, I did, but not garden variety threats, it's meant for national security threats." He slid the top photo to the side, and studied the next one of the girl strung up on the cross. "As horrible as *this* is, it's not a national threat."

"National threat or not, you should tell him because you could be in danger trying to stop this. You are an asset now. His asset. It's his job to keep you safe."

"He'll just tell me not to save the girl." He had come to respect Jim despite their rocky history where the other man had been head of the CIA team who had interrogated Mark for over a year. "He'll say it's not worth the risk."

"In a way he's right, you know. You could potentially save thousands if there is ever a repeat of 9/11, but if something happens to you...."

He blew out a breath in exasperation. "So you think I should just let her die? Is that what you're saying?"

"No, I'm just saying that you should get some help."

It was useless. At an impasse, Mark ended the

awkward moment. "I'll think about it. And Jess, thanks again."

"You're welcome. Just don't let on where you got the cult info, or I'll...I'll..."

Mark grinned, recognizing her playful tone. "You'll what?"

"You won't have to worry about the cult because I'll crucify you myself."

Mark laughed. "Thanks. I owe you one."

"You're damn right you do. More than one." Her voice softened. "And Mark? Stay safe, okay?"

CHAPTER TWO

The first warehouse Mark checked later in the evening was dark and locked up tight. It didn't look like anything could happen there anyway. At least, not in the time frame Mark had figured out. It was already eight-twenty and if a ritual was planned, it would have to get going pretty soon if it was going to happen tonight. If only he had a name. Why couldn't the dream have provided some clue as to who the girl was? Sighing, Mark pulled out his flashlight and checked the photos. He still had hopes that maybe, somehow, they had changed. Unfortunately, he still found grisly pictures of the soon to be dead girl.

The night was dark with heavy clouds scuttling across the sky and a cold, damp wind whistled through the alley. Mark hunched into his jacket and shoved his hands into the pockets as he hurried to the next address on his list. Approaching the building, he paused when he heard muffled voices, laughter and a popping noise float through a broken window. He peeked between the shards of glass and spotted a small group gathered around a burning trash can. The men passed a bottle around.

Mark turned back and leaned against the wall, willing his racing heart to slow to a normal tempo. He hadn't even known how keyed up he was until that moment. Obviously, this wasn't the right warehouse either. It was just a few homeless guys seeking shelter from the weather. He pushed away from the wall and headed back towards the street and his last address. His foot kicked a bottle, sending it clattering across the pavement, the sound loud in the stillness.

"Hey! Who's out there?" The voice was deep and rough.

He turned towards the door of the warehouse and saw a shadow moving towards him. As he spun to flee, his right foot hit a patch of something slippery and slid from beneath him. His knee cracked hard against the pavement and he fell onto his side, teeth clenched in pain as he rolled to a sitting position. Breathing deeply, Mark pulled his knee into his chest, rocking back and forth while the pain slowly abated. *Damn.* It hurt like a sonofabitch.

"You all right, man?"

Mark looked up to find one of the men from the warehouse leaning over him. His hair was matted and greasy and his clothes could probably walk away on their own, but the weathered face wore a look of concern. Mark relaxed slightly. Wincing, he nodded. "Yeah. I just slipped." Gingerly, he stretched his leg out and decided that it was in working order.

"Whatchya doin' out here?" The man held out a hand and Mark grasped it as the guy hauled Mark to his feet.

"Thanks. I was just...just looking to take some photos. I'm a photographer and need something edgy for a magazine cover."

Looking Mark up and down, the man said, "Where's your camera?"

Mark hesitated a second. "I left it in my car around

the corner. I didn't want to lug it around until I found a good site."

"Sure you did, buddy. Listen, this ain't a very good place for a guy like you to be wanderin' around at night."

Mark stiffened, not sure if he'd been insulted or not. "A guy like *me*?"

The man laughed, his teeth flashing gray in the faint light. "Yeah. You look like a doctor or lawyer or somethin'. And some folks in this part of town don't like your kind."

"I...I'm not a doctor or a lawy...look, I have a studio in the River North area. I'm just a photographer."

"And you came all the way out here to take some pictures?" He raised an eyebrow as he took a swig from his bottle then offered it to Mark.

"Uh, no, but thanks for the offer."

Shrugging, the guy took another pull.

Mark began backing slowly away. Time was wasting. "Well, seeing as how the full moon is hidden by the clouds, guess I might have to try another night." Mark didn't buy his own story and from the look on the other man's face, he didn't either.

"Do what you want, but while you're taking your pictures, steer clear of that warehouse across the street. There's some strange shit going on in there."

Mark whipped his head around. He strained to see the warehouse the man spoke of. "Strange...*shit*?"

"Yeah, the last few nights, we've heard chanting, screams and some creepy yowling."

His mind raced. That was the warehouse. "Thanks, I'll keep your advice in mind."

The man cleared his throat and spat before answering, "You do that."

* * *

Mark crept around the corner of the building and found an entrance. The door hung askew and creaked in the wind. He paused before entering. Maybe he should just call the police. But he shook off that plan. So far, he had nothing to tell them and with his lack of credibility with the Chicago PD, he doubted they would jump into action on his say so alone. He worried he might already be too late. Mark shook his head, trying to dispel the negative thought. Somehow, he would find a way to save the young woman.

Stepping over the threshold, he found himself in what he thought might be an office. It was pitch black, but he sensed walls instead of a large cavernous space like a warehouse. He shuffled his feet carefully, his hands held out before him as he tried to navigate in the darkness. Soon, his eyes grew accustomed to the lack of light, and he picked out dark shapes that appeared to be desks and chairs.

He stilled when he heard voices chanting. A chill swept over him. Something about the cadence of the chant sent a shiver of fear to his very core. Every cell in his brain screamed at him to turn and flee as fast as he could and he began to heed the order, but froze in his tracks when he heard a faint whimper of fear.

He couldn't leave--not without at least trying to help. His breathing quickened and his heart seemed to be beating loud that he was surprised the sound wasn't echoing off the walls. He advanced toward the chanting. He found a hallway leading out of the office and followed it around to the right. From the hollow resonance of his steps on the wooden floor, he figured he was in the warehouse now.

A mysterious glow emanated from the far corner. Mark couldn't figure out what caused it. He crept towards the light. It wasn't until he bumped into something that he realized that in front of him was a makeshift wall covered in a dark, rough cloth. Beneath the cloth, he felt a wooden framework. Pallets? Reaching up, he couldn't feel the top of the wall, but since the glow was visible above it, it couldn't have reached the ceiling. One hand skimming the cloth, Mark followed the wall until he came to an opening.

About a dozen people surrounded a naked woman who cowered on the floor--the photo come to life. They circled her, slowly, chanting words he couldn't decipher. Maybe it was a different language, but he wasn't sure. Every few seconds, a man holding a long pole, a staff of some sort, would poke her roughly. Mark noticed numerous bruises on her back and arms. The woman's eyes were huge and her bound hands lifted to try to fend off the staff, a gag choking off terrified sobs.

Bile rose in his throat.

The only illumination came from flashlights held by three people in the group. All wore the dark hooded clothing, masking their features. He thought he definitely heard at least a couple of feminine voices in the group. In the dim light, he could see a post rigged with ropes. He didn't want to think what they planned to do with that, but according in his dream, at some point the woman would be lashed to it.

His mouth felt dry as a desert and his mind raced trying to determine a plan of action. If he hurried, he could get help. That seemed like the wisest choice. He certainly couldn't take on a dozen people by himself. The thought of leaving the woman alone and helpless tore at his conscience, but what choice did he have? Mark backed away from the opening, but as he turned, he crashed into someone. A very large someone who shoved Mark away.

"Uh!' The push sent Mark staggering into the wall behind him. He reached out to catch himself, but his hand tangled in the fabric, and he bit back a cry of pain when something sliced his palm.

"Enjoying the show?" The man advanced and grabbed Mark by the shoulder of his jacket and yanked him towards the opening, sending him stumbling into the midst of the ceremony.

Mark regained his balance quickly and thinking fast, rushed to the woman before anyone could stop him. He had a certain element of surprise and hoped that by doing the unexpected, he might get them both out of this yet. He pulled her to her feet and tried to ignore the flare of hope in her eyes. Escape was far from a sure thing and already cries of protest arose from the gathering behind him.

A soft whoosh gave him a scant half-second warning, but probably saved his life as he ducked, huddling over the victim. The staff cracked across his head with a glancing blow.

Mark staggered. Shaking his head to clear it, he spun, catching the return swing of the pole and yanked it out of the wielder's hands. The suddenness of his movements caught the group by surprise. Mark chalked up his response to adrenaline and the instinct for survival. Sometimes, a bit of fear could work wonders.

One of the men charged him, but Mark held him at

bay by a sharp jab to the chest. "Get back!" He crouched, brandishing the staff, swearing when his hand slipped as the blood from his palm turned the pole slick. He tightened his grip. "What the hell are you guys doing in here? Are you people *insane*?"

"It's none of your business." The answer came from the behemoth who had grabbed Mark a few moments ago.

The man stepped towards the pair and Mark saw his eyes clearly for the first time, and he had to hold back a shudder. No human warmth or compassion showed in their depths, only a flat, cold blackness. Snake eyes...it was the closest comparison that came to Mark's mind.

"It's my business when you try to kill someone!" Mark swung menacingly and the leader stopped. The woman's hands clung to the back of Mark's jacket and he could feel her shuddering. He had to make a move, the longer the standoff went on, the worse his chances. "I'm sorry to spoil your little party here, but we're gonna be going now."

Still swinging at anyone who moved, Mark edged around the group to the opening. He didn't know why they didn't jump him en masse, but he wasn't about to question their motives.

Once Mark and the girl were out of the makeshift room, it was harder going in the dark. Mark tried to watch for pursuers while also attempting to guide the woman back towards the front entrance. They shuffled and stumbled their way out of the building. Mark dropped the staff and pulled the woman over to a nearby Dumpster for cover.

He tried to control his trembling hands as he fumbled with the rope around her wrists and finally remembered the little pocketknife he always carried. Digging it out, he sliced through the binding and looked over his shoulder when he heard shouting coming from the building. When he turned back, the woman was in the process of removing the gag. "Okay, let's go!" He grabbed her hand and pulled her behind him as he raced for the street and relative safety. It wasn't until the woman stumbled and Mark turned to see if she was okay that he realized she was still naked and trying to run barefoot over the pavement.

Mark shrugged out of his jacket. "Here!" He helped her into it, and then scooped her up in a cradle hold. "Hang on tight."

* * *

Mark trudged what seemed like miles, but was probably less than a half-dozen blocks, looking over his shoulder every time he heard a noise. Nobody followed, which was a relief, but Mark realized he was still in a bad neighborhood and there was nowhere he could call for help. He sagged against an iron gate protecting the front of a pawnshop and hiked the girl up higher. His arms ached, and she was now dead weight, having passed out at some point. A shiver shook his body, the cold, damp air chilling him now that he was no longer moving. Looking around, he got his bearings and was pretty sure that County hospital was only a block or so away. With a grunt, he pushed away from the wall. The girl was slight, but by the time Mark reached the hospital, his arms were shaking with the effort of carrying her.

"I...I need some help...please?" Mark gasped out his plea as he staggered through the automatic doors. "She was attacked...they had a...a pole. Kept jabbing her."

"Grab a cart!" Two nurses rushed up and relieved Mark of his burden and eased her onto the gurney. He stumbled at the sudden removal of weight and caught himself on a wall, his breathing ragged.

Hands on his knees, he bent over in an attempt to catch his breath.

"Sir?"

A hand gripped Mark's bicep, and he looked up to find a woman in blue scrubs regarding him with concern.

"Why don't you come with me and we can get you taken care of too." She tugged gently on his arm.

Straightening, Mark shook his head, trying not to wince. "Oh no, I'm okay...just out of breath. I must have carried her a half-mile. I'll be fine once I rest a minute."

"But your head is bleeding and you're dripping blood on the floor." Her voice held a note of amusement.

Mark glanced down and saw several bright red drops dotting the white tile. "Sorry about that. I cut my hand, but I just need a Band-Aid."

"Yeah, well, let's take a look and let the doctor decide, okay?"

CHAPTER THREE

"Mark?"

He groaned and opened his eyes, squinting up at the bright overhead light. Mark knew that voice. Jessie. The very last person he wanted to see at this moment. Sitting up slowly, he swung his legs over the side of the hospital gurney and reached for his shirt. The hospital gown he'd worn earlier had been removed after the doc had sutured Mark's head. Between the blood and the saline, it had been soaked. Unable to grasp the shirt with his still-numb fingers, it fell to the floor just as the curtain around his cubicle fluttered. A hand appeared from the other side and grabbed the material, yanking it back. The metal balls in the overhead track screeched in protest.

"I *knew* I shouldn't have told you anything!" She stood at the foot of the gurney with her hands on her hips and looking much fiercer than her slender frame had a right to appear.

Her eyes narrowed as she glowered at him.

"You know what I do, Jess. Don't think just because you're not part of it that I've stopped using the camera." Mark bent to retrieve his shirt, but a wave of dizziness swept through him and he almost fell off the gurney. Embarrassed, he eased back and tried to blink the room into focus again. The doctor advised Mark that he had a concussion, and he should take it easy for a week or so. It

happen to get her name?"

"Of course. I am a cop, after all. It's Judy." She pulled out a small notepad. "Judy Medea. She's a college student that somehow got mixed up with this group."

The nurse entered before Mark could ask any more questions. He wondered if Judy's family had been called and how she would get home. Tomorrow, he'd call and find out how she was doing and see if she needed anything. He sat up, dangling his legs off the side of the gurney and tried to listen as the nurse droned on about signs of infection, complications and to follow up in a week with his personal physician. After taking one last set of vitals, she gave him a sheet of instructions and released him.

Jessie followed him out to the waiting room, and he remembered her admonishment not to leave before she came back. He figured now was the time she intended to interrogate him. Before she could corner him, he sought a means of escape. Off to the left of the waiting room was a pay phone, and Mark veered towards it as quickly as his battered body allowed. He dug into his pocket and swore when he came up with a ten-dollar bill and no change. Maybe the desk clerk would let him use their phone to call for a cab. He didn't really feel like taking the 'L' home. Before Jessie could catch up to him, he approached the registration desk. "Excuse me? Ma'am?"

The woman looked up from her computer. "Yes?"

Mark held up his arm, showing the ID bracelet still encircling his wrist. "I was just released and wondered if I could use the phone to call a cab. I don't have any change on me."

"Sure, as long as it's local. Just dial nine first." The

clerk turned the phone so he could see the numbers. She pointed to a faded piece of paper taped to the wall on Mark's right. "There's some numbers up there, if you need them."

"Thanks so much." Mark picked up the phone and squinted at the list. The numbers wavered, and he rubbed his eyes in an attempt to clear his vision. Jessie, after detouring around a mom and three children, stopped beside him.

"Who are you calling?" Jessie craned her neck to see what Mark was looking at, her eyebrows knit in confusion.

Mark glanced at Jessie and pointed at the phone numbers. "I'm calling a cab."

"What for?"

"What for? So I can go home." He began punching the buttons, realized he'd made a mistake and hung up to try again.

Jessie reached over and took the phone out of his hands and set it in the cradle. "I can give you a lift home. I figured you knew that."

"That's okay. I can just take a cab." The prospect of being peppered with questions on the ride home didn't appeal to him in the least.

"Listen, you just got released from the hospital with a concussion. You can barely see straight. I can't let you take a cab home." She gently took his arm and as though she could read his mind, she added, "Come on. I promise not to grill you."

Too tired to argue, Mark let her lead him out to her vehicle.

True to her word, Jessie remained fairly quiet on the

32

ride home, just asking him about his injuries. "So, what's the tally?"

Mark fingered the lump topped with stitches behind his right ear. "Six in my head and four in my hand. The hand...that was just 'cause I caught it on a nail." He smoothed down a piece of tape over the bandage circling his palm. The cut wasn't that long, just wide and deep.

"Sure. It could happen to anyone." Jessie's dry tone as she pulled in front of the studio didn't pass unnoticed by Mark.

"What should I have done, Jessie? Just left her there?" He couldn't help the anger stamped onto his voice. He was so tired of the questioning and not just tonight's drilling, but every time something happened. He ground the heel of his hand against his forehead. Why was it that when he did something good, it practically required an act of God for anyone to trust in him?

"You could have called the cops!" She threw the car into park turned sideways in her seat and in the dim light, he could see the burn of anger in her eyes, but then her expression softened. "Do you have a death wish or something?"

Mark stared out the windshield, trying to recall exactly what had happened. Everything had transpired so fast, some of it was fuzzy in his mind. "No, I don't have a...a...I...I was going to call the cops. I swear it. You know, there were at least a dozen of them, and I knew I couldn't do anything on my own. I turned around to leave and that guy...the leader was there."

The recollection of the man's cold, almost inhuman eyes, elicited an involuntary shudder. Mark turned to find Jessie watching him, a thoughtful look on her face.

"What?"

"You okay?"

"Yeah. It's just that guy...he...gave me the creeps."

She nodded. "The officer's initial report has your description of what the leader looked like. Is there anything else you can tell me about him?"

"Um, nothing specific. The look in his eyes was...I don't know...cold and...and lifeless." Mark shook his head in frustration, knowing that the description wasn't very helpful. "And his voice was deep...like--never mind."

Jessie cocked her head. "Deep like...like what? You were going to say something."

"It's stupid; forget it."

"If it helps us catch the guy, it's not stupid."

Mark rolled his eyes, feeling ridiculous, but he finished his thought, "He...he sounded like Darth Vader." He grimaced and ducked his head at the snort of laughter from Jessie. "See, I told you it was stupid."

"I'm sorry, it's not stupid. I'm just picturing putting out an APB on Darth Vader." She grinned, and Mark couldn't help wondering when the smiles had stopped. Why hadn't he noticed? He'd give anything to make her grin like that more often. Especially if she directed it at him.

"Yeah, I guess that is kind of funny." Before he could suppress it, Mark let out a huge yawn. "Sorry." He rubbed the back of his neck and tilted his head to work out a kink.

She took the cue and turned to face the front of the car. "Go on. Get some rest and try not to think about it too much. The girl's okay and you're okay...for the most part, so everything came out all right." Jessie cleared her throat. "Well, take it easy, Mark. I'll probably have some more questions for you in the next few days."

"Sure. And, thanks for the ride, Jessie." His body aching, he pulled himself out of the car and trudged up to his loft.

* * *

"Adrian Kern."

Dan looked up from the report he was perusing. "What?"

"I have a possible name on that guy in the Medea case." Jessie circled the desk and showed Dan the file she had found buried in a drawer devoted to unsolved crimes. "A few years ago, a woman reported escaping from a group who had posed as a prayer group initially. After attending several sessions, she was pressured to sign over her bank account to the group. She was told it was something they all did and that pooling their resources was good for everyone. Besides, they said she wouldn't need it anymore because all of her bills would be taken care of. Apparently a group of them rented a big old house in Oak Park."

Dan sat back and raised an eyebrow. "And she believed them?"

Jessie shrugged. "I guess so. Anyway, after a few months, she balked and closed the account and left the group's home. One day as she was walking home, she was approached by members who were in a car and they lured her into coming with them. They told the woman that the group was dissolving and that she was owed a share from the group's savings."

"And she jumped at the chance to get her money

back."

Jessie nodded. "You bet. But, of course, that didn't happen. Instead, she was taken to a warehouse and beaten while the group chanted around her." Arching one eyebrow, Jessie looked at Dan. "Sound familiar?"

"Yeah, but what happened?"

"A passing squad is what happened. The officer on patrol noticed something out of the ordinary and interrupted the 'ceremony'. Unfortunately, there must have been a lookout, because the leader of the group and several of his followers escaped before back-up could arrive. The ones left were just low-level members who didn't really have much info. Just knew the leader as Adrian Kern."

"Okay, well let's go question this woman." Dan stood, stretching as he did so.

"Sure, let me just check for a current address first." Jessie sat and pulled her chair close to her desk and tapped the woman's name into the computer. Squinting at the small print, Jessie felt her heart sink. "Oh, damn."

Dan came around to stand behind Jessie. "What's wrong?"

Jessie pointed to the screen. "She was killed in a hit and run accident a month after this report was filed. Nobody was ever caught."

"What about Kern?"

Jessie typed the name into the database. While waiting for the computer to search, she drummed her fingers on the desk impatiently. In a few seconds she was staring into Adrian Kern's eyes. She shuddered as she remembered reading Mark's statement describing the leader's eyes as cold. And looking at the eyes in the photo, she knew instantly that this was the same guy that Mark had encountered. Averting her gaze from the man's picture, she read his history.

"Huh. It looks like Mark sure picked a winner to get messed up with," Dan commented dryly.

"Possession of drugs with intent to deliver, battery, extortion..." Jessie sighed. "You aren't kidding."

"But look, in every case, witnesses failed to show, resulting in a mis-trial, or the jury is dead-locked. In all the instances, the DA then reduced the charges to avoid another trial." Dan pointed to the outcomes of the charges. "What's his last known address?"

Jessie entered the request and then blew out a sigh of frustration. "Unknown. Figures."

"What about--" Dan began but was interrupted by the arrival of one of their fellow detectives. "Hey, Schmidt, what are you looking all excited about?"

The tall blond detective grinned as he waved a newspaper. "You guys aren't going to believe this! Look what the Chicago Tribune investigator wrote in her column today." He slapped the paper down in front of Jessie.

"Can't you see we're kind of busy here?" Jessie started to shove the newspaper back at the young man when a small picture of Mark Taylor on the upper corner of the front page caught her eye. Beneath the picture was a caption, "Fake, Flake or For Real?"

Puzzled, Jessie glanced at Dan, who looked as confused as she did. She turned back to Schmidt. "What's this about?"

"Well, the condensed version is this: The reporter, Denise Jeffries, claims your guy, Taylor, has some kind of divine powers." Schmidt rocked back on his heels, a grin on his face. "How funny is that?"

"Divine powers? What does that mean?" Jessie began flipping through the pages to find the article. Dan leaned over her shoulder to read it too. She began reading; dread building in her as Mark's past dealings with the police were summarized. It emphasized that each time, he had been cleared in each case. It detailed the year spent as an enemy combatant and how Mark's prediction of 9/11 had never been explained, but that Mark had been released just as suddenly as he'd been arrested. The reporter wondered if the government knew something about Mark Taylor that they were covering up.

Jessie glanced at Dan, and he gave her a warning look and a quick shake of his head then pointed his chin at Schmidt. Dan didn't know the specifics of Mark's secret, but Jessie had shown him photos that she had accidentally received after she'd used Mark's special camera--before she knew it was special. She'd even told her partner about Mark's claim that he dreamed the future after viewing photos from the camera. After Mark's release, she'd never mentioned it again, and had hoped Dan would forget about the camera. Obviously, he hadn't, but at least he wasn't going to spill the news to Schmidt.

Jeffries wrote that she had combed neighborhood police reports and Good Samaritan stories going back five years and Taylor's name kept popping up. Most of the time, it was just a brief mention in a report, as if his involvement was minor, but when the reporter called to verify, she got a much different picture. The people all remembered Mark being the chief peace negotiator, risk-taker or just the one to give a word of warning.

Below the article was a list of more incidents and eyewitness accounts. The last third of the article was devoted to wondering how Mark ended up in the middle of everything. It said repeated calls to Taylor had been unreturned so the reporter admitted that all of her ideas were mere speculation. Her top two ideas were true psychic abilities or prophetic knowledge. The column ended with an invitation to readers to voice their opinion via email to the reporter.

"You've got to be kidding!" Jessie fumed as she jumped up from the desk, causing Dan to step back quickly or have his nose smashed. "What a load of--"

"Hold on now. Jeffries is only voicing what we've all been wondering for a long time."

"Divine intervention, Dan? You really think Mark is some kind of what? Prophet? Real-life angel?" Jessie smirked.

Dan chuckled. "Okay, I see your point, but do you have a better explanation for how he seems to know things before they happen?"

Jessie glared at him and began putting a folder together with Kern's picture and then opened a file behind the desk, quickly rifling through and selecting several other photos of other men, stuffing them all in the folder. She'd never give details about Mark's secret but couldn't bring herself to outright lie. Instead, she simply raised an eyebrow at Dan and grabbed her jacket off the coat rack in the corner of the office. "I'm going to lunch." She shoved her arms into the sleeves and opened the drawer to her desk, removing her purse. "I'll be back in a bit." Fishing in her pockets for her keys, she pulled them out and snatched the folder off the desk.

Dan grabbed his own overcoat, his eyes dancing mischievously. "I have a taste for a big juicy burger. You know, like the kind they have at the place on the way to the studio."

Jessie shook her head and sighed. "That wasn't where I was going."

"Yeah, right."

"Besides, they're known for their hot dogs, not burgers." Jessie grinned over her shoulder at her partner.

"Have you ever tried their burgers?"

* * *

"It'll blow over. Just give it some time."

"What do I do in the meantime, Lily? Just ignore the camera?" Mark ran his fingers through his hair in frustration and winced when he snagged a stitch behind his ear. Standing, he stalked to the office door and opened it a crack. He'd wanted to close up for the day, but Lily was against the idea. Mark understood her reasoning that they should ignore the article, but that didn't make it any easier. "There's a little kid who falls off his balcony in an hour. How am I going to go save him if I'm being followed by a pack of reporters?"

"Can't you call his home and warn them?" Lily clicked the mouse several times as she edited photos on the computer.

Mark shook his head. "No, I thought of that, but they're unlisted. I'm gonna have to go there myself." He scowled at the crowd outside the studio.

The clicking of the computer paused. "You know, you could just go talk to the press. It's possible once they see you're just a regular guy, they'll leave."

"Hmph. Maybe." Mark was about to shut the door when he noticed the reporters all turn towards something. He couldn't see what they were looking at, but something or someone definitely caught their attention. Curious, he heard the reporters address someone as 'detectives'.

Groaning, he leaned his forehead against the edge of the door. Just perfect. He didn't even need to hear the familiar voices to know which detectives had entered. Mark could practically see the reporters salivating at the prospect of having something, anything to add to their story. So far, he had given them nothing.

"What is it, Mark?"

"The dynamic duo is here."

Lily smiled. "Don't sound so gloomy. At least *they* know you're not the second coming."

"That's for sure, Mark," Jessie remarked with a smirk as she approached him, obviously having overheard Lily's remark. He rolled his eyes and sighed, gesturing for them to enter. Dan sported a big grin but didn't comment and for that, Mark was thankful.

"Looks like you're a popular guy." Dan held out his hand.

So much for being thankful. Mark clasped hands with the detective. "Yeah, I guess so." He glanced at Jessie, but her expression was all business. He masked the sharp stab of disappointment and directed his question to Dan, "Is there something I can do for you two?"

With a quick look outside, he shut the door, but that made the small office feel crowded. Lily looked tense; she still hadn't forgiven Jessie for dumping Mark.

"Hello, Lily." Jessie smiled, but it faltered when Lily

gave a brief nod in return.

Mark felt a slight easing of the pain when he noticed the blush creep up Jessie's face. At least it wasn't any easier on her.

Dan didn't seem to notice the tension and stuck out his hand to Mark's partner. "Lily, right? We met at the Christmas party."

Lily's anger apparently didn't extend to the tall detective as the corners of her mouth turned up in a grin. "Good to see you again, Dan."

Mark raised an eyebrow at the spark that passed between the two. At least they were enjoying this.

Lily's smile stayed in place as she edged toward the door. "I have a shoot I have to prepare for, if you'll excuse me." She pushed open the door, but turned at the last second to add, "Oh, and don't forget that errand you have to run, Mark."

"No, I won't. Thank you for reminding me." Mark knew the reminder was for the benefit of the detectives, to give Mark an excuse to cut any inquiry short. Bless her. He circled his desk and motioned for his company to sit in the chairs opposite. He waited.

Jessie glanced first at Dan, who shrugged as if to say, go ahead. She pushed a strand of hair behind her ear and scooted to the edge of her seat. "We think we might have a name to go with the description you and Medea gave us." She opened a manila folder she had brought with her and withdrew several photographs, lining them up on the desk. "Do any of these people look familiar?"

Mark barely glanced at the other five pictures, honing in on the third one. Too bad his own photos had reverted to an innocuous photo of a dark alley. Otherwise, he could have used them to identify the man. Even though the picture Jessie showed him appeared to be several years old, he'd recognize those eyes anywhere. He tapped it hard with his finger. "That's him." Tearing his gaze away, he glanced up to see Jessie and Dan exchange a look. "What?"

Dan turned to him, his eyes steady and serious. "His name is Adrian Kern...at least, that's the name he went by last time anyone heard from him. He's bad news, Mark."

"How's that?" Mark remained stock-still, eyes wide, awaiting the answer. Somehow, he just knew he wouldn't like the detective's reply.

Jessie pursed her lips and then spoke. "It seems that he has a long history, but nothing ever seems to stick to him. He has a whole string of mis-trials and dropped charges attached to his cases."

Mark remained silent, unsure what that implied in regards to him.

Dan stood and jammed his hands into his pockets. "There was a case very similar to what happened to Judy Medea." He stepped around the desk then sat on the corner, one foot on the floor, the other dangling. "The victim was saved by a passing police officer, but Kern wasn't caught at the time, only brought in for questioning. Before enough evidence could be gathered, the victim died in a hit and run."

"The driver of the car was never caught," Jessie added quietly.

Mark felt a chill run through his body, and he shot a look at Jessie. He wasn't reassured by the worried expression in her eyes. "So, are you gonna set some protection up for Medea?"

Dan shook his head and clasped his hands in his lap. "There's not enough evidence linking that victim to Kern or even to the prior incident. It's all just speculation, which isn't enough to justify the expense of posting a guard for anyone, including you."

"Me? I...I don't need a guard. I mean, the guy doesn't even know who I am."

"Have you forgotten about the Trib article?" Dan asked, his expression grim.

"Damn!" He had to think, but was finding it difficult. His head still ached from the concussion, and he massaged his brow.

Why did that reporter have to write that story now? Why did she have to write it at all? How was he going to take care of things with the camera if he had a media entourage? He swallowed a groan but pushed that problem aside for the moment. Right now, he needed to figure out what he should do about the cult guy, Kern.

Mark tilted back in his chair, letting a sigh escape. "I don't know what to do. Maybe I can just hope he doesn't read the Tribune?"

"Well, then he'd have to avoid TV and radio too. Seriously. You're a huge story right now and the guy would have to be living under a rock to not know who you are." Jessie's voice held a touch of anger, but Mark couldn't tell who it was directed at so he ignored it for now, wondering about something else she had said.

He leaned towards her. "Television and radio?" Mark hadn't tuned in to either yet today, and dread at her reply began to build.

Jessie exchanged a look with Dan, and Mark felt a flicker of irritation. What was with all the secret looks?

She turned to him. "It's true. We had the radio on in the car on the way over, and a least a couple of shock jocks were talking about you. One referenced something he'd seen on TV already."

Mark bent forward over the desk and wrapped his arms around the back of his head, unable to suppress the groan this time. Things just got better and better all the time.

"Speaking of the Tribune...do you have any plans to respond to the accusation--or whatever you want to call it?" Jessie asked.

He wanted nothing more than to keep hidden in the safety and darkness of his arms or better yet, crawl back into bed and pull the covers up. He raised his head and scrubbed his hands down his face. "No."

"No?" Dan's eyebrows shot up in surprise.

Mark shrugged. "What's to be gained by responding? It would just add fuel to the fire. We all know it's just a reporter exaggerating stuff for the sake of a story. If I ignore it, it'll just die away sooner." He looked at his watch and jumped up. "Damn! I have to get going. Hey, I wonder if you guys could do a favor for me?"

"Maybe. What kind of favor?" Dan exchanged yet another look with Jessie. Mark envied their unspoken communication

Snatching his jacket off the back of his chair, Mark shrugged into it. "I just need a diversion so I can get out of here without attracting a whole slew of media. I have that errand to run."

Jessie arched an eyebrow in his direction while gathering up the photos and putting them back in the folder. "What kind of errand is it, Mark? Do you have another damsel in distress to go rescue?"

Mark paused while straightening his collar, and then resumed the act with a casual air. He didn't want to discuss anything in front of Dan. Jessie had mentioned telling her partner about the camera and dreams at one point, but it had been while Mark had still been locked up. He didn't know if Dan knew the full story. "Not exactly. It's more like I have to go pay my ER bill--hate to let those things linger--and maybe run up and see Judy, if she's still a patient." It was the truth even if it wasn't the whole truth.

"No problem, Mark. Come on, Jessie, let's go out there and create a ruckus." Dan wiggled his eyebrows at Jessie. "I know what we can do to divert their attention. I can make a pass at you, and you can slap me!"

"Oh, you'd like that, wouldn't you?" Jessie smirked. "I have a better idea. Let's just go tell them that Mark is resting after an ordeal last night."

Mark waited a few moments until he heard a loud commotion in front of the building. Hoping that was his cue, Mark opened the back door a smidgen and peeked out just in time to see a reporter running from the back door around the side of the studio to the street in front.

He took the opportunity and raced out the door as quickly as he could. After a couple of minutes of brisk walking, he dared to sneak a look over his shoulder and was relieved to see that nobody was following him. Sighing, he pulled out notes he'd made upon waking this morning and re-read the details of the child's impending fall.

CHAPTER FOUR

Adrian Kern read the article for the fifth time then slammed the paper onto the table. "What a bunch of shit!" He sneered at the smiling photo of Mark Taylor. "Damn do-gooder."

First, this Taylor guy disrupts last night's ceremony and now the man was all over the news, taking headlines that should rightfully have belonged to him. How was he going to gain any power and prestige if nobody knew what he was capable of doing? Of course, if he'd been successful last night, only his accomplishment would have been in the news, not his identity, but, that wasn't the point. Now, he looked like a failure to his followers.

Last night was supposed to be a punishment for the girl, but more importantly, it had been meant to show his absolute power over the group--the guild--as he liked to think of them. It had taken months of careful preparation to set the stage. He'd had to find the perfect sacrifice. Someone who appeared pure and innocent. If he could get the guild to sacrifice her, he could get them to do anything and claim it was Satan's command.

How many times had he warned his followers of Satan's disappointment and need for retribution? The groundwork had been laid with the precision of a master architect building a monument.

Judy Medea hadn't been a random recruit, although

she didn't know it. Kern had set out months ago to find the right person. She had to be young and at least give the impression of innocence. When he'd spotted Medea working at a coffee shop near the university, he just knew she was the one. After striking up a conversation with her, he realized just how perfect she was. Estranged from her family and struggling to make it through college on her own, she was desperate for money.

It wasn't long before he had her running a few errands for extra money. After that, he'd convinced her to move into the guild's quarters and save money. Soon, she was a devoted member, her college aspirations put on hold.

Just when she was content, he'd planted the seeds of doubt in her mind. Just a comment here and there about how it was too bad she wasn't going to get her degree.

It all fell into place when she told him she wanted to go back to school. All he had to do was bait the other members with examples of everything they had sacrificed for the good of the group. After all they had done for her, how dare Medea think she could just walk out and take what they had so generously given?

Kern smiled at the memory. Oh, he had been in top form and the guild had devoured his speech like a pack of wolves feasting on a downed deer.

The drums and chants had built the cult's frenzy to a fever pitch and just at the moment when justice would have been served, Taylor had spoiled it all. Kern had considered killing the man right then, but the ritual had already been ruined.

Everything had to be just right during a ceremony or the group members would lose faith in him. There was no way he'd let that happen. On the spur of the moment, he'd decided to allow Taylor and Medea to go free, confident that he would exact his revenge in the near future. He always did.

One of his followers had shown him the Tribune article first thing this morning and later a local morning show had discussed Taylor. The story seemed to have been picked up fast by other news sources as well. Kern snatched the newspaper off the table and strode to the door leading to the common room, scowling when the door emitted a loud creak as he opened it. This place was a dump. The group's former residence in Oak Park had been much nicer.

He missed the spacious old Victorian set well back from the road. It had afforded them the room and privacy they needed to operate. With five large bedrooms, it had housed twenty members. If only he hadn't been forced to abandon it and lay low for a while.

Kern knew he'd been lucky to get this one cheap because the prior owner had defaulted on the loan, but even so, he cursed the leaky plumbing, warped floors and dingy walls. The home had been listed as a two flat with three bedrooms per flat. Kern had taken over the top flat and allowed his two bishops to occupy one of the rooms, the third room became his office. Six other group members lived in the downstairs flat while the remaining five occupied a rented apartment next door. Lack of room had caused half the members to leave. He didn't have the funds to provide anything bigger just yet, but he had a plan.

The girl had been the first major step on the rung of the ladder. He intended to climb that ladder of notoriaty to the top rung--the head of Chicago crime. For too long, the gang-bangers had occupied the top, controlling all the good business areas. But soon he'd have members flocking to him, and not poor ghetto kids either. No, he'd have angry, disenfranchised and most importantly, well-monied followers who weren't looking to make a quick buck. Kids who would never consider joining a gang, but who wanted to be a part of something. He had only to persuade them to believe in something more powerful than they. Something dark and mysterious. He grinned. He could be very persuasive when he wanted to be.

Soon he'd be living in a place more suitable to a man with his power. His followers worked hard bringing in money. Donations were down but the escort business was proving lucrative. He smiled when he thought of last month's receipts. All of it untraceable to The Guild of the Rose. At least something was going right. Kern stopped in front of the television. Taylor's picture filled the screen for a moment before the newscast switched back to the anchorperson. Jesus, could Taylor look any more innocent? He practically screamed boy next door.

Kern jabbed the off button with his finger and shook his head in disgust. While he didn't outright forbid television viewing by the members, he didn't encourage it either. He preferred to distribute information in a way that meshed with his own thinking. That lessened the confusion and helped maintain the harmony of the group. Harmony was everything. The guild depended upon the members giving up their own identities to form a cohesive unit that functioned as one.

The wall clock chimed the hour and Kern was surprised at how much of the morning had already passed. There was a lot of work to do to mitigate last night's disaster.

He glanced around his office, relishing the sense of calm that washed over him. This was his refuge. The few outsiders who had been allowed inside were always surprised at the room's decor. He guessed they expected something dark and sinister, but here, he preferred light walls, wooden trim polished to shining amber and colorful abstract art adorning the walls.

The chair creaked under his weight, the rich leather scent enveloping him as he focused on the problem at hand. It was the smell of riches and power. He basked in it.

An idea began to form. What if he used this news of Taylor to his advantage? He tapped a pencil on the desk. There was still the need to complete the ceremony anyway, as it was a major one.

First there was the problem of Medea. She had been a promising member until she had questioned Kern's authority and defied him in front of the group. She'd been openly repulsed at the two animal rituals, not believing that the chickens represented the guild. She'd balked at the idea that their sacrifice had been necessary to open the pathway to salvation and to assure the guild's place of favor with Satan. Only blood would sate their master's demands. Kern sighed. He guessed he'd have to amp up his teachings. Somehow this important piece of information had eluded Medea.

In order for Kern to achieve his full divine power, he needed to make an offering to Lucifer. If he reached his full potential, then so would the guild. Why was that so difficult for people to understand?

Medea hadn't understood the concept that it was for the good of the group. Behavior like hers couldn't be tolerated, and so, her punishment had been planned. Adrian smiled. It had been easier than he had thought it would be to get the rest of the members to go along with the ritual. He had done a great job preparing them for the possibility of harsh punishment, and with a little encouragement on his part, the group had practically thought the ritual had been their idea and Kern was going along only to appease them. Yes, he'd agreed with them. A human sacrifice was an even greater tribute, but were they ready for something that serious? He'd pretended to seem worried and they had assured him that they were more than ready. That Lucifer would reward Kern and the guild with tremendous power afterward. It had worked out perfectly. Or would have until Taylor ruined everything. Now, the boy next door would have to pay the price.

Rifling through his desk drawer, he pulled out a notebook and began outlining a new ritual. He didn't think it would be too difficult to adjust last night's plan to include Taylor. A few adaptations needed to be made. Kern set his pencil down and stared out his office window.

They could probably use that warehouse they had used a month ago for one of the animal rituals. It was surrounded by industrial buildings and at night, the area would be almost deserted. They still had their cross, and Kern made a mental note to praise Joshua for his quick thinking last night by dismantling it and stashing the two parts in the back of a neighboring warehouse. It wouldn't take much to get it up at the other warehouse. They would need something, a stand of some sort, to hold it because

Kern was pretty sure that the floor was cement, not wood. Well, they had plenty of tools and a couple of the members were really handy with them. He'd let them devise a way to make it work.

Kern leaned back and kicked his feet up on the corner of the desk, crossing his arms. As the details fell into place, he began thinking of what he wanted to incorporate into the ritual itself. It needed to be even bigger, harsher than what he'd planned for the girl. Suddenly, he became aware of the tall church spire a block away. It was an appropriate visual for his thoughts. Topping the spire was a cross.

CHAPTER FIVE

Taylor was famous now. They had to honor him with something really great; something befitting the man that the press was calling a prophet. Kern lurched forward in his chair. He had an idea. It wouldn't even take much tweaking to put it into place. Kern felt a thrill of excitement. It was a win/win situation for him. If Mark Taylor really had some kind of...power...then it was possible that power would transfer to Kern upon Taylor's death. Or maybe he'd be able to absorb it with the right kind of ritual. If Taylor was a fake, then his death would only demonstrate Kern's power to the guild. Maybe last night's ritual was meant to be interrupted. Smiling, Kern nodded, maybe instead of punishing Medea, he should reward her.

The doors slid open and Mark raced out of the 'L' car, dodging commuters as he bolted down the platform steps to the street. Hardly missing a step, he got his bearings and ran north towards Foster Avenue. He hadn't planned on cutting the timing so close but the late start due to the visit from Jessie and Dan had thrown him off schedule. The condo should be right on this block, and he just hoped he reached it in time. His lungs burned and little stabs of pain shot through his head in time with the pounding of his footsteps.

The neighborhood was a mix of new condos and

older two-flats, but the child was going to fall from the second floor balcony of one of the condos. Pushing his legs to their limit, he skidded around a corner and into a parking lot behind the address that had been listed. Mark stopped and scanned the half-dozen balconies above the U-shaped lot. Motion on the third one caught his eye, and he started in that direction. His heart jumped into his throat when he saw the toddler, his blue shirt bright against the red brick as he balanced precariously on a stack of cardboard boxes. Mark wracked his memory for the boy's name. Timmy? No, but it was something with a T, then it came to him. "Thomas!'

Faintly, he could hear another voice echoing his own. "Get down, Thomas!'

There was a flash of blue as the boy lost his balance and tumbled over the railing. Mark's final burst of speed put him in the right spot at the right time, and the little boy fell into his arms. The impact against his chest knocked Mark onto his back, his head thumping against the asphalt as his breath whooshed out.

He had tried to soften the fall for the child and managed to cradle the boy's head in the crook of his arm, his other arm beneath his knees. Dazed and the breath knocked out of him, Mark lay still, vaguely aware of the sound of feet running towards him. Thomas rolled out of Mark's arms and stood, and a second later, the child's wail sliced through Mark's head.

He knew he shouldn't let the boy wander off but was powerless to prevent it. His lungs still refused to work, and for what seemed like an eternity, he fought to take a breath, feeling for all the world like a fish out of water.

"Thomas! Oh, thank God!"

Out of the corner of his eye, Mark saw a man with sandy brown hair sweep the boy up and bury his face against Thomas's neck. A woman, only a step behind, rushed up, her eyes wild with terror. He wanted to reassure her that her son wasn't hurt.

"Is he okay? Is he *okay*?" Frantically, she sought to hold Thomas. "Oh, my baby." Her arms went around the boy and the man wrapped one arm around her, encompassing them all in an embrace. Her shoulders shook with sobs as she clutched her son.

"He's fine. Shhh...it's okay, hon. He's fine."

Finally, Mark was able to take a shaky breath. He reached around to rub the back of his head. Drawing another deep breath, he moved to sit up.

"Wait! Don't move! You could be hurt." The man relinquished his son to the mother and knelt at Mark's side. Putting his hand on Mark's chest, he gently held him down. "Do you have any pain anywhere?"

"I'm okay. Just had the wind knocked out of me." Mark shrugged off the restraining hand and sat up, but he had to blink hard when everything tilted crazily. He sagged back onto the ground and threw his arm across his eyes. Maybe he just needed another minute or so.

"Jen, call 911!"

Mark's eyes snapped open. *"No!"* This time, he sat up and ignored the spinning. The last thing he needed to do was go to the hospital. If the press got wind of that...well, it hurt his head to even contemplate what would happen then.

"I don't know, buddy. I saw you fall and it looked like you took a heck of a knock." The man cocked his head. "Do I know you?"

This was Mark's cue to leave. "Ah, no, I don't think so." He stood, trying his best to pretend his knees weren't wobbling. "I'm sure I'd remember if we'd met before."

He started edging towards the street. If he could have, he would have bolted, but he was afraid he'd fall flat on his face after two steps.

The man scratched behind his ear. "But I'm sure I've seen you before." He turned towards the woman. "Doesn't he look familiar, Jen?"

Jen stopped examining her son long enough to look at Mark and he knew the instant she recognized him from the way her eyes widened and her mouth rounded into an 'O'.

"You're the guy in the newspaper today! I read about you over breakfast! Scott, remember I showed you the article?" She hiked her son up on her hip and then swept a wayward strand of hair out of her eyes. "You're Mark Taylor, right?"

Mark darted a look around to see if anyone had heard her and was thankful that no one else was nearby. "Yeah, but that article...it isn't true...I'm just..." He backed away, trying to come up with a graceful exit.

"Hold on, don't go yet. We didn't get a chance to thank you." Jen approached him, hugging her child close. Thomas's thumb was planted in his mouth, and he regarded Mark with large brown eyes.

"That's okay. No thanks are necessary. I'm just glad Thomas is okay." Mark smiled and began to turn away. He was almost home free.

The dad stepped close and tugged on Mark's arm. "Wait! How did you know my son's name is Thomas?"

Mark stilled then slowly turned back. "I guess I heard

you calling him." His reply came out sounding more like a question.

Scott shook his head. "I heard you call him first. That's what got my attention."

At a loss, Mark ran a hand through his hair and scratched the back of his neck. He was not up to this today. Usually he was good at making up stuff on the fly, but right now, his head felt about ready to explode and he'd give anything for a couple of aspirin. He sighed. "I just...knew."

Jen's eyes softened. "It's all true, isn't it? The stuff in the paper?"

Mark looked at her and tried to come up with a reply. She was watching him with a mixture of awe and compassion. Uncomfortable with the scrutiny, he shifted his focus to the boy's father. The man gave him a speculative look, but his eyes too, held a hint of...what? Sorrow?

Mark couldn't figure it out, and dropped his gaze to the ground. He didn't know how or why, but somehow all of his normal defenses and walls had come crumbling down and he was left with no protection. He shoved his hands in his jacket pockets and swallowed hard, unable to speak.

The dad moved up beside him and threw an arm over Mark's shoulders. "You know what? I don't care how you knew any of this. I'm just *so* grateful that our son is still alive thanks to you." He gave a friendly squeeze. "My name is Scott Palmer and this is my wife, Jen. Have you had lunch yet?"

Mark shook his head, careful to keep it lowered, embarrassed at the sudden emotion that had welled up.

What was wrong with him? He hoped it was just a side effect of the concussion.

Jen took up a position on his other side and put a hand on his arm. "We were about to eat lunch just before-" She broke off and shuddered. "Well, lunch is almost ready. Please join us?"

All he could do was nod.

* * *

"Please don't mind the mess. We're in the process of moving." Scott entered and motioned for Mark to come in. Jen followed and set Thomas down just inside the door, and then headed through the living room, the boy toddling behind her. A sliding glass door at the end of the dining room stood open to the balcony and, with a shake of her head, she closed and locked it.

The condo was narrow, but stairs led up to another level and down to another floor below. One wall was a deep earth-tone red that complemented the polished wooden trim. It gave the room a homey feel. Mark noted boxes stacked along one wall, and several opened boxes scattered around the living room. Piles of old newspapers sat beside the boxes, and items wrapped in the paper lay ready to be packed, or maybe they had just been removed from the boxes. "Moving in or out?"

"Out. In fact, the reason we're moving is because we want a home that's more kid-friendly." Scott nodded towards his son. "Ever since Thomas began walking last year, it's been a nightmare." He took Mark's jacket from him and hung it on a coat tree beside the door. "This place has four levels; do you know how fast a two year old can go from the ground floor to the fourth?"

Mark smiled and shook his head. "Not really, but pretty fast I imagine."

"In the blink of an eye!" Scott snapped his fingers to illustrate his point then walked through the living room into the kitchen, waving for Mark to follow him. "Do you have children?"

"No." It was too complicated to explain that about the time he was ready to settle down and have kids, he'd been locked away as an enemy combatant. His eyes fell on Thomas, now parked in a high chair and banging away with his hands on the tray.

The child turned to him and grinned. "Eat! Hunggy!"

Laughing, Mark reached out and tousled the boy's hair. "Me too, buddy."

"Why don't you have a seat, Mark, and lunch will be ready in just a couple of minutes. Scott, could you get out another plate, please?" Jen bustled around the stove and looked at Mark over her shoulder. "I hope you like macaroni and cheese."

"Sure, that's fine." His leg bounced under the table, and he tried to control it. Why had he accepted the invitation? They seemed like nice people but with everything going on, he knew they would start asking questions. At least he'd only had the one dream about Thomas's fall. Sometimes, the camera surprised him with more than one tragedy. Good thing today hadn't been like that. The way he felt, he wouldn't be good for much more, anyway. He rolled his shoulders and tilted his head to work out a kink.

Scott opened the fridge and bent to look inside. Bottles clinked and scraped before he pulled his head back out. "Would you like something to drink? We have milk, lemonade and apple juice."

"Milk is fine." Mark made a silly face at Thomas and was rewarded with a whoop of belly laughter. The kid was cute. Slowly, Mark walked his fingers across the child's tray, watching as the brown eyes became bigger and bigger as the hand approached, then suddenly, Mark swooped in and tickled Thomas's ribs much to the child's delight.

"You're good with kids," Scott said as he tugged out a chair and sat opposite him. He placed a tall glass of milk in front of Mark and handed a sippy cup to his son.

Feeling self-conscious, Mark pulled his hand back. "I like kids, but the only ones I see are in front of my lens usually.

Scott shrugged. "Still, you're good with 'em." He cleared his throat. "I hope you don't take this wrong, because I mean this in the most sincere way, but there is some truth to the article, isn't there?"

He knew this was coming and probably should have declined their invitation to lunch. Mark sighed and glanced at Jen, who was standing with the serving spoon frozen above the pot of mac and cheese, awaiting his answer. "It's not like the article says. I sometimes get a little...warning of some things that will happen, that's all. If I can, I try to change things to prevent the bad stuff."

"Like Thomas's...fall?" Scott and Jen exchanged a look and remnants of their recent terror still lingered in their expressions.

Mark nodded unable to meet their eyes when he knew that right now they were imagining what would have happened if he hadn't been there. Even though he had prevented the tragedy, he was sure they would be haunted by the sight of their son falling and being too far away to help.

Some of the dreams he had haunted him even after he'd prevented the tragedies. If only he could have gotten here sooner, he could have just gone to the front door and let them know that the balcony door wasn't shut all the way. They could have shut it and never known what would have happened.

"I'm sorry. I should have been here sooner." A drop of milk traced a path down the side of his glass, and Mark wiped it up with his finger.

"Sooner? What would that have mattered?" Jen set plates piled with gooey pasta in front of each of them and a small plastic bowl of the same in front of Thomas before taking a seat at the other end of the table.

"I could have warned you and you'd have just locked the door. That would have prevented the...the fall." Mark shrugged, still feeling too guilty to look at the couple. He picked up his fork and ate a bite. It was good, but his appetite had dwindled as his guilt increased.

Scott regarded him for a long moment, his brown eyes thoughtful then he set his fork down and leaned towards Mark. "Maybe there was a reason you were late. Perhaps you were meant to catch our son not just prevent the accident."

Mark thought of the media circus back at the studio and smiled bitterly. "Yeah, there was a reason all right, but I don't think there was a purpose to it."

"Everything happens for a purpose, Mark." Scott said quietly. "I truly believe that."

Mark's head shot up, and he met Scott's eyes. "You

sound just like my partner, Lily. She says that, too."

"You should believe her." Scott took a bite of his lunch, nodding. "She sounds like a wise woman."

"If you hadn't been late, we wouldn't all be eating lunch together. You would have warned us and then gone about your day, wouldn't you?" Jen smiled at Mark. "So, see? There was a purpose. You were meant to meet us." She winked at him to lighten the mood. "And eat this delicious meal."

Mark shrugged, a reluctant smile escaping as he conceded the point. "This is good. I haven't had homemade mac and cheese since I left for college." He took another bite, his appetite suddenly returning.

The rest of the meal was filled with stories of the other situations the couple's son had managed to get himself into. Mark snorted with laughter when they told him about the time Thomas had gotten into the fridge and threw one egg after another on the floor. Before each throw, he had said, "Ball!" They had heard him, but just thought he was playing with his favorite toy. It wasn't until they went to investigate the funny noise that followed each 'ball' declaration that they discovered a slimy mess all over the floor.

For dessert, Jen brought out a package of cookies. "I know it's not fancy, but with the move and all, the pickings are slim."

"Hey, nothing wrong with store bought cookies, is there, Mark?" Scott snatched a cookie off the plate and handed it to Thomas. "There you go, little man."

"Oh, Scott! I was going to give him an animal cracker. He's going to be a mess after eating that."

Mark glanced at the boy, who had cheese smeared

from ear to ear and several pieces of macaroni stuck in his hair. He guessed mess was a relative term when it came to kids.

"Sorry, hon." Scott grinned at her and looked anything but sorry. Jen just shook her head and playfully punched him on the shoulder.

"That's okay. Today is special so he can make a mess if he wants." She stood and crossed to a drawer, pulling out a package of baby wipes. "At least I can keep the damage to a minimum."

After eating a second chocolate sandwich cookie, Mark looked at his watch. "Wow! I had no idea it was this late." He pushed away from the table and stood. "I have a couple of errands to run, but thank you for the great meal."

"It was our pleasure. Really. I'm so glad Scott and I got to meet you, Mark." In that way mothers had, Jen seemed to focus on Mark, but all the while, she swiped at her son's face and hands with the baby wipes, somehow managing to efficiently clean the little boy in just a few quick passes. Finished, she pulled the now sleepy Thomas out of his chair. "Can you say good-bye to Mark?"

Thomas smiled, his head resting on his mother's shoulder, but he stretched a hand out to Mark. "Bye, Mawk."

"Good-bye, Thomas." Mark reached out and squeezed a little toe. He felt a lump come to his throat as the little boy popped a thumb into his mouth and turned to rub his nose on his mom's shoulder. Mark shifted his gaze to Jen, catching her watching him with a soft smile turning up the corners of her mouth. Embarrassed, he shrugged. "He's a sweet kid."

She smoothed back Thomas's hair. "Yes. We're very lucky." She looked at Mark. "Thanks to you. You'll be in my prayers tonight."

Surprise flooded him. He wasn't the religious sort, but he was deeply touched at her sincerity. "Thanks. I could use all the help I can get."

Scott clapped him on the shoulder. "Here's your jacket. Do you need a ride? I can give you a lift wherever you need to go."

"Oh, no. That's okay. I'll just take the 'L'; it passes right by where I'm going. Besides, you're in the middle of packing, and I've already taken up too much of your time."

"You didn't take up any of my time." Scott walked with him to the door and once outside, his mood became quieter, pensive even. They stopped in front of the building. Scott reached into his back pocket and pulled out his wallet. For a horrified moment, Mark thought he meant to offer him money, but all he did was pull out a business card.

"Here, Mark. Take this. If you ever need anything, don't hesitate to call me."

Mark glanced down at the card. Dr. Scott Palmer, Board Certified in Psychiatry. "You're a psychiatrist? I...I don't think I need one just yet." Humiliation burned through him. He had thought they were different. That maybe, for once, someone had believed him with no questions asked. He tucked the card in his wallet. "I'll do that." He stuck out his hand, barely able to suppress the hurt he was feeling. "It was nice meeting you and your wife. You have a great family."

Scott shook his hand, but regarded Mark with

concern. Instead of letting go of Mark's hand he tugged on it until Mark met his eyes. "I didn't give you the card because I think you're crazy. I gave it to you because, with the move, it's the only number that won't be changing soon." He released Mark's hand. "I want to keep in touch and if you ever want to talk, officially or unofficially, please call me. God only knows, you probably need someone to talk to."

Mark nodded, feeling stupid that he had misinterpreted Scott's motives, but also relieved. "I'll remember that, Scott. And if you're ever in the River North neighborhood, stop in the studio and say hello."

CHAPTER SIX

The Chicago cityscape slid by in a blur but Mark didn't notice. His mind wandered back to the time he'd spent with the Palmers. Their home, even with the mess created by moving, was comfortable and inviting. It was the kind of home he'd always imagined he would have one day. A home filled with love and laughter and kids. At least a couple of them. And a dog. Gotta have a dog. He shifted on the hard train seat in an attempt to ease the discomfort in his back. When he thought of the reason for the soreness, he smiled. Thomas's face, with his big eyes and mop of sun-streaked hair, popped into his mind. A little stiffness was a small price to pay.

"Polk Street!"

The announcement pulled Mark from his reverie, and he stood and headed for the doors. Several other passengers also prepared to exit and he noticed a few studying him curiously. He zipped his jacket higher and turned up his collar in hopes that it would conceal a bit of his face. He'd tried on a baseball cap, intending to use that to help hide his identity, but the edge of it rested right on the place he'd received his stitches and he couldn't tolerate the irritation. Maybe he should have worn sunglasses. He glanced up at the steel gray sky, the clouds threatening to either deposit snow or rain any minute. Sunglasses would have just called attention to him.

Ignoring the stares of the few that seemed to recognize him, he exited and headed the short distance to Cook County Hospital. He wondered if the girl was still a patient and if she was, if they would even let him up to see her. The automatic doors slid open, and Mark approached the information desk.

The volunteer manning it looked up. Her tight curls had a blue cast but her eyes weren't the least bit dimmed by age. "May I help you?"

"I sure hope so. Could you please tell me what room Judy Medea is in?"

"Let me just check." She pushed a couple of buttons on her computer and leaned forward to read the screen. "It says here that she has to be notified before any visitors are allowed." The woman picked up the phone and punched in a few numbers. "Hello. This is the information desk. I have a young man here to see you."

The volunteer looked Mark up and down. "Yes, he's kind of tall...no...no, not that tall."

Mark shuffled his feet, feeling a flush of embarrassment as the older woman continued to relay his description to Judy Medea. "He's a very nice looking young fellow."

His face heated with a full-fledged blush. "Um...just tell her it's Mark Taylor; the guy from last night."

The woman's mouth dropped open as her eyebrows shot up. Mark straightened and shook his head with indignation. "Not like *that!*" Sheesh.

The woman relayed the information and finally hung-up. "She's in room 207. Second floor."

Mark found the room without any trouble and knocked lightly on the open door as he entered. Judy looked a lot better now than the last time he had seen her. Her blond hair hung limply around her face and dark smudges stained the skin beneath her eyes, but her smile was bright.

He stopped a few steps inside the door, feeling awkward now that he was here. "Hi. I just wanted to stop by and see how you're doing. "

Judy pulled the covers up to her chin and swept her hands through her hair. "Hello. I'm doing okay." She shifted in the bed and bit her lip. "Mark...your name *is* Mark, right?"

He nodded and stepped to the side of the bed, his hand out. "Mark Taylor. Nice to meet you."

She shook his hand. "I'm Judy, nice to meet you too." Judy smiled, then burst into giggles and covered her face with her hands. The gesture made Mark realize just how young she really was. She couldn't be more than twenty-two years old. After a moment, she stopped laughing, but her smile remained. "Gosh, this is so embarrassing. You've seen me in the altogether, and we're just now introducing ourselves."

Mark dipped his head and jammed his hands in his pockets. "I wasn't looking... I mean, I don't really remember any details or anything." His face heated, and he was sure even his ears were red.

Her face became serious, and she averted her eyes for a moment before meeting his gaze. "I didn't get a chance to thank you last night for what you did. For saving me."

"I'm just glad I was able to help, and that you're okay."

"Are *you* okay? I sort of remember you got hit with the staff." She grimaced and rubbed her temples. "It's all kind of fuzzy in my mind."

"I'm fine. Couple of stitches is all." Mark glanced around the room, noticing a lack of cards or flowers from anyone. "I was just wondering if you need anything. One of the detectives said that you used to be part of that cult--"

"It's not a cult." Her chin rose and she glared at him. "It's a guild."

Mark snapped his mouth shut in surprise and rubbed the back of his neck. "Oh. Sorry. I just thought--well, that's what I was told." He took a step backwards. "I guess I'll get going. Take care now."

"Wait, don't go yet. I'm sorry I snapped at you."

He paused at the doorway and looked over his shoulder to see Judy sit up and swing her legs off the bed as though to stop him.

"Don't get up." Mark stepped back into the room and held his hand up in a stop sign.

"It's just that our leader is normally so wonderful. Last semester, I was struggling at school. I had no money, I was behind on my tuition payments, and the leader paid for it all, and gave me a place to stay. I was treated like family."

Mark bit back a response about how if that's how they treated family, he'd hate to see how they treated their enemies, but he didn't come to upset the girl, so he kept his thoughts to himself. "I'm sorry. I didn't know that the group wasn't a cult, and it's great they helped you out. All I was trying to say is that if you need anything, just give me a call." He pulled a business card out of his wallet. "Here's the phone number of the studio."

"Thanks." She glanced down at the card and then up

at him, her eyes wide with hope. "Are you hiring?" Her voice held a note of desperation. "As much as I love the guild, I'm not sure I can go back there, but I don't have a job."

Mark scratched his cheek as he tried to hide his surprise. "Um, I hadn't really thought about it. It's just Lily, my business partner, and me running the studio. I'd have to discuss it with her first."

Judy leaned forward. "I know how to edit photos! I took a few classes as electives. I'm good at it. Or I can be a receptionist, answer the phone, set up appointments — whatever you need."

Things had been getting busy, and someone in the studio all day answering the phone could be a distinct advantage. It would mean potential customers would get a live person to ask questions instead of having to wait for a return call from either Mark or Lily.

Lily probably wouldn't mind if he offered her a job, but on the other hand, he didn't know that much about the girl. He couldn't help the sense of responsibility he felt for her now. "I'll tell you what. When you feel up to it, come on down to the studio and talk to Lily. I'm sure we can work something out."

The brilliant smile returned. "Thank you so much! I'll do that. I'm getting out of here later today and I'll come by first thing in the morning."

Mark chuckled at her enthusiasm. "Great! Lily usually gets there around ten. I'll let her know you're coming by."

* * *

"You offered her a job?" Lily stood in the doorway of

71

his kitchen, her expression bordering on annoyed.

Mark poured coffee for each of them. He handed Lily hers and took a sip of his own before answering, "Not exactly. I just said she should come by and talk to you." Placing his mug on the counter, he rummaged in his fridge looking for something to eat and had to settle for an apple and yogurt. Everything else was spoiled or a condiment. Someday soon he'd have to do some shopping and buy some real food. He thought about ordering a pizza a little later.

"I don't know, Mark. She seems to have an awful lot of baggage."

Speaking around a mouthful of apple, Mark defended his offer. "Aw, c'mon Lily. She's practically a kid. A desperate kid." He gathered his meager meal and went to the sofa and sat gingerly, a sigh escaping. It would be a miracle if he managed to stay awake long enough to wait for a pizza delivery.

"I know, it's just that all that cult stuff makes me nervous." Lily followed him and took a seat on the chair beside the couch. "What kind of monsters would do that to a woman?"

"Sick twisted ones, that's for sure, but Judy insisted that they weren't a cult." Mark downed the yogurt in record time and polished off the rest of the apple, sticking the core in the empty yogurt cup. He thought about going around the corner to the hot dog place to get something more substantial, but hated to risk seeing any more media. The horde had continued hanging out front and he had no idea what they hoped to learn by loitering. The most tantalizing tidbit would be what he preferred on his pizza.

Lily's brow furrowed. "How could she say that?

Normal people don't treat someone that way."

Mark leaned back into the sofa, stifling a groan. His back had stiffened already. "I don't know. Could be she's embarrassed that she ever became involved with them."

"I suppose."

They fell silent for several minutes, and Mark almost dozed off when Lily broke the silence. "Hey, how did it go with the little boy today? I'm assuming you were there in time?"

Rubbing his eyes, he nodded. "Yeah. Just barely. The little guy landed like a sack of potatoes right in my arms."

"So he was okay?"

"Oh, sure. Shaken up a bit, but fine." Mark touched the back of his head, feeling a raised swelling where he'd thumped against the pavement. It was tender, but the ibuprofen he'd taken earlier had helped with the headache.

Her eyes narrowed as she watched him. "And you? Did you get hurt?"

Mark shot her a look. "Not really. Just a little sore. But...the parents recognized me from the Tribune article."

"Yikes. What did they say?"

"Actually, they were surprisingly calm about it all. The dad heard me call the little boy's name before the kid fell, and questioned how I knew his son's name." Mark paused, feeling a lump rise in his throat as he remembered his near breakdown. "I...ah..." He swallowed the catch in his voice. "I finally said I just knew." Mark tried to chuckle but the sound, when it finally squeezed past the lump, was harsh. "Pretty quick thinking on my part, don't ya think?"

Lily sat forward and put her hand on his knee, giving it a slight squeeze. "Mark, are you all right?"

Leaning into the corner of the sofa, he stretched his arms over the rear and side and let his head fall back against the top. He didn't answer for a long time. When he finally did, his confusion and anger escaped. "Why is this happening, Lily? What's the point? I have this camera that has some spooky power from...God only knows where... and I try to do my best, but it seems like every time I turn around, someone is...is throwing marbles in my path."

"I don't know why that reporter decided to write an article. She was probably just looking for a story and your name popped up." She shook his leg. "Listen to me, Mark. I know everything happens for a reason. God doesn't do things on a whim, without a plan. He just doesn't. There's a purpose for all of this."

Mark rolled his head to look at his friend; amazed to hear Thomas's dad's words coming from Lily. He narrowed his eyes. "Did Scott Palmer call you today or something?"

Lily straightened and pulled her hand away, her expression confused. "Who?"

Shaking his head, he pinched the bridge of his nose. "Thomas's dad. The kid I caught today. His dad's name is Scott Palmer, and he said the very same thing to me over lunch. He said I should listen to you."

Her shoulders went back, and she beamed. "I've never spoken to him, but I can tell he's a *very* wise man."

He laughed. "Of course he is."

Lily chuckled, but then turned serious. "Have you ever tried asking God what his plan is for you?"

Mark squirmed on the couch, then sat forward. With

a drawn out sigh, he rubbed his hand over his face before resting his forearms across his knees. "How am I supposed to do that, huh? It's not like I can just call him on the phone or...or send him an email. I can ask it in my head but...God's not there...he's...I don't know *where* the hell he is..."

He stood and stalked to the window, bracing his arms on either side of it. Maybe if he just looked really hard, he'd see God down there strolling the streets of Chicago.

Why couldn't he feel the same sense of certainty that Lily felt? She just seemed to *know*. He thought of the Tribune article that suggested that he, Mark Taylor, might be the second coming. His mouth twisted ruefully. Even thinking something like that made him feel uncomfortable. If only they knew. Not only was he a far, far cry from the second coming of Jesus, but, he wasn't sure he even believed in God.

CHAPTER SEVEN

Kern motioned to the chair opposite his desk. "Please, have a seat, Judy."

The young woman scuttled from the door to the chair and sat with her hands clasped, head bowed. A large bruise marked her pale neck. Was she trembling?

He'd made sure to send the most nurturing member in the Guild, Claire, to pick Judy up from the hospital this morning. His instructions were to act as if it had been the plan all along for Judy to escape from the ceremony. Not only had he advised Claire to be comforting and supportive, but gave her money to buy a complete outfit for the poor girl.

"Have you recovered from your unfortunate ordeal the other night?" The concern he poured into his voice did the trick. Judy looked at him, her eyes brimming.

She nodded.

"Do you understand why the unpleasantness had to happen?"

Her gaze slid to the right, and she shrugged.

He leaned towards her. "I understand you're confused. I'm sorry about that. You are a valuable member of this Guild, and I couldn't stand that you thought we wanted to hurt you. I was trying to capture that special quality you possess. Your innocence and absolute certainty of what is right and what is wrong. I still want to capture it."

Her eyes flew back to his, fear making them wide.

Adrian reached across the desk and held his hand out, beckoning for Judy to take it. She hesitated, but put her hand in his and allowed him to clasp it gently. He stroked his thumb over her cool skin.

"I was testing you with the ritual, and you passed. Very few members are ever deemed worthy enough to be put through the initiation rites. Consider yourself truly special. You've made it into the inner sanctum of the Guild. From now on, you must be very careful because people on the outside will try to question you, make you doubt, but now I know that you can remain strong."

Her face relaxed, her mouth turning up at the corners. He almost had her. The next part would be critical. "I'm planning another ritual, only this time, it won't be an initiation. This time, we carry the sacred ritual through to the end."

Her hand stiffened in his, and he gave it a gentle squeeze. "Don't fear, Judy. You are the key to this working, but you are not the subject of the ritual."

A muscle twitched in her neck, and her eyes remain glued to his face.

Adrian patted her hand with his other one, then released her. He unfolded yesterday's newspaper and spun it so she could read it, but she only seemed to glance at the photo. "I don't know if you're aware that you hold the key for us. Here is our subject, and you are going to deliver him to us."

"Mark Taylor?" It was the first words she'd spoken, and her voice wavered. "I don't understand what you want me to do."

"Claire told me she found Taylor's business card on your hospital table with today's date and a time written on it."

Judy nodded. "Yes, that's true. I was going to go over to his studio today and talk to his business partner about working there, but now that you want me back, I'll cancel it."

This was better than Adrian had hoped. They had a legitimate way of getting inside. "No, keep the appointment. I've done some research and found out that Taylor lives above the studio. I want you to keep your eyes open and find a way for us to get inside. If you get a chance to unlock a window, that would be great. I want to know the layout, alarms, anything so that we can get inside."

"Why? And what do you want to do?"

Adrian bit back the anger that surged when she questioned him. He pasted on a smile. "He's been chosen. You are the messenger that delivered him to me once. Now, you will deliver him again. It's your destiny."

Her back straightened as she nodded. "I'll do whatever it takes."

His smile became genuine. "I'm sure you will, but remember, it has to be done carefully. Look for opportunities, but be subtle. If you arouse suspicion, it would ruin everything." He allowed a tinge of menace to color his voice, and by the way a muscle jumped in her throat, he knew she recognized it. "I'm sure that you will use the utmost care."

She nodded. "Absolutely."

* * *

"Mark! Mark! I'd like to talk with you a moment."

"Mr. Taylor! Could you comment on the speculation about how you get your information?"

"Are you the second coming?"

Mark rolled his eyes and shouldered his way through the throng of reporters, keeping his head down all the while. The camera had delivered more than one incident today. It didn't do that often, but when it did, it made for a crazy night of dreams. He yawned and rubbed the back of his neck.

The first save was only a mile or so away. A grandmother was going to accidentally give her little granddaughter too much cold medicine because she had forgotten her reading glasses and misread the label. He hoped that the magnifying lens he had would do the trick. The other saves were minor and involved little more than making sure that he was in the right place at the right time. He hoped he'd have enough time to make it back between saves to meet with Judy and Lily and ease the introduction.

"Hey, Taylor!"

He looked up, recognizing the voice and blinked as a series of flashes went off in his face. Squinting through the spots in his vision, his mood brightened when he saw George Ortega move through the horde, his camera held high in one hand, his other out-stretched.

Mark reached out and shook hands with the man. "How are you doing, George?" It had been ages since Mark had seen the other man, but at one time, they had been pretty good friends.

"I'm good, I'm good. But how about you, man? I see

you're making headlines again." His friend wore a hat at a jaunty angle, his dark eyes dancing with humor.

Mark glanced around at the other reporters eagerly listening for any scrap of information. He shook his head and said, "I have no idea why. Is that what you're doing out here?"

George shrugged. "Sorry, amigo. I got a job to do." With a sly smile, he added, "You know, being a friend and all, you would be doing me a big favor if you gave me an exclusive."

"Exclusive what? There is no story." Mark turned and began walking away, deciding that taking the 'L' would be his best bet. If he walked where he needed to go, he'd probably end up looking like the Pied Piper with the media trooping along behind him. Lily had taken the van this morning because she needed the portable lights which were too big to take in her own vehicle.

George fell into step beside him. "For someone without a story to tell, you sure do manage to get involved in a lot of stuff."

Before Mark could reply, one of the reporters called out sarcastically, "Are you giving your story to him but not us?"

George turned around, walking backwards. "We're friends, dude. Understand? Friends from way back, now shut up and give my friend a little breathing room!" Spinning back around and hardly missing a step, George continued, "So, what about it, Mark?"

Mark turned to go up to the 'L' platform. "Look, George, I'd help you out if I could, but I don't have a story. If there ever is one, you'll be the first person I tell." Hearing a train rumbling down the track, he waved. "See ya! Gotta go!"

It took a mad dash up the steps and being fortunate enough to find a fare card in his pocket that still had a couple of rides left to make it on the train just in time.

* * *

Jim Sheridan finished reading the article and shook his head. If Mark Taylor kept racking up mentions in the news, Mark would be no good as an asset, but he felt a stab of guilt. It was his job as a CIA officer to protect his asset, and this article meant he'd done a piss poor job of it. It didn't matter that he'd had no way of knowing the article would appear. He chuckled, unable to escape the irony that if he had a magic camera like Taylor, he might have known of this in advance. Even if he had, what could he have done? Ordered the reporter to drop the story? If only he could. Jim stared at the picture of Mark on the page. It was undated, but it had to have been taken before Jim had ever met the man. He was smiling at something off camera, and the wariness which always lurked in Taylor's eyes ever since Jim had known him was absent.

Mark Taylor's unique ability was something which made him special. It wasn't just the camera and the dreams. Jim never knew exactly how to treat the guy, and that made him uneasy. His training had covered how to deal with people who were never quite trustworthy. Anyone who was close enough to the enemy to provide information had to be looked at as somewhat suspect. Someone in that position might drop five great tips, but then clam up, or the tips could turn out to be bait, drawing a CIA agent in, gaining their trust while biding their time to strike when the stakes were high.

It was a risk that Jim had taken before with other assets. Some paid off, others didn't, but in his long stint in the CIA, more often than not, he managed to contain or avoid any damage to himself or more importantly, anyone else. In all that time, not one of his assets had ever been outed. Until now.

Jim leaned back in his desk chair and put his feet up on the corner of his desk, arms folded. He knew he was getting ahead of himself. There was no mention of Taylor linking him to the CIA. If anything, the enemy combatant mention would throw a smoke screen up, but this article could be the stick that pokes the hornet's nest.

He scanned the article again. There were no direct quotes by Mark, so Jim was fairly confident that the reporter hadn't actually interviewed him, but had just drawn conclusions based on some in depth research. What had Jim curious was why the reporter was curious about Taylor.

So far, Jim had kept his nose out of what Mark did with his future photos. If it didn't involve national security, he remained uninvolved, preferring not to know what the guy did. This article popped the bubble of ignorance that Jim had willingly hidden inside. *Damn it.* He pulled his legs down, his feet hitting the floor with a thump that would tick off the FBI agent on the floor below him. Jim smiled. It was the little things in life that gave him pleasure.

He reached for the phone and dialed Mark's cell number. The cell phone was special issue, as safe as current technology could make it, and Mark was to carry it at all times. It was the only stipulation that Jim had insisted upon. Taylor hadn't been thrilled with having a cellular leash, but start-up money for the photo studio had been on the line, so he'd conceded.

After the tenth ring, Jim hung up. So much for the leash. He looked up Jessica Bishop's number. While he stayed out of Mark's business, that didn't mean he didn't know that Taylor and Bishop had parted ways. However, he had a feeling that if anyone would know where Mark was, it was Jessica.

"Detective Bishop."

"Hello, Jessica. This is Jim Sheridan."

She groaned. "Oh no. You saw the paper?"

He broke into a grin at her weary tone. "I sure did. As a matter of fact, I was wondering if you had any idea where the blessed one is right now?"

"Cut the crap, Sheridan. I'm neck deep in it already, and don't need more heaped on. And no. I saw him earlier today, but he didn't give me his itinerary."

While Jim had counted on them remaining in touch, this news came as a surprise. "You saw him *today*?"

"Come on, it's not every day that an ex-boyfriend is accused of being the Second Coming. I had to see firsthand if I'd missed something in all the time I've known him."

"And did you?" Jim asked, intending the question to be sarcastic, but it came out sounding serious.

"What?"

"Miss something."

"Look, Jim. You know Mark. He's about as honest as they come, and, I admit, he's a good guy, but he's not perfect."

"Nobody is."

"I would think the Messiah would be pretty damn close to perfect, wouldn't you?"

Jim looked at the photo of Mark. No, the guy wasn't perfect, that was for certain. Someone who was accused of being the next Jesus wouldn't have the temper that Taylor had shown on more than one occasion. Most of all, he would have had the power to prevent 9/11.

"I'm just giving you a hard time. However, it is important that I reach him. With his name all over the news, he could be in jeopardy." He traced a pencil line around the photo, darkening the edges.

"You mean his status as your asset?"

Jim would never acknowledge that kind of question, but he couldn't stop her from guessing. "I mean, there are a lot of nuts out there. I'm concerned about his well-being and if there's anything I can do to help keep him safe, well, I guess I owe it to him."

"Unfortunately, you're a little late on that."

The pencil traced through the paper. "What do you mean?" Had something happened and he hadn't been notified? He had contacts in the Chicago P.D. and other places. Someone should have informed him.

"He had a run in with some cult. He's okay, just a few cuts and a concussion, but it wasn't a good situation."

"What the hell happened?"

Jim rubbed his forehead as she related the details. Just what he needed, a loose-cannon asset who thought he could save the world all by himself.

* * *

The minor saves took longer than he'd anticipated because someone would recognize him on the street and try to question him. Mark tried to be polite, but he was sure that many of the people were left in no doubt that there was nothing saint-like about him after the encounters.

He entered the studio through the back door, shutting it in the face of another reporter. The smell of burgers made his stomach growl, and he hurried into the office.

"Hey Mark. I hope you haven't eaten because I ordered you a burger from next door. With your fan club camped outside the studio, I thought I'd save you the hassle of wading through them to get dinner." Lily lifted a bag from her desk, the scent wafting to him hinted of a side of fries.

Mark gleefully rubbed his hands together and took the bag. "Thanks. I'm starving! I didn't have time for lunch." He reached in and popped a fry in his mouth. It was hot and greasy with just the right amount of salt. Pure heaven.

Lily nodded and pulled out her top drawer, rummaging around for a few seconds before shutting it. She gave a delayed, "You're welcome," while lifting a stack of photos. She checked the spot beneath them, and did the same with the appointment book, her brows knit together. "Do you see the spare keys lying around here somewhere?"

Mark set his burger down, and rolled his chair back to check under the desks, then stood and turned in a circle, scanning the floor and the top of his own desk. "Nope. When did you have them last?"

"I can't remember." Lily put her hands on her hips in

exasperation. "Where could they have gone? I was going to lock them in my desk drawer. I don't put it past one of those reporters out there getting it in their head to sneak in and bug the office or something when nobody is around."

"Bug the office?" He couldn't help laughing. "Isn't that just a *little* paranoid?" He sat and resumed eating his burger.

She crossed her arms. "That's easy for you to say. You've been gone all day and haven't had to deal with keeping the pack at bay."

"Sorry." He swallowed. "I'm sure the keys will turn up."

She sighed. "Yeah, I hope so."

He dipped a fry in ketchup and ate it, thinking back and vaguely recalled using them a few weeks ago when he'd left his own keys in his kitchen and used the spare keys to lock up rather than run up to get his own. It's possible that he left them up in his loft. "I think maybe they're upstairs."

"Oh, okay. Well, as long as you have them."

"So, how did the interview with Judy go?"

Lily's brow furrowed. "Strange."

Mark paused with the burger half-way to his mouth. "Strange? How?"

"I don't know. I just...sensed that she really wasn't all that interested in coming to work here." Lily turned in her chair and began re-organizing her desk. Everything had a place, and she knew exactly where it all went.

Mark was always amazed at how organized she was. It was at total odds to the edgy look she preferred. "Could she have changed her mind and just didn't know how to tell you?"

She shrugged. "Possibly." In less than a minute, her desk was in perfect order. "So, are you done for the day?"

Full, he pushed his wrappers away. "Pretty much. I thought I'd tackle some photo editing this evening. I'm almost caught up, then I have to develop my other film."

Lily shook her head. "No."

"Excuse me?"

"Mark, when was the last time you had a night off? A night to just relax and not think about anything?"

He scratched the back of his neck. "I don't know." Probably before Jessie had left, but he didn't share the thought with Lily.

She tilted her head, her expression softening. "You've been really stressed with all of this attention lately, and you haven't even had a chance to recover from your concussion. Will the world end if you don't develop your film tonight and just got a good night's rest for once?"

"I'm fine, Lily."

"So you say, but it couldn't hurt to take it easy tonight. Aren't you a classic film geek? I saw a commercial for some old black and white movie on tonight. I think Jimmy Stewart was in it."

It sounded tempting. Really tempting and, as though to seal the deal, he was overtaken by a monster yawn.

Lily smiled and raised her eyebrows.

"Fine. You don't have to convince me anymore. I'll see you tomorrow." Mark gathered his trash and deposited it in the garbage can. Now that he was on his way to his loft, the fatigue that he'd kept at bay by sheer willpower swept through him. Maybe he'd just go straight to bed. He glanced at his watch. It was only seven o'clock, but he was beat. Before he could put the plan into motion, his cell phone rang. He glanced at the number and groaned, wanting to ignore it, but knew he couldn't. He'd agreed to this arrangement.

"Hello, Jim."

"Why aren't you carrying the phone I issued you? I tried calling you earlier."

Mark entered the loft and kicked his shoes off. "Now you're starting to sound like my mother. Yeah. I guess I forgot to grab it this morning. I had a lot on my mind." He refused to apologize -- not when he'd never wanted the damn secure phone to begin with.

"Yes, I saw that. All the more reason to keep the other phone handy. You're supposed to avoid attracting attention. I would hardly call this article as keeping a low profile."

"I had nothing to do with the article. I spoke briefly to the reporter, but I told her nothing that she didn't already know." He eased down on the couch and let out a sigh as he relaxed. His back was still sore from yesterday's adventure.

"Why didn't you tell her to forget the story?"

"Listen, Jim, the last time I checked, the press had the right to free speech, or is that is that not true anymore?"

Jim was silent for so long, Mark pulled the cell from his ear and checked to make sure they were still connected. He knew it still rankled Jim that judicial process hadn't been followed with the enemy combatant thing, but Mark didn't care. It was nothing compared to the anger he'd been forced to bury away.

"Nobody is talking about taking away any rights. It's not even about free speech, it's about maintaining national security. Do you have any idea how valuable your 'gift' could be? But that's beside the point. If you didn't cooperate, where did she get the photo of you? It's an old one, so someone had to give it to her."

Mark stifled a yawn and scrubbed his fingers against his scalp. "I have no idea. It's kind of funny, actually. The picture is one of the first taken with the camera."

"You mean the special camera? I thought only you used it."

"Not long after I came back from Afghanistan, I had the camera sitting on a counter in the studio while I was doing a commercial shoot with a few kids for an ad. One of the kids picked up the camera and caught me off guard. I meant to send that picture to my mom because she complained that I'm a photographer, but she never had pictures of me." He shrugged even though Jim couldn't see him. "I never got around to giving it to her though." He put his feet up on the coffee table, crossing them as he searched for the TV remote in the cushion of the couch.

"So how did the reporter get it?"

Damn, Jim was like a dog with a bone. "How the hell should I know? I haven't seen the picture since I got out. I figure it disappeared with just about every other thing I owned." He couldn't resist that last dig.

"Mark, I'm sorry if this is coming off like I think this is your fault. I know it's not. It just makes me really nervous to have one of my guys in the spotlight."

CHAPTER EIGHT

Mark felt their presence before he heard them. He bolted awake. Hands--it seemed like dozens of them-- yanked him to the floor. The covers tangled around his legs and a vise-like grip in his hair immobilized his head. He lashed out with his feet and arms, feeling impacts and hearing grunts, but there were too many hands.

Panting, he swore, the torrent of words erupting as a harsh growl. The blows landed on every part of his body, but he ignored the pain as terror fueled his efforts. A hand brushed his face and he lunged at it, biting hard. The metallic tang of blood washed over his tongue, but he only released when forced by a hard kick to his ribs. Frozen in agony, he couldn't resist as they dragged him away from the bed and hauled him to his feet.

His eyes grew accustomed to the dark, and he flinched when three shadowy forms swarmed on his right and grabbed at his arms. The shadows, loose hoods hiding their faces, surrounded him. More of the hooded figures converged on his left and slammed him against the support beam in the center of his loft. They held him tight.

"It's no use, Taylor. Stop fighting, and it'll go easier for you." A face loomed above his own and Mark recognized it. Pale light from the streetlights reflected off the snake eyes.

"No! Let me go!" Mark arched his back, every muscle

straining to escape, but the intruders didn't relent. "Uuuhhhh!" He sagged, his breathing ragged and harsh. It filled his ears. "Wh...what do you...want?"

Kern laughed. "We want to see if it's true, Mark."

A bright light shone in Mark's eyes and he squinted against the intensity. "See if...if what's true?"

"If it's true that you're the second coming."

A soft chortle followed the comment, but the flashlight prevented Mark from seeing anything except vague shadows. He picked out the tallest one and tried to focus on him. "What? That's...that's crazy!"

"Oh, but is it? See, I've been doing some research on you, Mr. Taylor." He paused to smile, his teeth gleaming in the darkness. "It seems like you have saved a lot of people. Hundreds, if the tally is right. You have a 'gift' for saving people." Crossing his arms, the leader leaned back slightly. "And isn't that what Jesus did? He saved people? He's the Savior, right?"

Mark shook his head back and forth. "No! It's not like that! Th...that's insane! You're *all* insane!"

Grinning, the man stepped close to Mark. "We shall see. I have a little...test for you. Just to see what happens."

"I'm not doing any damn test!" In blind panic, he fought to escape. His muscles screaming in protest as he raged against the arms that held him. His tee shirt ripped, and he could feel fingers and sharp nails biting into his skin. In his frenzy, he managed to free one arm and used it to claw at the nearest person, grabbing onto the hood. The dark cloth fell back and even the darkness couldn't hide the bright blond hair or the delicate features.

Stunned, Mark's arm dropped and someone immediately grabbed it and restrained him once more.

"Judy? I... don't understand."

"I'm sorry, Mark, but it's beyond my control. This is where I belong." And then she smiled. "It'll be okay."

"Let's get on with it people," Kern snapped.

Mark's hands were wrenched behind his back and bound. Another rope circled his neck like a noose. He tried to resist again, but a sharp tug on the rope tightened it enough that, instinctively, he stilled.

His captors urged him forward with a pull and he had no choice but to comply. He stumbled down the steps and out the back door of the studio. A light snow drifted down, and he gasped at the pain of the snow on his bare feet. The rear doors of a large van opened and the holder of the rope stepped in, yanking Mark in behind him. The rest of the group piled in the side door. Mark knelt on the floor while one of the members held his leash.

Chills wracked his body, and he fought to control his trembling. He remembered the horrifying details from Judy's ordeal. There had been that pole, and he recalled the ropes attached to it. Feeling sick to his stomach, he swallowed hard.

Far too soon, the van pulled into a deserted alley behind an old building. Mark had no idea where they were and he tried to look for landmarks when he staggered out of the van, but a jerk on the rope tugged his head forward.

"Ahhhhgh!" He struggled to breathe and sank to his knees as his vision dimmed. A roar filled his ears.

"Loosen the rope! We can't have him dying out here. That would ruin everything."

A rush of air poured into his lungs and Mark sucked it in as fast as he could. Hands clamped onto his shoulders and pulled him to his feet, the lead rope left mercifully slack this time. A door opened and the group quickly entered, maintaining their almost complete silence. With the exception of Judy and Kern, no one had uttered a single word during the whole ordeal.

A long hallway opened into an empty warehouse. A bonfire blazed in the middle of the room. A half dozen black clad members of the cult greeted the new arrivals with bows of their heads. Someone threw a piece of wood onto the fire, sending a cascade of sparks shooting into the air. Broken windows high on the walls ventilated the room and the fire flared as a cold breeze swept the space.

A make-shift wooden cross loomed over the room. A small ledge jutted out from the bottom of the pole. Mark stopped in his tracks and even the tugging on the rope couldn't get him to budge. His trembling intensified, and he uttered a hoarse, "No."

Kern approached him. "Oh yes, Mark. How else can I test my theory?" He looked to the cross and back at Mark with a mocking smile. "Be grateful we didn't make you haul it in here."

Hands tightened on his biceps and jarred him into action. Spinning suddenly, the grip on his arms slipped and he lowered his shoulder, plowing his way through the group. Two people fell and Mark made a break for the hall. He hadn't gone three steps when the rope tightened, snapping his head back. His legs flew out from under him and he crashed hard on the cement floor, his skull cracking with a dull thud on the pavement. Sparks shot through his sight. The impact knocked the wind out of him and pain rocketed through his back and shoulders. The rope bit into his neck and when he tried to breathe, his diaphragm spasmed.

There was nothing left to do but pray.

The cult members dragged Mark, face up towards the cross. He closed his eyes; barely registering the movement. Flashes and snippets of his childhood and adolescence played in his mind like a movie on fast-forward. His thoughts filled with images of his parents. It bothered him that he couldn't remember exactly what he had said in his last conversation with them. Had he told them he loved them? Maybe he'd told his mom, but probably not his dad. His dad didn't go much for expressing his feelings. What his dad lacked in verbal expression, he made up for with handshakes and claps on the shoulders. Mark's mom had no qualms about telling Mark she loved him and no visit ended without lots of hugs and kisses.

Vaguely, he heard clatters and clanks, but ignored the intrusion into his thoughts. He concentrated on the kaleidoscope of images swirling in his brain; his first bicycle, first home run in Little League, and later, the first time he ever made love. All his friends and loved ones made their appearance in his parade of memories.

Several people rolled Mark onto his side, rudely yanking him from his reverie and thrusting him into the present. They tore off the remains of his shirt and cut the rope around his wrists. Before he could breathe a sigh of relief, they pulled him onto the long vertical part of the cross, which now lay on the floor. Gasping, his eyes darted around him and his heart beat at breakneck speed. This can't be happening! His terror ratcheted up another notch when a drum started pounding and the cult began chanting.

Stretching Mark's arms wide, they held him down. He tried one more time to get free, kicking with his legs, but within seconds, he felt his arms and legs lashed to the wood. Another rope circled his chest, holding him fast. The drum tempo increased and the chanting matched it beat for ominous beat. Then, silence.

Kern bent over him, a wicked gleam in his eyes. "Are you ready?" He placed a hand on Mark's chest. "Hmm... your heart seems to be beating pretty fast. Are you nervous? If you'd like, I could convert this to a different kind of ritual."

Mark couldn't answer, his whole body felt paralyzed. Why the hell didn't they hurry and just get this over with? His throat spasmed several times before he managed to respond, "Why can't you just shoot me?"

Kern threw his head back and laughed. "But that wouldn't serve our purpose, now would it?" He drew a sharp knife out of a leather case attached to a belt around his waist. "What I could do, though, is make this into more of an Aztec sacrifice than a Christian test of faith. Hmmm...I've always been intrigued with a culture that was so advanced and yet, worshiped in such a blood-thirsty way. Utterly fascinating."

The gleam in his eyes was replaced with a cold, flat effect, and he touched the tip of the knife against Mark's upper abdomen. "Are you familiar with their rituals?" Without waiting for an answer, he continued, "They would cut the heart right out of a person, and while it was still beating, show it to the poor victim."

Mark could only gape at him in mute horror.

"It could be all over in a matter of seconds if I just plunge this in right...here!" Kern shoved the knife in and

Mark cried out, his whole body writhing as he tried to get away from the pain.

"You're lucky. I held back or you'd be dead."

Slowly, he withdrew the weapon and Mark groaned. He went on as though carrying on a casual conversation. "No, I don't think we'll go the Aztec route. I'm too curious about you, Mark. I've always despised the Church and its silly belief that the son of God walked amongst ordinary men, performing miracles and healing the sick." Kern paused for a long moment, his eyes took on a faraway expression before snapping to Mark's. "Do you heal the sick?"

Mark moaned, his head lolling in pain and shock, Kern's question barely registering. For a minute, the only sound in the room was his ragged breathing. He almost wished the knife had gone deeper--just to end the whole thing. His eyes opened wide and he gave a hoarse cry when Kern poked his finger into his wound and then held it up, the blood dripping down.

"Apparently, I've answered my question. If you could heal the sick, self-preservation would demand that you heal yourself first. As you can see, that is not the case." And then he laughed as though he had told the funniest joke in the world. "What I want to see is if your God can save you. Do you have faith, Mark?"

With a short nod to the cult members restraining Mark, he turned abruptly and strode away. The chanting renewed; the members' voices louder, more insistent.

They began with his right hand. Mark didn't want to look, but he couldn't tear his eyes away. "No...don't...don't do this...please...stop...*oh God!*"

Nobody looked at him; every person who held him

kept their heads bent, ignoring his pleas. They forcibly pried his fist open, spreading his fingers and scraping his knuckles against the wood. The drum increased its tempo and a hooded figure held a long, thick nail to Mark's palm. He could feel the cold metal point digging into his flesh. The chant surged in time to the beat of the drums, and the firelight flashed off the hammer as it slammed down.

Mark never heard it connect with the nail head. He stiffened, his back arching in pain and shock. Before he could catch his breath, they moved to his left hand. He didn't look this time. Instead, he closed his eyes, his lips moving in prayer.

"Our father who art in heaven, hallowed be thy name. Thy kingdom come, thy will be done, on Earth as it is in heaven..."

He felt the bite of the metal against his left palm; heard the chanting reach a crescendo. Mark raised his voice, hoping to drown them out.

"And bless us oh Lord, with these, thy gifts which we are about to receive through Christ our Lord, Amen."

The hands holding him tightened, and his heart raced, the beat pounding in his ears. Any second, the hammer would fall.

"And yea, though we walk through the valley of the shadow of death --"

A bolt of pain shot through his palm. When he could breathe again, he licked his lips and swallowed. Mark had lost his train of thought and began again with the first prayer that came to mind.

"Holy Mary, Mother of God, pray for us sinners now and at the hour of our death --"

They held his feet, one over the other, distracting him. He raised his head to look down at them, feeling sick fear at the spike held over his left foot. He couldn't look any more and turned his head as acid burned the back of his throat. The drums increased the tempo, matching the staccato rhythm of his pulse. The chanting reached a frenzy while embers from the fire drifted in the air above him, like pieces of hell.

The last prayer was silent, his breathing too harsh to give it voice.

Forgive me, Father, for I have sinned...

They drove the last spike home and mercifully, darkness claimed him. When Mark roused again, the cross was upright, and he hung above the cult members. He didn't know how long he had been there, but the room was dimmer. The drums still beat, but the tempo had changed. The earlier frenzy had been replaced by a slow erratic beat. Kern held up a staff and the cult members bowed to him.

The pain in his hands went beyond anything he had ever felt. His weight hung on them, only the ropes binding his arms helped ease the burden. He almost didn't notice his difficulty breathing until he had to consciously make an effort to take a breath. Mark could feel his throat closing, the abuse his neck had taken earlier taking its toll. Sweat dripped down his face, the stress causing him to shiver and perspire at the same time. Each chill that shook him increased his agony until finally, his mind shut down.

* * *

"No! Oh God!"

Jim started awake and shot out of the recliner. "Taylor?" He glanced around his living room. The voice had been so clear, as though spoken by someone in the room. Mark's voice. He was sure of it. He'd heard that panic once before when Taylor had been water-boarded. Had he flashed back to that interrogation? Why would he re-live it? While unpleasant, he'd never felt terror during them.

Grabbing the remote off the floor where it had fallen from the arm of the chair, he pointed it at the television and clicked off the infomercial that droned on about a miracle weight loss solution. It couldn't have been the source of the voice he'd heard.

His shoulders ached, and he grunted and rotated one as he made his way to the kitchen. He must have slept on it funny. Instead of the pain decreasing as he tried to work out the kink, it intensified, and he gasped and sank onto the nearest kitchen chair. Cold sweat popped out on his forehead. Was he having a heart attack? He was only 48 and in good shape. His heart thudded, resonating in his ears, the sound deafening in the silent house.

Holy Mary, Mother of God, pray for us sinners now and at the hour of our death...

Jim staggered to his feet and spun in circle. "Mark? Where are the hell are you?"

The kitchen was lit by only the light from the oven clock. The green glow created a surreal atmosphere as the beating in his ears grew. After a moment, he realized it wasn't his heartbeat. It was a drum. No...drums. He checked the radio on his counter to make sure it was off.

Forgive me, Father, for I have sinned...

Jim stumbled back, bumping into the counter. The kitchen dissolved and instead of his table, chairs, stove and refrigerator, he was in a room. A huge room. To the left, in front of him was a bonfire. The wood smoke stung his nose, and he rubbed his eyes. Chanting kept time to the drums, but Jim couldn't decipher what was being said, and as he tried to filter it from the rhythmic pounding, he picked out the dark hooded people kneeling on the floor before him in a half-circle. A shadow crossed the floor between him and the worshipers, and he turned to see the source. Looming to his left rose a cross. Jim blinked. *A cross? Holy shit.*

Hanging from the cross, as real as the kitchen stove that should have been there, hung Mark Taylor.

Stunned, Jim stared. Was Taylor dead? The drums increased in volume, resonating through Jim's body. The sour taste of bile rose in throat. It was so vivid, so real but it couldn't be. He was in his kitchen, not standing in some warehouse. The hairs on his arms stood on end as a chill shook him.

He tried to rush towards Mark, but his feet seemed nailed to the floor. No matter how hard he tried, he couldn't reach the cross. While only appearing a scant ten feet away, it might as well have been an ocean that separated them.

The drums reached a crescendo, and stopped. The fire crackled and snapped, breaking the silence.

A man in a black robe lifted a staff, the others bowed to him. His mouth moved, but Jim had to strain to hear him as he mumbled, *"Satanus, non sum dignus... sed tantum dic verbo."*

For a moment, the black-clad figure seemed defeated, but then his head rose, and he boomed, *"Levate. Evenit diabolus.*

An instant later, the scene was gone. It didn't fade, it

was just there one second and gone the next.

A sense of impending doom raced through him. It was a dream. It had to have been. He probably just hadn't quite woken all the way up before coming into the kitchen.

Despite his confidence that he'd just had the strangest, most realistic dream ever, a sense of urgency prodded him to action. As though released from a spell, his feet felt light, and his shoulders no longer ached as he sprinted to his bedroom and grabbed his cell phone. Flipping it open, he found Mark's number and called him.

Voice-mail picked up and Jim snapped the phone closed. He dialed again, hoping that Mark hadn't reached the phone in time. Still no answer. He plopped on the edge of the bed and glanced at the bedside clock. Two-thirty in the morning. Where would Mark be at this time?

His car keys and wallet sat on the night table. At this time of night, he could get to Taylor's place in less than fifteen minutes. By three, he'd be back home and in bed. He felt silly enough calling Taylor, but he couldn't shake the sense of urgency that screamed inside of him like a banshee from the Irish legends his grandma used to tell him.

Jim grabbed his keys, stuffed his wallet in his pocket, and headed for the door before he could convince himself he was acting irrationally.

CHAPTER NINE

Fifteen minutes later, Jim pulled up in front of the studio and then wondered how he'd get Taylor's attention. He hunched into his jacket and shuffled a path through the light snow to the front door of the studio, hoping to find a doorbell for the loft. Having only been to Taylor's apartment a couple of times, he wasn't sure of the layout. He thought there was probably a back entrance in the alley behind the building.

The alley was dark and Jim hesitated before rounding the corner. He quickly peeked around the building, relieved to see that the alley was empty. Still alert, Jim faced the back door and jumped back in surprise when the door swung open. "Taylor?" There was no answer, and in fact, taking a step closer, Jim realized that there was no one there. The wind must have blown the door. The hair on the back of Jim's neck prickled. Taylor might be a little odd, but he wasn't stupid. He'd never leave the back door to his business open all night.

Jim rapped on the door. "Hello?"

Nothing. A soft glow from an exit sign threw off just enough light to illuminate the entryway. Not seeing anything amiss down here, Jim cautiously climbed the steps, noting lots of little puddles scattered on the stairs, as though someone, or lots of someones had entered recently with wet feet. At the top, his stomach tightened when he saw the loft door gaping open. He paused outside it to listen. All was silent, and with a deep breath, he crept around the threshold wishing he'd thought to bring his weapon. He'd gotten out of the habit of carrying it since he spent the majority of his time behind a desk.

Jim felt around for a light switch and swore when he found it and illuminated the room. His jaw clenched in reaction to the scene before him. It was obvious from the disarray, that something had happened here. The bedding hung off the mattress, the bedside table was completely overturned, and loose change dotted the floor. Stepping quickly over to the bathroom, he hoped maybe Taylor had felt ill and in a mad dash to the bathroom, had created the mess. It was a stretch, but he wanted to be sure. It was empty. *Damn it.*

Careful not to disturb anything, Jim pulled out his cell phone and called Jessica Bishop.

"Hello?" She sounded sleepy and confused.

"Jessica, this is Jim Sheridan. I had a dream about--."

"Jim? What in the world? It's almost four in the morning."

"I know what time it is. Could you let me finish?" Jim continued surveying the loft, his gaze landing on Taylor's black leather jacket in a heap on the floor near the end of the sofa.

"Okay, so what's the problem? I would kind of like to go back to sleep, if you don't mind."

"Do you know where Mark is?"

"Didn't we already cover this earlier today?"

"Listen to me, it's important. I need to know where Mark is, and if you know, could you please enlighten me?"

"And I told you before, he doesn't fax me his plans.

Did you try calling him?"

"I tried, but it went to voice mail. His loft isn't too far from my place, so I decided to drive over." He took a deep breath, and let it out before continuing, "Something's happened here."

"What do you mean?"

"I was greeted by the back door flapping in the wind. Then I found Taylor's apartment all torn up. He's nowhere around." He could hear a soft sigh and creaking through the phone.

"Sometimes he had trouble sleeping at night. He'd have flashbacks, and to forget about them, he'd go out for a run. That's probably what happened tonight."

Mark had never told him about the flashbacks, and he felt a twinge of guilt, but nudged it aside for the moment. "Look, I suppose that might be possible, but I think I'm smart enough to recognize a crime scene when I see one."

He paced from the side that contained the sleeping area to the kitchen at the far end. On his second pass, he halted suddenly, his attention zeroing in on several red smears on the sheets and more drops leading towards the living area. "There's blood on the sheets and floor."

She swore, and even through the phone, he heard the worry in her voice. "Yeah, that doesn't sound good. I'll be right there."

* * *

Jim tried not to disturb anything while awaiting Jessica's arrival. A quick scan of the kitchen area didn't turn up anything out of the ordinary. A couple of dirty dishes in the sink and a nearly empty refrigerator all indicated nothing other than a typical single guy's apartment. He followed the blood trail to a pillar and circled the brick support looking for any abnormal findings. About four feet up, he spotted a small piece of white fabric caught on the edge of a brick. Peering more closely, he guessed that it was part of a t-shirt. Higher up, Jim saw several strands of dark hair and a small red stain. A feeling of dread washed over him with the realization that something violent had happened here.

Unwilling to risk contaminating the scene, he stepped back and glanced at his watch. Mentally, he calculated how long it would take Jessica to jump into some clothes and drive here. At this time of night, the roads were practically empty, but it wouldn't be long before the morning rush began. He crossed to the window and watched, trying to piece together a scenario. Best case, Taylor had tripped into the pillar, cut himself and fell against the bed. The cut had needed stitches, and so he'd gone to the ER. Plausible, but improbable. Besides, Taylor's van was still out front.

"Jim?" Jessica burst into the room a few minutes later, her long coat billowing out behind her. She came to an abrupt stop when she saw the mess and turned to Jim. "Is this how you found it?

"Yes. And look here." He pointed to the evidence on the pillar. "There's more blood over there on the floor." He tried to ignore the way her face blanched and her eyes welled. Jim bent and pretended to examine the dry drops of blood dotting the hardwood; allowing her a moment to regain control of her emotions.

A few seconds later, he straightened and asked, "What do you think?"

She glanced at the blood on the floor and then over to the pillar before answering. "What I think...is that Mark didn't leave here of his own volition."

"I agree, but who could have come in here and where could they have taken him?"

With a short laugh, Jessica shrugged. "Well, with Mark, who knows? A month ago, I would have said no one, but now? With everything that's going on in the media?" She sighed and shook her head, meeting Jim's worried look with one of her own. "We need to call this in and get an evidence team out here."

For some reason, he'd held out hope that she would have a rational explanation for this, something a lot more logical than what he'd seen in his dream. An explanation like Mark was a sloppy housekeeper or he had a new girlfriend he'd been staying with. Not that either scenario sounded like Taylor, but it was a lot more likely than what he had. He gave a short nod of agreement, and pinched the bridge of his nose. As stupid as it sounded, he had to tell her about the dream.

"Wait, Jessica. I came by because--damn, this sounds ridiculous--but I had a dream. A nightmare, really, and it involved Mark. Something bad was happening to him and it was as if I was right there watching it happen. Only it didn't feel like a dream." He hoped the last bit didn't sound as lame to her as it did to him.

She stilled. "A dream? Like the kind Mark gets?"

"I don't know." He rubbed a circle on his temple as the images from the dream flashed through his mind. "Maybe. In the dream, he was in trouble."

"Trouble?" She moved towards him, her expression confused. "What kind of trouble?"

He hesitated as the sick fear that he'd felt in the dream claimed him again, forming a ball of dread that lodged in his throat. His tongue felt thick as he said, "Mark was...they had him in a warehouse, and there was a bonfire. There were at least a dozen people kneeling in front of him. I couldn't see them clearly because they wore some kind of dark robes or something with hoods."

The next part was the hardest, and as she came right up to him, he wished he didn't have to tell her.

"Jim..." she pleaded.

"First, just remember, this was only a dream, so don't get too upset, okay?"

Her eyes narrowed.

He sighed. "He was on a cross."

She stepped back, her brows knit together. "What?"

Jim fumbled for a way to explain it. It was too absurd to make it sound rational. "It was a cross, you know, like...Jesus."

"You mean he was crucified?"

The ball of dread dropped with a crash to his stomach. He nodded.

"Oh come on. That's crazy." Her mouth twisted into a sickly smile.

"I know. It's just that I've never had a dream like that in my life. I can recall it as clearly as if I just re-wound the tape and hit play."

Understanding dawned on her features. "Mark describes his dreams like that."

"Yes, I know." Jim wandered to the window and rubbed his forehead. Behind him, he heard Jessica's footsteps approach, and he glanced over his shoulder. "I never dream. Not that I can remember anyway, but tonight, it was vivid-- like I was part of it."

Remembering how he'd been paralyzed in the dream, he added, "I was there, but nobody acknowledged me. I couldn't act on what I was seeing, but I could hear and see everything."

Jessica touched his arm, her hand tightening. "Was Mark alive?"

It was the one piece of good news he could give her. "Yes. At least, he was in the dream."

She released his arm with a shaky breath. "I'm going to call this in."

While she called 9-1-1, Jim tried to make sense of what he had dreamed and what they had found in Mark's loft. The time he had worked closely with Mark had been the Wrigley Field case, and Mark had been able to relate the details of his dreams in a straightforward manner. Plus, he had the photos to back up what he said. Jim had no photos so his dream was just that. A dream. A very realistic one, but the chance of it coming true was about as likely as Jim shooting fire out of his fingertips.

"I had a hard time convincing them to send a car. Only when I mentioned the blood did they consent to take a look." She looked around the room, and he saw uncertainty on her face. "You know, I should call Lily Martin. She might know where Mark is."

Jim did a double-take at the tone of her voice, and when her cheeks pinked, he understood. "Do they have a relationship? I mean besides that of business partners?"

She shrugged. "It's none of my affair, but it just occurred to me, he's probably there all snug as a bug in a rug, while we're here worrying about him because of a dream you had. That isn't exactly something I want to put in a report."

Jim had to admit, the evidence of foul play was less than overwhelming, especially if someone didn't know Mark. A messy room and a few drops of dried blood. Taylor was a grown man and Jim had spoken to him less than ten hours ago.

"Mark sees the future in his dreams, right? So all of this should happen tomorrow, not now--if it's even true-- which I highly doubt." It all sounded so preposterous he couldn't believe he was even discussing it.

"The problem, Jim, is that Mark is gone now, not tomorrow. We need to find him before what you saw in your dream takes place." She had her cell phone open. "I think I have Lily's number on here. Yeah, I knew it." She pressed a button and held the phone to her ear, but spoke to Jim, "I can't believe I'm hoping he's there."

He nodded and stopped suddenly when he spied the phone he'd issued Mark. It was half beneath the sofa, a scattering of coins around it, as though all had been knocked off the coffee table. From the worried look on Jessica's face, he guessed Mark wasn't at Lily's. With a quick glance over his shoulder, he strode to the sofa and snatched the phone and slipped it into his pocket. It wouldn't be a good idea for police to find it. Everything was encoded and scrambled, but they'd wonder why a guy like Mark had a secure phone.

"She hasn't seen him since he went up to his loft shortly before seven p.m."

Red lights flashed against the windows, and a minute later, two police officers entered the loft.

Leaving Jessica to explain the situation, he headed towards the door. "I'll go downstairs and get out of the way." The last thing he wanted was to be identified as a Fed. It was better to keep a low profile and let Jessica do all the talking. Within ten minutes, the studio was crawling with police officers. Within twenty, the media had gotten wind that something was up and a half-dozen news vans were parked around the building.

Jim walked through the office, noting that all looked in order as far as he could tell. He knew Mark kept his special photos in a file cabinet down here, but to anyone looking, they would appear to be just random photos, and not very good ones at that.

He opened the file drawer and flipped through the photos, checking the dates Mark had written on the back. There wasn't one dated today. That meant he hadn't used the camera today, or at least, he hadn't developed the film. It was a long shot, but maybe there was a photo depicting the horrifying scene Jim had dreamed. He raced back upstairs and nearly crashed into a police officer coming down the steps.

"Whoa there, buddy. This is a restricted area now as a possible crime scene."

He had to get to that camera, no matter the obstacles. Not only could it hold the answer to where Mark was now, if it went into a police evidence locker, it could disappear forever. With a hard stare, he pulled out his wallet and flashed his badge.

Technically, this wouldn't be considered his jurisdiction, but there were ways around that. "I'm a Federal officer with an interest in this case. Right now, I have to get back in there to check for something."

The officer glanced at Jim's badge and hesitated. The guy wasn't a young rookie and Jim could see that the man wasn't intimidated, but probably just running through his options in his mind. Before he could come to some conclusion, Jim blew past him and ignored the call to stop.

Jessica was in the kitchen nodding to something a uniformed cop was saying, her arms crossed as she watched the activity in the apartment.

Jim motioned to her, his manner urgent. Her forehead knit in confusion as she waved off something the uniform was asking and crossed to Jim.

"What?"

"Where does he keep his camera?" The uniformed cop appeared at the top of the stairs.

She turned and pointed to the bed in the far corner. "On his bedside table."

Damn. The only thing he saw was a clock radio blinking at the floor. "Distract the cop coming in, okay?"

Jessica seemed to know the officer, and with her running interference, he hurried to the bed and knelt, not caring if he destroyed evidence. The comforter hung on the floor and he lifted it out of his way and almost shouted with relief. The camera appeared intact under the bed. He snagged it and tucked it inside his coat, then tightened the belt, hoping the cut of the trench coat would hide the bulge.

Jessica pointed to the pillar and the cop approached it. While the officer's attention was diverted, Jim sauntered towards the door.

* * *

As Jim waited, he listened to the chatter of the cops as they hurried in and out of the studio and loft. The evidence team had found tire tracks in the snow behind the studio along with dozens of footprints. What had everyone really worried were the faint prints of someone who was barefoot. Measurement of that print corresponded to the size of Taylor's shoes up in his loft. That, along with the blood and hair had been ample enough evidence that the whole building was now cordoned off with yellow police tape.

A uniformed officer poked his head into the studio. "Officer Sheridan, there's a Lily Martin outside; says she needs to speak to you."

Jim glanced around, ready to have the officer bring Lily back, but then thought better of it. The fewer people who entered the room, the less chance of destroying any evidence that might turn up. He stood and circled the desk. "I'll go outside to talk to her. Could you let Detective Bishop know that I'll be in my car?"

The young cop nodded. "Yes, sir."

Walking through the studio, Jim exited the building, squinting in the glare of the bright lights from the television news cameras. Lily stood off to Jim's right.

"Excuse me, sir. Can you state who you are and what can you tell us about the disappearance of Mark Taylor?" A slew of microphones were shoved in Jim's face. He blinked against the lights and batted away a microphone.

"Do you think this has anything to do with all the talk about Taylor's claim to have divine powers?"

"Is it true that the police believe Taylor was kidnapped? What did you find?"

Jim held up his hands. "You need to direct your questions to the Chicago P.D. I'm not affiliated with the department."

March Into Hell

"Is it true that you're with the CIA and why is the CIA involved in this investigation?"

Jim found the reporter who voiced the question and pinned him with a hard look. "No comment."

"Is there a government cover-up going on?"

Jim ignored the question and elbowed his way through the throng and moved towards Lily. The comment about divine powers bothered him. In all the articles he had read, and news stories he'd seen, never once had Taylor claimed anything and he just couldn't let that reporter's question pass as though it was fact.

He turned back and said, "One thing, though. You're wrong to say Taylor ever claimed to have any powers, divine or otherwise. It was all you guys...the media, who made up all that crap. If something has happened to Mr. Taylor because of all your speculation..."

Jim had wanted to end his comment with a bang, but instead, it petered out as what he said hit him. Something bad had happened to Taylor. He'd seen it already. Time was wasting and the reporters were just in the way.

He caught Lily's eye and inclined his head towards his vehicle, "Why don't we go sit in my car and talk? It's a zoo inside and it's not much better out here. Besides, I'm cold."

* * *

"...so that's pretty much it. Jessica and I called it in after that." Jim sighed and rubbed his eyes.

Lily brushed away a tear that raced down her face. "All these...lies people have been saying about Mark have really had him down." She repeatedly wrapped and unwrapped her purse strap around her hand.

"Has he had any threats? Did anyone call or approach him? Anything?"

Lily shook her head and dug a tissue out of her bag, dabbing her nose it. "Not really, but I did have to put the business phone straight to voice-mail. I'm not sure Mark knew about it though. He's been kind of busy the last few days."

Jim noticed Lily shiver and so he turned the car on and cranked up the heat.

"Busy doing what?" From what Jim had heard the other day, most of the customers had been media and Taylor had been trying to avoid them.

"You know what he does so take a wild guess." Lily rubbed her forehead as though trying to ease the pain of a headache. "Besides, what does it matter?"

Jim looked out the front window, noting the arrival of even more news vans. He drummed his fingers on the steering wheel. "It could matter a lot. We should know all of his movements from the time the story broke. I just have a feeling the story is connected somehow to Taylor's disappearance." He turned to her. "Did he do anything unusual in the last few days?"

Lily let out a snort. "By Mark's standards, no. The only thing he even mentioned was the lunch he had yesterday with a family on the north side. It wasn't anything bad though. At least, that's not the impression that I had."

Jim rummaged in his glove box for a notebook and pen. "Do you have a name?"

"I think the man's name was Scott something...oh,wait, it was Palmer. Scott Palmer. But, like

I said, Mark didn't say anything bad about them, just that they were nice people and I think they did ask Mark about the stories in the paper."

"Did you get the impression that Mark was afraid of him?"

"No, not at all. If anything, their questions seemed to make Mark wonder about something in his own life and how to handle it."

"You mean the camera?"

She slanted him a glance. "So you know about that too?"

Jim pulled the camera out from beneath his coat and gestured toward the second floor of the building. "I took it from upstairs. I was hoping it could hold some answers for us."

Lily frowned and looked from the device to him. "How? Without Mark here to dream--"

"I dreamed," he cut in. He set the camera in her hands. "I'm hoping that there's a picture on it that could correspond to what I dreamed." Aw, hell. It sounded as stupid as he feared, but he had to take the chance.

"That's not how it works though. Mark dreams *after* seeing the photos." She checked the film counter. "He didn't develop this one." Tears filled her eyes again. "I told him not to. Told him he should get some rest instead. What if there's a picture of whatever happened to him on here and he could have stopped it?"

He didn't want to be cruel, but there was no time for guilt and recriminations. "Listen, Lily. We can't do anything about the past, we can only worry about now." He tapped the top of the camera. "I want you to develop this film."

"Right now?"

"Yes."

"But where? The dark room is in there," she pointed to the studio, "and I doubt they'll let me in to process film."

She was right. He thought about going back to his office building. If he recalled, there was a photo lab to process crime scene photos, but he wasn't sure he wanted to use that lab. It would involve red tape that he didn't have time to deal with right now.

There came a sharp knock on his window, and he started. Jessica. He motioned for her to get in the back seat.

Once she was in, he turned around. "Anything new from the police?"

"No. Just that there was no forced entry."

"Oh my god!" Lily nearly dropped the camera as she whirled in her seat to face Jessica.

"What?" Jim and Jessica both asked.

"The keys. I couldn't find the spare keys this afternoon."

"Do you know when you had them last?" Jessica asked before he could get the same question out.

"I never use them, but Mark said he thought he might have left them up in his loft a few weeks ago."

"Why were you looking for them today? I mean, if you never use them."

Jim caught the hint of suspicion in Jessica's voice and wondered if Lily had also heard it.

If she did, she didn't let on. "I was afraid a reporter might get a hold of them and bug the place."

"Are you serious?" Jessica shook her head and rested her brow on top of the front seat.

Lily's eyes narrowed. "You were here yesterday morning. You saw the chaos outside the studio. Besides, it looks like I had the right idea. Someone found the keys and used them, only for something much worse than bugging the place."

Jessica took a deep breath and nodded. "You're right. I'm sorry. It's no excuse, but when I'm scared, I get angry. Usually at the wrong people and at--"

Jim cut the apology short. "Right now, we need to find Mark, and our best lead could be sitting on that film right now. We have to find somewhere to develop it ASAP."

The three were silent for a moment. Finally Jessica said, "Why don't we take them to that lab we used before?" She looked at Jim. Lily focused on him as well, her face full of confusion.

It took him a second to understand what Jessica meant. "The one we used when Mark was locked up still?"

The fact that the photos Jim had taken that day with Jessica had caused Mark to dream his own water-boarding still caused Jim to shudder when he remembered it. At the time, he thought it had been a leak on his team, not evidence of a magical camera. Now he knew better.

A plus was that Mark had ended up working there after he'd been released. It was the perfect solution.

He glanced at the dashboard clock. It was close to five-thirty. "They won't open for hours."

Jessica shrugged. "So we call Gary and tell him to open up. He doesn't know about Mark's camera, but he's afraid of you, Jim. He'll do whatever you want." A trace of smile turned up the corners of her lips.

Gary wouldn't be the first person to fear him, but for

once, maybe that fear would work for him. "Good. Call the guy."

"I hope I still have his number." Jessica pulled out her cell and it cast a glow on her face as she scrolled through it. "I had to call a few times when Mark had problems that caused him to be late to work."

An hour later, he, Jessica and Gary waited while Lily developed the film. Gary had offered to run it through his machines, but Lily had said she preferred to develop it herself. Now, her choked scream from within the dark room told Jim and Jessica exactly when the film was done processing, and that whatever was on it wasn't good.

She came out with the still damp prints. Jim hated to look at them, but he had no choice.

Lily visibly trembled as she laid the photos out on the counter. Gary hurried over from where he'd been sitting half-asleep in a corner, Jim froze him with a look. "Sorry. These are classified."

Gary held up his hands. "Fine. I'll just go in my office and take a nap, since I was awakened so early this morning."

Jessica rearranged the five photos, her face stoic. Jim knew she was used to these kind of photos, but recognized that she was trying her best to detach, to gain emotional distance. He couldn't blame her. It was a survival mechanism for one in her profession. He'd learned it early on in his field as well.

One photo showed Mark half in his bed, half on the floor as dark clad figures held him. Another showed him entering the back of a van, and Jim swallowed hard at the rope around Mark's wrists and neck. He was clad in only a tattered t-shirt and sweatpants.

"Plates."

Jim tore his gaze from the photo and looked at Jessica. "What?"

She already had her phone out. "We can see the plate number as well as the make and model of the van. It's a start."

The third photo showed Mark on the ground in what appeared to be an alley. The scene was dimly lit, but his white t-shirt stood out in the darkness. The building they were behind had several doors visible and Jim squinted, making out a partial word and a complete second word. "It says, something son Textiles". He looked at the women. "Does that sound familiar to either of you?"

Lily shrugged helplessly, while Jessica looped her hair over her ear and peered more closely at the photo. "The warehouse district has a few used by textile manufactures, and Mark had the run in with the cult in that area. I bet they wouldn't stray too far from their home turf, so to speak."

The fourth photo showed him tied to a cross, his eyes screwed shut. The fifth showed a window with sunlight streaming in. It made no sense

.

CHAPTER TEN

"This area matches the photo, I think." Jim put the car in park.

Jessie angled her head and looked up at the old building. The sky was just beginning to turn pink in the east, but the side street was still very dark. "Lily, why don't you stay here while we check it out?"

Lily looked like she was going to argue, but instead quietly said, "Should I call an ambulance?"

"We don't know if one is needed. Remember, all of the images in the photos might not have happened yet." Jessie tapped Jim on the shoulder. "You have your weapon?"

Jim nodded and opened the center storage compartment, withdrawing his own gun. "This place looks deserted, though."

"Still, better to be prepared." Jessie exited the vehicle, scanning the alley for any movement. "What do you think, Jim? I don't see anything except some trash bins that need emptying." She looked around then squatted and pointed to the ground. "Lots of footprints here though. With this new snow, they can't be more than a few hours old."

The door closest to them had the faded words they had seen in the photo except now it was open a crack. Jim put his hand in the slit and pushed the door wider. He turned to Jessie and whispered, "I'll go first. Cover me."

Jessie nodded and pulled her gun. Ordinarily, she

would have rolled her eyes at his chivalry, but she was too keyed up and barely noticed it. "Right."

They slipped inside and paused to let their eyes adjust. Jim pointed at his nose, indicating that he smelled something.

She mouthed the word, 'Fire?' at him.

Jim nodded and pointed in the direction he was going to go. Swallowing hard, Jessie motioned for him to move forward. She followed behind him, her eyes darting around. There was a short hallway that opened into a warehouse. The windows on the opposite wall faced east, and a dim golden light illuminated the room. Jessie looked to her right, into the darkest corners, senses alert for danger. No matter how hard she tried to walk quietly, her footsteps echoed off the walls and she cringed. A beam of sunlight illuminated dust motes, turning them golden. The beam ended in a rectangle of light on the far end of the room.

"Good God! Taylor!" Jim stopped suddenly and Jessie stumbled into him. She looked over his shoulder, seeing nothing but the glowing remains of a fire. She raised her eyes.

A wave of shock and horror exploded through her. Mark was suspended by his hands...on a cross--just as Jim had said. His head hung, and Jessie couldn't tell if he was still alive. Frozen, she barely heard Jim tell her to call for an ambulance and back-up.

She fumbled for her cell phone, but training took over as she relayed the need for help. Even as she gave the dispatcher instructions, she hurried towards Mark, but stopped several feet away as the need to vomit overwhelmed her. She bent and swallowed convulsively, fighting it down.

"Jessie, I need your help!"

Jim's sharp, commanding tone snapped her out of her immobility and she rushed to his side. He pointed at the base of the cross, and she saw what she could only describe as a giant Christmas tree stand. The vertical part of the cross stood inside the holder and long curved legs angled off and were bolted onto the floor. Whoever had done this had planned well in advance.

"We need to try and lift this up and lay it down!" Jim had his shoulder against the vertical part, his arms wrapped around it. Jessie shuddered as her gaze fell on Mark's feet on the small platform just above Jim's head. She didn't know where to grab, and finally snaked her arm behind Mark's knees, the other at the small of his back. His skin was cold and she recoiled for a split second, terrified that he was dead. Swallowing down bile, she regained her hold at his back.

They grunted and strained, but after the wood swayed precariously and threatened to topple, they stopped, afraid that the pole would crash down and crush the suspended man.

Jim swiped his arm across his brow. "We need more people."

Mark's head lolled and a groan slipped from his lips. Jessie could have cried in relief. He was alive! Her elation dimmed when she took a closer look. Barely alive, from the looks of it. Blood ran down his arms in a thick trail and the floor beneath each hand was marred with large puddles. Just beneath his ribs, another wound bled freely, soaking into his sweatpants. Despite the chill in the air, sweat dripped and his hair was wet with it. A coarse rope circled his neck, and Jessie could see ugly purple bruises spreading out from beneath it. She touched the part that dangled down, wishing there was some way she could take it off him.

"Jessica, why don't you go show the fire department where we are?"

Jim's voice held a note of sympathy and she knew that he was trying to spare her witnessing Mark like this. But, he was right, the crew might waste time looking for them, so she turned and raced out of the building. In the far distance she heard sirens and willed them to drive faster.

Lily was pacing the sidewalk, her back to Jessie. At the noise of the door hitting the wall, she spun. "What?"

"We found him and he's alive. Whoever took him is gone, though."

Lily's shoulders sagged as she sobbed, "Thank God!"

She turned to enter the warehouse, but Jessie put out a restraining hand. "Wait! He's not in the best shape and we can't get at him until the fire department arrives."

Lily straightened and lifted her chin. "I'm going in there. I saw the pictures too. If they were right, and I can see by your face that they are, then he's going to need all the friends around him that he can get." With that, she shrugged off Jessie's hold.

"Okay, Lily. You're right, but at least hold on until the rescue squad gets here, then I'll go back in with you."

Lily opened her mouth to protest, but Jessie cut her off. "Look, I want to be there with him as much as you do, but there's nothing we can do until help arrives!"

They waited in silence, the sirens growing closer. Just before the rescue squad reached the building, Lily asked, her voice full of dread, "Are you sure he was alive?"

Jessie hesitated before answering. "Yeah, he was...but the bastards left him in bad shape."

* * *

Mark sensed movement and strained to lift his head. What did they plan to do to him now? Thirst overwhelmed him and his tongue felt thick. He'd give anything for a drink of water. Maybe they would give him one. If nothing else, it would prolong the fun they were having. Mark's last memory had been of the cult milling beneath him. Chanting and drumbeats had echoed in the warehouse, but they had seemed distant and disorganized. Someone had wondered aloud about breaking Mark's legs but Snake Eyes had told them no, because things would go too fast then. Mark hadn't been sure what he meant, but was thankful that he didn't have that added misery.

He arched his back in a futile attempt to relieve the strained muscles and pressure on his hands, but that movement intensified the pain in his palms. Mark couldn't help uttering a deep moan. The smallest movements sent shards of agony through his hands and so he stilled, his breathing rapid and shallow. Blinking, he tried to focus on the blurry forms in front of him. The room was lighter and a slow glance to his left showed sunlight beginning to spill into the room. The pink and gold looked beautiful and he tried to block out everything except the sunrise. His last sunrise.

How long had he been here? It seemed like days had passed since he had gone to bed, and he wasn't sure what time they had come for him, but his impression in the van had been that it was around two or three a.m. Very few cars had been on the streets. He guessed it was now almost seven. There was a sudden lurch and the cross swayed. Mark groaned, dropping his head and closing his eyes. The pain in his hands became exquisite. He whole being; his awareness telescoped down to the his palms. Nothing else existed.

* * *

"Hurry! He's in here!" Jessie pointed the way for the paramedics as they exited their squad, then motioned for Lily to follow her. The paramedics rushed in ahead of them, loaded down with their supply boxes. The first one stopped abruptly.

"What the hell?" He turned to look at Jessie. "What happened here?"

The second paramedic looked beyond his partner and his eyes widened. "Jesus Christ!"

"No, he's Mark Taylor and he needs your help," Jessie snapped and pushed the man firmly towards the cross. She turned and grasped Lily's elbow. "It might be best if you stand over here, okay?" Lily began to protest, but Jessie put her hands on the other woman's shoulders and gave her a squeeze. "We have to stay out of the way for now. It's going to get crazy in a minute, with a whole slew of people running around."

"But I feel like I need to *do* something." Lily shrugged Jessie's hands off and crossed her arms.

"I know. I do too, but we have to let the paramedics do their job, okay?"

Lily let out a deep breath and swiped at a tear at the corner of her eye. "You're right. That's the most important thing. I'm fine."

"Thank you." Jessie turned to see more help pouring into the room. "Come on." She put her hand on Lily's back. "Let's get a little closer." They moved to where Jim stood, his arms crossed, his expression hard.

Jessie watched silently while the firemen rigged ropes and first lifted the cross out of its stand and eased it down onto the floor. Even though the men did their best to be gentle, the cross jolted slightly as it met the cement, eliciting a strangled moan from Mark. Her stomach twisted.

Jessie tried not to focus on him, and on the horror she felt every time her gaze was pulled to his limp figure, but found it impossible to look away. She had a constant taste of bitterness in the back of her throat and swallowed audibly.

"You okay, Jessica?" Jim searched her face, concern in his eyes.

Jessie nodded and cleared her throat. "Yes. I just...this is..." She gave up, unable to form a coherent sentence about what she was feeling at that moment. Her revulsion at what was done to Mark almost overwhelmed her and her throat tightened. She crossed her arms. Lily rubbed her back, and Jessie felt grateful for her presence and silly for any jealousy she'd felt earlier. It was trivial now.

Jim looked at the flurry of activity and nodded. "I know what you mean. I think this ranks up there as one of the sickest things I've ever seen."

At that moment, something caused Mark to start thrashing his head, his back arching. His mouth opened and a hoarse series of protests mixed with moans poured out. Jessie hurried closer, feeling a need to do something. Jim and Lily only steps behind, but they had to stop short of reaching him as the paramedics surrounded him, and two more entered the warehouse, muttering curses and dragging a gurney behind them.

Lily's face was still wet with tears, but there was a desperate note of hope in her voice as she said, "He's going to be okay, right?"

Jim sighed. "I wish I knew."

One of the paramedics stood arms outstretched and bellowed, "Stop! Everybody just *stop* for a second!"

All activity ceased and they turned to the paramedic for direction. Mark quieted as well, his head turning weakly from side to side.

"Listen up. We all want to help him, but we have to do this right, okay?" The paramedic scanned all the members of his team, "We need to be very careful because we don't want to cause more damage. Do not pull the nails out. They need to do that at the hospital. What we have to do, is somehow get the nails separated from the wood while keeping his hands and feet as still as possible."

Another paramedic nodded and spoke up. "I think the eight inch bolt cutters will fit in between the victim and the wood. They shouldn't have any trouble cutting through these nails."

The first one nodded. "Good idea, John. Let's try it."

Jessie watched the one called Luke turn to a toolbox and pull out the tool. He moved to Mark's left arm. "Mark? Can you hear me?"

Mark's eyebrows raised as his head turned towards

the voice. "That's it, buddy. I'm going to insert a bolt cutter beneath your hand here, and snip that nail. It might hurt a bit, but I need you to try and hold still and not pull away. Do you understand?"

Mark opened his eyes and turned his head, looking up at the ceiling. For several seconds his eyes roved the upper reaches of the building before drifting closed. His lips began moving but only a whisper of sound came out. Luke leaned closer and turned his head to hear, holding his hand up for quiet from the rest of the crew. His eyes squinted in concentration then an expression of disbelief washed over his face as he sat back slowly.

"What did he say?" Jim stepped forward and Jessie realized that Mark might have told the paramedic something important that would help them catch the bastards who had done this to him.

Luke looked at Jim. "I...I think he said, 'Our Father, who art in heaven.'...and then he started saying something else. It might have been a prayer too, but it's all mixed up and jumbled."

"Oh." Jim sounded nonplussed and crossed his arms. Out of the corner of her eye, Jessie saw one medic make the sign of the cross.

The paramedic motioned for his crewmates to hang on tight to Mark's arm and then he leaned in, cutters in hand. "I need some more light!"

Someone aimed a bright flashlight on the trapped hand and Luke spoke once more to Mark "Okay, here we go, Mark."

He wiggled the tool into the slight gap and took time to assess his placement, peering into the tiny space he'd squeezed out between wood and flesh. "Looks good. Hold him tight!" His forearm muscles flexed as he exerted pressure on the handles. The nail snapped with a soft pop accompanied by a low moan by Mark.

Luke backed away and allowed another paramedic to ease Mark's arm down and Jessie shuddered at the agonized cry that the movement elicited from Mark. She turned away and in her haste, bumped into Lily. "Excuse me," she choked out as she side-stepped the other woman. Jessie didn't know where she intended to go, but she knew she couldn't watch any more of this. Lily's hand on her arm stopped her.

"Don't go. He needs us here." Her voice was calm despite the tears running down her face.

Jessie turned back, seeing that the paramedics were about to free the other hand. She quickly glanced away. "He doesn't even know we're here, Lily."

Lily's chin quivered in an instant of uncertainty before her resolve returned and she squared her shoulders. Her grip tightened on Jessie's arm. "I'm going closer."

Before Jessie could reply, Mark cried out again and this time, he began flailing his right arm at the paramedics, catching one on the jaw and leaving a bloody trail. Lily stopped in her tracks.

"Mark! It's okay, we're trying to help you!" Luke grabbed the flailing arm and tried to wrestle it back down, but was having a hard time of it. Despite Mark's injuries and weakened condition, his fear and desperation lent him extraordinary strength.

The other paramedics tried to help, but they literally had their own hands full. One man had been trying to start an IV on Mark's free hand, and was now leaning back, bloody IV needle held out of the way of the other paramedics; a thin stream of blood flowed from the attempted IV site. Two other firemen maintained their grip on Mark's legs, trying in vain to hold them completely immobile and the man who had been hit by Mark was swiping his jaw on his shoulder.

"Hold still, buddy!" Luke sounded frustrated and Jessie stepped forward, pulling Lily along with her. She nudged the man holding the needle out of the way.

"Let me through. I have his friend here. She might be able to calm him." She ached to be the one to calm Mark, but worried she might do more harm than good. They hadn't parted under the best circumstances.

The paramedic nodded and scooted back. "Go for it."

Lily sank to her knees and touched Mark's shoulder then moved her hand up to rest on his brow. "Mark? It's me. You're safe now." She stroked his hair back and he stilled. "Shh...that's it. Relax."

His head turned, and Jim saw him struggling to open his eyes. "Lily?" The hope in his voice tore at Jessie's heart.

"Yes, it's me. And Jessie and Jim too. Whoever did this is gone, okay?" Lily continued the rhythmic motion of feathering his hair back and Jessie could see the tension in Mark's body begin to ease. "There's a whole lot of people here trying to help you. Let them help you, Mark."

He blinked and his eyes roamed, seeking but unfocused, his brows knit in confusion. "Jessie's here?"

Jessie knelt beside Lily and put her hand lightly on his shoulder, surprised at how cold and clammy his skin felt. "Yeah, Mark, I'm right here. Hold still now and they'll have you...free... in just another minute. Got it?"

He nodded obediently. " 'kay". Mark sighed and his body went limp as he gave in to his exhaustion.

Jessie nudged Lily and motioned for them to step back to allow the medics more room to work. In a matter of minutes, his feet had been freed, but the medics taped them together, opting to allow the doctors to remove the long nail. They moved him to a gurney, hung bags of fluid and placed an oxygen mask over Mark's face.

He never stirred throughout the rest of the treatment and Jessie didn't know if that was a good sign or bad. She heard a blood pressure number tossed out by one paramedic and saw another quickly adjust an IV bag until what had been a slow, steady drip of fluid into the the line became a fast stream.

Luke swore and tossed a blanket over Mark, tucking it around him; the paramedic's hands a blur as he secured Mark to the gurney. "Let's wrap and run, guys!"

CHAPTER ELEVEN

The ambulance sped away leaving a spray of slush in its wake. The scene inside the warehouse had been so surreal...so bizarre that Jessie felt like she needed to re-orient herself. She leaned against the wall of the building, aware of Lily's impatient pacing. She was sympathetic to the other woman's desire to rush to the hospital, but she needed just a a minute to process everything that had happened. Jim was still inside talking on his cell phone to someone so they had to wait anyway.

She let her head fall back, closed her eyes and took a deep breath. She let it out slowly. After repeating the exercise five times, she opened her eyes. Above her, the sun glinted off icicles forming on the downspouts and eaves of the building. Last night's snow was already beginning to melt as the early spring warmth battled with the retreating winter over which season would hold Chicago in its grip for the day.

Excited chatter and the idling of engines caught her attention. A half-dozen reporters and photographers milled at one end of the alley along with a network news van.

Jessie pushed away from the wall and glared at the offending van. She saw the disgust that she felt mirrored on Lily's face.

"Can you believe those vultures?" Lily moved a step

ahead of Jessie and stepped towards the crowd, but Jessie took her arm.

"Listen to me Lily. The last thing you should do is talk to them."

"I don't care. I need to rip them a--"

"I get it. I do. But they'll start grilling you about what happened to Mark, and in the emotional state you're in now, you are easy pickings."

Lily's chin came up. "I don't think so, but you're right. It would piss them off if I don't talk to them at all."

"There you go." Jessie steered her towards Jim's car. "Why don't you wait in the car, and I'll go see what's keeping Jim. Then we can head to the hospital."

Lily nodded, her eyes still reflecting her anger, but she agreed. "Try to hurry."

As Jessie returned to the warehouse, a television reporter called out to her and tried to flag her down.

"Detective! Will you come and talk to us for just a minute?"

Jessie wondered how they knew her, but in her experience, reporters seemed to have even more sources than cops. She ignored the reporter and practically ran back into the warehouse.

She spotted Jim in a group with a couple of uniformed officers. As she approached, she noted the remains of the fire still glowing faintly and had a vision of what the scene must have looked like to Mark. It stopped her in her tracks. Medea's description of her similar ordeal filled in some of the details in her mind and Jessie's imagination completed the picture.

The cult circling and swaying in time to their Satanic chants would have been eerie and frightening. In the scene she created in her head, the red glowing fire crackled and popped, the sounds echoing in the far reaches of the warehouse. Mark must have been terrified. Her stomach rebelled at the images and she bent; her hand to her mouth, afraid she was going to vomit.

"Jessie? Are you okay?"

She turned to find Dan approaching her.

Not sure if she was or not, she didn't answer him at first and had to swallow several times before she felt it was safe to speak. She straightened. "Yeah. I think so. I thought I was going to be sick there for a minute."

Dan nodded. "Well, you wouldn't be the first."

Jessie glanced sharply at him. "You too?"

It was hard to see in the dimness, but Jessie was pretty sure the man's face had a tint of red staining his cheeks. He cleared his throat and looked down, his hands buried in his pockets. "Just don't go over to the far corner. I've already investigated that spot."

Jessie glanced in that direction and wrinkled her nose. "Right." Looking back at Dan, she said, "I didn't know you were here."

"You were pretty preoccupied, but I arrived about the time they put Taylor on the gurney."

She shivered. "It was horrible, Dan."

"I know. As soon as I heard it come over the radio, I headed over."

Jessie sighed. "I came back in to find Jim. Have you seen him?"

"He was over there a minute ago." Dan pointed to a door behind the spot where the cross had stood. "There's evidence the cult left through that door, probably only minutes before you guys got here. We think they had someone monitoring a police scanner."

"Great." She shook her head, wishing she hadn't called in the silent alarm. "Once I find Jim, we'll be taking Lily to the hospital or to get her car at the studio, whichever one she wants, and then I'll be back to help with the investigation."

Dan shook his head. "No, you won't."

"Excuse me?" She wasn't sure she'd heard him right. It was her case. She'd been the one to track down the plates and the van, had called in to find the address of possible textile warehouses. Plus, she had been handling the Medea case, which bore striking similarities and was sure to be related.

"You're too close to this one, Jess. I think you should take yourself off it."

"How am I too close?" She glared at him, practically daring him to mention anything about her relationship with Mark.

"Come on. You know I'm right. Are you going to make me say it?"

She narrowed her eyes. "Say what?" Her hands rested on her hips.

Dan took a deep breath and looked away for a brief moment before meeting Jessie's eyes. "You still have feelings for Taylor." He put up his hands in a stop motion. "Look, I don't care, but it might hamper the investigation or, even worse, when we catch the guys who did this, it could come up at the trial. You wouldn't want to jeopardize the outcome, would you?"

Crossing her arms, Jessie remained silent for almost a minute. Did she still have feelings for Mark? She felt her face heat up. If she were honest with herself, she'd admit it was possible.

On the other hand, a defense lawyer could twist all kinds of innocent things into something sinister. Like how she and Mark had lived together for six months.

Or worse, what if they brought up Jessie's role in Mark's imprisonment? How she had ultimately been the one who had listened to Mark and dug deeper, proving his innocence? It had been the right thing to do, but would she have put her career on the line for just anyone? A smart lawyer would draw connections and let the jury think there was more going on between her and Taylor than a past relationship.

Was she willing to take that risk? Jessie thought of all Taylor had gone through and decided that she wasn't. She sighed. "Fine. You'll keep me updated?"

Dan nodded. "Of course."

Jessie nodded and turned away.

"Oh, and Jessie?"

She stopped and looked over her shoulder. "Yes?"

"You'll let me know how he's doing?"

She couldn't help smiling. Dan might tease her about Taylor and all the scrapes he got into, but Jessie had always suspected that deep down, he liked the guy. "I'll call you on your cell as soon as I hear anything."

* * *

Mark felt himself lifted, the movement wrenching a hoarse groan from him. He shivered. For a few minutes, he'd felt a little warmer, but now all the blankets were gone. Maybe he'd kicked them onto the floor. Conversation swirled around him and he tried to follow it.

He struggled to open his eyes, but even as the thought occurred to him, he felt himself drifting, his mind jumping to something else. Was he still in the warehouse?

"What the hell happened to him?" The voice was deep and Mark had the impression of someone big. Kern? The voice didn't sound menacing enough.

"It's crazy, Doc. Some bastards crucified him. Be careful, the nails are still in his hands and feet."

"You've got to be kidding."

"Look for yourself. See his hands?"

Mark felt his hand raised and unwrapped.

"Ouch." It was the deep voice again, this time, sounding sympathetic.

The manipulation of his hand hurt and he attempted to withdraw it, moaning softly. As soon as he did, whoever held him released his wrist and loosely re-wrapped his palm. "It's okay, Mark." An annoying beep sounded at regular intervals.

"Hey, Doc, did you see his blood pressure? It's only eighty-two over forty-six."

"Is the IV wide open?"

"Yes. Both of them. We started another in the squad on the way in."

He remembered hearing that voice before. It had told him to hold still and then his hands had been freed. It was a voice he could trust. It just occurred to him that the voices were talking about him. About what had happened. He flashed on the memory of the nail being held to his palm and he instinctively tried to move his hand. A wave of pain washed through him as his stomach roiled and he tasted bile. Intense agony radiated from his left shoulder, and his belly burned. His head and his feet added their own melody to the symphony of pain.

"Has he been conscious at all?" Hands skimmed over Mark's head, pausing on a tender spot on the back. "We'll need some x-rays of the head and a c-spine. Maybe a CT too."

"He sort of woke up at the scene, spoke to a friend and the detective who was with her. Other than that, he's been out of it."

The hands continued their exploration, and Mark tensed as they rested on his left shoulder.

"Well, that's obviously dislocated."

Mark wanted to talk to one of the voices, ask what was going on, but his throat didn't cooperate. Once, as a kid, he'd had strep throat and that misery paled in comparison to the raw, bruised feeling he was experiencing now. He had the sensation of trying to suck air in, but never getting quite enough. Exhaling was even harder, and in his mind, he pictured a blown up balloon with the neck pinched off. A little air could get out, but not all of it. He had the urge to sit up.

"Whoa! Lay back, Mark!"

"Can't-" Pressure on his chest prevented him from sitting. He gasped, "Please..." The voices began fading and he struggled to listen to them.

"Sats are dropping."

"Yeah, I know. You have him on a hundred percent?"

"Yep. But he has audible stridor. He's not moving much air."

"Yeah, he's working pretty hard."

Mark lost track of what they said next, his sole focus getting the air in and out.

Next, he heard a metallic click as his head was tipped

with his chin pointing toward the ceiling. The position made him feel like he was strangling, but he had no energy left to fight them.

"Let me take a look here...I need some suction."

Mark felt cold hard metal against his tongue. He gagged, tasting blood and renewed his efforts to sit. The guy with the deep voice had to be another one of Kern's followers. It was the only thing that made sense. Kern must have thought up another form of torture.

Someone grabbed Mark's right hand, and another set of hands held his head still. Yet another invaded his belly, pushing and prodding. Someone or something was squeezing his throat. Was the noose still there? He panicked.

With a strangled cry, he bucked his hips and shoulders in an attempt to escape the hands. A heavy weight across his legs kept him from leaping off whatever he was lying on. Ignoring the pain and the shouts to calm down, he twisted and turned; using his head to try to bash anyone who was within reach.

The metal disappeared from his mouth and a mask with cool air covered his nose. He dimly wondered why they had stopped, but decided he didn't care why. All he wanted was more air.

"We going to have to sedate him. Give him two milligrams of Versed."

* * *

"I'm looking for a patient by the name of Mark Taylor."

A nurse at the desk looked up, snapping a chart

closed. "Are you family?"

Jessie flashed her badge. "I'm part of the investigation and I need to speak to the doctor as soon as he or she is available." Technically, she was still on the case since she hadn't officially taken herself off of it.

The nurse glanced at the badge, unimpressed. "There's a waiting room down the hall to the left. Doctor Jenkins will be out as soon as he can." She turned and put the chart in a slot on the wall.

Jim leaned over the desk and gave the nurse a polite smile. "Listen, Carol, I know you aren't allowed to tell us anything. That's fine. It's just that Mark's only family, his parents, are out of the country right now. We're the closest thing he has."

"Can you tell us anything?" Lily added her own plea and the fear and desperation it contained softened the nurse and she stepped close to the desk again.

"I know that they were getting ready to put a tube down his throat to help him breathe." The nurse touched Lily's arm. "I'm sorry I don't know more, but don't worry, Dr. Jenkins is the best." Coming around the desk, the nurse said, "Won't you all come with me? There's a quiet room you can wait in. I heard one of the paramedics mention lots of press were already at the scene, so it would probably be better for you to wait somewhere private."

The nurse led them to a small room with two love-seats and an easy chair. "There's coffee across the hall in the lounge; feel free to help yourself. I'm pretty sure it's even fresh."

Jim nodded. "Thank you."

"I should call Mark's parents." Lily sat on the edge of

one of the loveseats, worrying the nail on her thumb. She put her hands to her temples. "I should have paid closer attention when Mark mentioned something about them going on a vacation. I'll have to check his desk and see if he has their contact information anywhere."

"Why don't we just wait and see? Maybe it's not that bad and he can call them himself later today."

Lily glanced at Jim, but she didn't appear to have heard him.

Jessie stood, too keyed up to sit still for more than a minute. "I could really use some of that coffee. How about you?"

Lily shrugged. "Sure."

"Jim?"

He nodded.

"Okay, I'll be right back."

Thirty minutes later, Jessie tossed a half of a cup of cold coffee in the trash. They hadn't heard anything yet and she opened her mouth to tell Lily that she was going to go demand some information when the door to the room opened.

A tall distinguished looking man with dark hair, graying at the temples, entered. He stopped a few steps in, his blue-eyed gaze touched on Lily and Jim and then swung towards Jessie.

"Hello." He stuck out his hand. "I'm Doctor Jenkins. I'm sorry I haven't had a chance to get back here to let you all know what's going on until now."

Jessie shook his hand. "Detective Jessica Bishop, Chicago PD, and this is Lily Martin, friend and business partner of Mark Taylor's and Jim Sheridan...a friend."

Lily stood. "How is he, Doctor?"

The doctor cleared his throat. "I take it none of you are family?'

Jessie shook her head. "No."

Lily took a step closer. "We're the closest he has right now. His parents are on a cruise...I think in the Mediterranean. I'm not even sure how to contact them. Mark and I have been business partners for five months now. We're good friends."

Dr. Jenkins sank onto the easy chair with a sigh and then shrugged. "Well, he's stable for now. His most serious injuries are to his throat and the stab wound in his abdomen. I had to insert a tube to keep his airway open, but in a few days, the swelling should go down and that will come out. He's breathing entirely on his own, so no worries there."

No worries? Jessie dropped onto the edge of the love seat. She'd seen enough severely injured people in her line of work to know what a breathing tube was and what it meant. They were never good.

The doctor continued, "His abdominal wound is a little more troublesome. He seems to have some internal bleeding from that so he'll be on his way to surgery for an exploratory laparotomy-they're going to take a look around inside his belly and see if he has any active bleeding. I don't expect there to be too much damage from the location of the wound. It missed everything vital."

He clasped his hands and paused. "Right now, his blood pressure is our biggest problem. He lost quite a bit of blood through his various injuries and was rather traumatized. His body temp is low and he's shocky. We've given him warmed fluids along with medications and we're monitoring his blood pressure closely. The thing he has going for him is he's young and looks to have been in excellent health. Those factors will hopefully work in his favor to overcome that."

Lily voiced what Jessie was thinking, "Hopefully?"

"I'm fairly confident that he'll be fine. I have to tell you that in addition, he has a probable concussion, lots of bruises, a dislocated shoulder and, of course the injuries to his hands and feet. None of those are life-threatening, but they're painful and it's going to be awhile before he's back to normal." He stood and tried to stifle a yawn. "I'm sorry. I just finished up my shift."

"Thank you, Dr. Jenkins. I know you must be tired, but we appreciate that you took the time to tell us all of this." Jim stood and clasped the doctor's hand again while Jessie did her best to pull her scattered emotions together.

"You're welcome, Mr. Sheridan."

CHAPTER TWELVE

"Morning, Tina. How's he doing?" Matthew Jenkins greeted the nurse as he breezed into his patient's room.

Since he had admitted Mark Taylor three days ago, the papers had been full of stories on the man and Matt was fascinated, but also worried for his patient. Not just for his physical condition, but for his mental state as well. It had been almost a blessing that Taylor had required sedation due to the breathing tube. Matthew hoped that by the time Mark was alert enough to be aware of the media circus that things would have calmed down.

At first, the stories in the news had been full of wonder, but now the press was beginning to turn against the guy. Some radio personalities wondered if Taylor had arranged the whole thing, pointing to his visit to the Medea girl and the job interview as evidence. The rumors had fired up the airwaves with debate. Matt felt guilty, but he found himself tuning in every chance he got, which, with Chicago's traffic, meant at least an hour every day during his commute. Most of the callers had silly conspiracy theories, but occasionally, a caller would get through who would tell a story of Taylor doing some good deed for him or her. Matt was sure that not all of them actually had a tale to tell, but some of the stories rang true.

One in particular stood out because the caller claimed

it had happened only the day before the incident. That man spoke of Taylor catching the man's child and then having lunch with the caller's family. The man insisted that he'd called the radio station to defend Taylor more than to relate any heroic deeds and seemed reluctant to give too many details, but he did mention that Taylor had hit the back of his head against the pavement. That interesting detail matched a bruise Matt had found on the back of Mark's head. It had the characteristics of an older bruise, with yellowing at the edges. The one beside it was obviously new and the injury that had required stitches a few days prior had been to the right side of the head.

In fact, the reason that Matt had remembered the bruise at all was because when he'd initially seen it, he wondered about possible complications to having three head injuries in such a close period of time. It was fortunate for Taylor that he'd had no brain swelling or bleeding.

Matt supposed that there were some crackpots out there who might go to such extremes to garner attention, but after speaking to the people who actually knew Mark Taylor, he found it hard to believe the speculation that the whole thing had been staged.

Cards, letters and flowers had poured into the hospital for their famous patient. So many, that his business partner advised the hospital to give most of the flowers away to other patients.

Matt stood at the foot of Taylor's bed and glanced at the windowsill to where a small sample of the gifts were displayed. For the most part, his patient had been kept too sedated to notice any of them. A couple of times they had tried to decrease the sedation but the results had been scary. The poor guy had awakened extremely disoriented and fighting. They'd had to restrain his right hand and his left was in a sling due to the dislocated shoulder, but that hadn't stopped Taylor from straining to get free. At the moment, Mark was still, his breathing unlabored and his color good, but the livid bruises on his neck had taken on an even more colorful hue as the edges began fading. The yellow contrasted sharply with the still vibrant purple that circled his neck like a morbid tattoo.

"Good morning Doctor Jenkins. Mark's doing a bit better. His blood pressure has been stable and all his labs came back within normal limits. Oh, and the radiologist's report says that the laryngeal swelling is down." Tina adjusted the flow rate of the IV.

Matthew Jenkins grinned. "Great! I'm going to take a look at his chart, and then we'll see about waking him up and pulling that tube."

He couldn't help feeling a little excited about finally being able to meet the man.

* * *

Mark blinked several times and tried to focus. Above him were white ceiling tiles with little tiny holes in them. A faint water stain darkened the corner of one. His eyes felt gritty and dry and he gagged on a hard plastic thing in his throat. It hurt. Lots of things hurt. He reached to remove the object, but found that his hand was tied down. Panic raced through him and he pulled as hard as he could against the bonds. The effort made him gag again and he tried to call for help. Nothing. The only sound he could make was an awful raspy whistling as his breath moved inside the tube.

What the hell was going on? Mark quit fighting, but his chest heaved as he tried to take stock of the situation. He turned his head, wincing at the stab of pain as the tube shifted in his throat, gagging him again. Bright sunshine streamed into the room hitting his eyes like shards of glass. He felt foggy and muddled and wondered about all the plants on the windowsill. This room definitely wasn't his loft. A dark-haired woman dressed in pink scrubs crossed in front of his vision and closed the blinds. Bless her, she must have read his mind and at least now he knew where he was.

Mark relaxed and let his head fall back against the pillows. Snatches of memory from his ordeal played in his mind; memories of Kern, the chanting and the warehouse. He closed his eyes and tried to push it all out of his head. He saw again the large wooden cross and his breathing quickened. How had he made it out of there? His last coherent memory was of seeing the sun rise. He had thought for sure it was his last.

"Good morning, Mark. I'm Tina, I'll be your nurse today." She checked the tubing on an I.V. in his arm. "Do you remember what happened to you?"

Mark looked at her eyes, saw the barely concealed pity and turned his head. Slowly, he nodded.

* * *

"Now take a big breath!"

Mark tried to obey the nurse's request, but choked as the tube scraped up and out of his throat. He coughed hard and followed by a groan when the coughing caused the pain in his belly to flare. Lying back against the pillows, he closed his eyes, starting when he felt a cool washcloth wipe against his mouth. He swallowed. There was still pain, but the removal of the tube was a big improvement.

"Mark?"

He opened his eyes. "Yeah?" It came out more as a croak than an actual word, but it was the first word he'd spoken in three days.

"Are you having any trouble breathing?"

Mark took a deep breath. Except for some abdominal pain caused by inhaling so deeply, he didn't have any trouble. "No." He tried to clear his throat; grimacing at how raw it felt-- like someone had taken a metal grill brush and swirled it around down there.

Tina swiped the damp cloth along his neck, a dry towel following behind. The personal care embarrassed him and he didn't want to think of what else had been wiped and cleaned while he'd been out of it. Her brown eyes lifted from the task and met his gaze. "Try not to talk too much. We'll see how you do and if everything is good, I'll get you some ice chips in a little while, okay?"

It crossed his mind that if she didn't want him to speak, then she shouldn't have asked a question. Especially since nodding his head wasn't something he was eager to do either, but if a cup of ice awaited him at the end of the line, he'd do whatever she wanted. "Okay."

He didn't have a whole lot he wanted to say anyway. The last three days had been a blur. Mark vaguely recalled waking up a few times, but the details were sketchy. He remembered the blind panic he'd felt one time when he'd found that he was unable to free his arms. The room had been dark and he had thought he was still in the warehouse. When he'd tried to call for help, he'd gagged on the tube and tried to bend his head down to his hand to pull the offending object only to be firmly pushed back against the mattress. It embarrassed him now to think of how he must have behaved, all wild and fighting everyone.

* * *

Although he was more awake than he had been, Mark spent most of the day sleeping. Lily had come by. He remembered that, but it seemed like one minute she was there, the next she was gone and the clock had skipped ahead several hours. The biggest event had been the ice chips. After keeping those down and not having any trouble swallowing, he'd graduated to a small cup of lemon-lime pop. He figured he hadn't eaten since the night before he'd been abducted from his loft, but found he didn't have much appetite. The pop had been enough to fill him up.

The room grew dimmer, the bustle outside in the halls settled down, and Mark shut his eyes once more, wondering just before he drifted off, how he could still feel tired when he'd done nothing but sleep for three days.

A hand shook his shoulder, and Mark's eyes flew open as he gasped and blindly swung his arm in that direction. Dimly it registered that soft cloth brushed his fingertips and there was a clatter as someone stumbled. The room wasn't completely dark; light from the hallway spilled in and he blinked when he recognized his surroundings.

"Hey! Take it easy, Mark! I'm just here to check your vitals." He recognized Brenda, the nurse from the night before, as she stepped close to the bed, her expression wary.

Embarrassment flooded through him even as he sank back against the raised bed. "Sorry. I didn't hurt you, did I?"

"No, I'm fine, don't worry about it." She reached up and angled the I.V. bag, peering at the fluid level before meeting Mark's gaze and folding her hands on the bed-rail with a sigh. "And I'm the one who should be sorry. You'd think I would know by now to make a little noise and to call your name before touching you."

Her reminder of the previous night and the similar incident only served to further embarrass him and he felt his face burning. At least the room was still very dim. Unable to look her in the face, he mumbled another apology and closed his eyes, hoping she'd hurry and finish what she had to do. He was okay in the daytime when they would wake him up because the room was light and it was immediately apparent where he was, but night was harder. Even without someone touching him, he frequently awoke in a panic, his heart racing.

Brenda took his blood pressure reading, popped a thermometer in his mouth, and stuck a clip on his finger. Various beeps sounded and the devices were removed. "Hmm... looks like you're running a little temp. I'll get some acetaminophen for you."

Mark sighed, wondering if the fever was going to delay his discharge. He'd hoped to go home in a day or so, but at least he was no longer on a monitor.

Images from that night would flash through his mind

at random times... even when he was thinking about something else entirely and at night, with no distractions, it was even harder to keep the nightmares at bay. If he could, he'd just stay awake all the time. As much as he wanted to leave the hospital, the thought of sleeping in his loft made his skin crawl. Mark shuddered. Somehow, he'd have to get over it.

"Are you cold? Getting chills?"

Mark started at the sudden question, not realizing that Brenda had returned with his medication. Now that she mentioned it, he became aware that he was shivering and it wasn't just from the images in his head. "Yeah, I guess it is a little cold in here."

Brenda frowned. "Here, take these and I'll be back in an hour or so to take your temp again."

He tossed the pills back, and fumbled with the water glass. After washing the medication down, he took a few more sips. His throat still hurt from the tube and the water felt cool and soothing. Tugging the covers up, he settled down to try and get a little more sleep before the nurse returned, and then shortly after that, if he had their schedule figured out, the lab rats would come and draw blood. He yawned and wondered how doctors ever expected anyone to get better when the patients were continually awakened.

* * *

In the morning, his temp was near normal and he felt half-way human again.

"Good morning, Mark." His doctor swept into the room, his white coat flapping behind him. "I'm Doctor

Matt Jenkins. I doubt you remember me very well." He laughed and his eyes crinkled into a pleasant expression. "How are you feeling?"

"Okay. Better than I did." Mark only vaguely recalled the man coming into his room yesterday after the tube had been pulled. The doctor had tried to ask him some questions, but Mark hadn't been able to keep his eyes opened.

"You sound a lot better too. I think we'll advance you to a soft diet. How does that sound?" He jotted something down on Mark's chart then set it on the bedside table and stepped right up to the bed.

Mark would have shrugged if he could. It didn't matter to him. He nodded instead. "Sure."

"Let me take a look at your incisions." Dr. Jenkins untied the back of Mark's gown and eased it down. Quickly, he pulled the tape off one side of the incision in Mark's shoulder. "It looks good." He removed the entire dressing and tossed it into a trash can. "You don't need that anymore."

His exam moved down to Mark's abdomen and Mark tried not to wince when the doctor's fingers lightly pressed near the wound. He didn't say anything this time, and his mouth set in a grim line before he re-tied Mark's gown.

Sitting in the chair Lily had used earlier, Dr. Jenkins grabbed the chart and began writing again. Idly, Mark watched him, wondering at the other man's expression. Was something wrong? He looked pissed off.

Sighing heavily, the doctor stood again. "Okay, now let me just take a quick peek at your hands and feet." He unwrapped the bandage and Mark watched the other man's face instead of looking at his wound.

"Can you make a fist?"

Mark grimaced and clenched his right hand as hard as he could, which wasn't very hard at all. He could barely hold a paper cup and even that was a challenge.

The doctor ran the tip of his pen along Mark's pinky finger and Mark pulled his hand back at the sharp sensation. Jenkins glanced up at Mark and smiled. "That's good. I was testing for sensitivity there. You're very lucky. You could have wound up with permanent nerve damage."

Mark shook his head and remarked dryly, "Yeah. I'll try to remember how lucky I am."

Dr. Jenkins glanced up sharply, not missing Mark's sarcasm but choosing to keep any comments he had to himself as he re-wrapped the wound.

Mark tried to smile to take the bite out of his previous comment, but he was incapable of forming his mouth into a curve and closed his eyes in embarrassment instead, feeling like a first class jerk. None of this was the doctor's fault. He opened his eyes but kept his gaze fixed on the sheets bunched around his waist. "Sorry about that, Doc."

"No need to apologize. I'd be pretty pissed too if I were you." He walked around to the other side of the bed. "Let's take a look at this hand." He repeated the thing with the pen, and this time, Mark didn't feel the need to pull back. He could feel it, but it was more distant, a pressure more than anything sharp.

"Hmmm... it could be temporary. Can you make a fist?"

Mark tried and his fingers curled, but it was even weaker than the other hand. His little finger didn't curl as much as the others. His eyes flew to the doctor's. "It's not working as well as the other one." He tried to keep the fear out of his voice.

"No, it's not, but it could be temporary and with some physical therapy, you could regain all or most of your normal function."

Mark absorbed that and prayed that the doctor was right. Then he wondered why he bothered to pray at all. He'd prayed before and it hadn't stopped the crucifixion from happening. His jaw clenched and he felt bitterness rise up within him. At the very least, there could have been a hint of what was going to happen in the camera. He'd done so much for that damn camera and now, when he needed help, it had abandoned him.

The doctor moved onto his feet and seemed satisfied with the results of those tests. "I'd like to get you up walking today. It's going to hurt a bit, but you'll recover faster from the abdominal surgery if you're up moving around." Jenkins moved over to the sink, washed his hands, and dried them with a paper towel as he returned to the chair. He crossed his legs and opened the chart once more. "As long as you don't try running a marathon, your feet should be okay."

Mark barely heard the joke and only glanced at the doctor in confusion.

Apparently realizing his attempt at humor had fallen flat, Dr. Jenkins leaned forward, his expression serious. "Mark, would you like to talk to someone? A psychiatrist? Or clergy? We have a fantastic chaplain here at the hospital. I could send him in later."

Mark shook his head. "I don't think so. I'm okay." He avoided the doctor's eyes and leaned back, his gaze fixed on the water stain. Maybe he wasn't completely okay, but he would be. Eventually.

CHAPTER THIRTEEN

Sweat popped out on Mark's forehead and he dipped his head to swipe the moisture with his shoulder. Gritting his teeth, he took another step. Every time his foot made contact with the floor, it felt like stepping on an upturned knife. He swallowed hard and bit his lip in determination. He couldn't remain sitting for the next few weeks while his feet healed.

"That's it! Good job, Mark." Wayne, his physical therapist, smiled in encouragement. "Just a little bit more." He gripped Mark's right elbow with one hand and his other reached for a nearby chair, angling it to make it easier for Mark to sit down. "Here you go." Wayne stepped aside to allow Mark access.

Heaving a sigh of relief, Mark sat and attempted to catch his breath. He looked at the ten feet he'd covered between the chair and his bed and shook his head. "Jeez, how pathetic is it that I feel like I just ran a marathon?"

The therapist laughed. "Well, you've been flat on your back for about four days. It doesn't take long. Add your injuries to that, and it's no wonder you're short of breath."

"Believe it or not, I was in decent shape before...before...." Mark floundered, seeing something flicker in the other guys eyes. He'd seen similar looks flit across several other people's faces. It was a look that said they were uncomfortable with the subject. Mark averted his gaze. That was okay; he wasn't comfortable with it either.

Wayne stepped over to the computer in the corner of the room and began charting. Every few seconds, Mark would catch the man tossing a glance his way and Mark supposed he was commenting in the chart about how the session had gone.

Uncomfortable with the scrutiny, he looked out the window and his mind flashed back to the warehouse. The images springing up vividly, so strong, he could almost smell the fire, hear the chanting and feel the scratch of the spikes against his skin. His foot twitched. He stared through the glass, not seeing anything, his thoughts still mired in the past nightmare.

With an almost physical effort, Mark shoved the memories into a corner of his mind and took a deep breath. He searched for something else to focus on and spotted a man and dog across the street in a park. That was safe. He wondered what kind of dog it was. It looked like it might be part Lab, but the ears were wrong.

Whatever breed it was, it was definitely energetic and obviously enjoyed being outdoors as it raced around. Occasionally, the man would throw a stick for the animal to fetch. Mark smiled when one attempt at retrieving ended with the dog skidding through a pile of dirty snow and sliding on his side in a patch of mud. The dog scrambled to his feet and shook his fur. Even from his distance, Mark saw water and bits of mud fly in every direction. Then the dog, without missing a beat, found the stick and returned it to its master.

Sunlight flashed off something and Mark blinked at

the glare. Several news trucks had pulled into the circle drive, and it was the sun's reflection off of one of the satellite dishes mounted on top of one that had distracted him. A crowd of people hovered near the front entrance to the hospital so he rose up a little in the chair and squinted, wondering what was going on.

"Hey, Wayne, did something big happen?" Mark raised an eyebrow at the therapist and nodded at the crowd outside.

Wayne stepped over to the window and glanced out, then shot a look at Mark before looking down at his feet and clearing his throat. "Uh, no. They're just here to find out stuff about...ah, about one of our patients."

Mark took in the scene and then Wayne's demeanor and the way he didn't quite meet Mark's eyes when he announced that he'd see Mark tomorrow for their next session.

That was when Mark knew. Until that moment, he'd hoped...prayed... that his experience hadn't made the news. He clenched his jaw and swallowed, his focus dropping to his hands.

"Do you want to stay up in the chair awhile?" Wayne's voice was bright. Too bright.

"Sure." Whatever. It didn't matter. Mark plucked at a loose piece of tape.

"All right then, well I guess we're done for today. When I come back tomorrow, I'll give you some exercises you can do with your hands to help strengthen them too."

"Great. Thanks, Wayne." Mark tried to force some cheer into his voice and failed miserably. He kept his head lowered, barely aware of when the therapist left the room. Did everyone in the world know? How was he ever going to face anyone again? What about his parents? Had anyone reached them? He couldn't imagine how they would feel when they found out what had happened. Mark began to run his hand through his hair and realized that he couldn't do that with the I.V. and bandage. He dropped his hand with a growl of frustration.

"Mark? Are you okay?" His day nurse appeared at his door.

He took a deep breath and lifted his head, pasting on a smile. "Yeah. I'm fine." He couldn't remember her name and the energy required to look over at the dry erase board to find out didn't seem worth the effort. Her name tag was attached to her scrubs, but he couldn't read it from this distance.

"Since you're up, do you want to try taking a shower?"

That idea appealed to him and he sat a little straighter. He felt grungy and the thought of feeling clean, truly clean, sounded wonderful. "Yeah. I'd like that."

* * *

"There, that should do it." The nurse taped the plastic bag around Mark's arm, protecting his IV site from water and then untied the back of the hospital gown. She had helped him into the bathroom and he sat on a plastic chair trying to act like he didn't hate needing help to do something that he'd been doing alone since he was six years old.

"We can leave the bandages on your hands and feet and I'll change them when you're done. I left the shampoo and soap in the stall and I'll put some clean towels on the chair when you get up. If you feel dizzy or have any problems, use the pull string to call for help, understand?" She threw some extra tape in the trash. "And don't forget to let me know when you're done so I can re-connect your IV. You're due for your antibiotic in a little while."

Mark nodded. "Yeah, I will. Thanks." He stood and waited a moment to get used to the pain in his feet. It was the bending of the foot that caused the most pain, so in an effort to minimize the discomfort, he shuffled, sliding one foot a few inches and following with the other foot.

The top of the shampoo was tricky to get off with only one hand, especially since that one was only partially working. His left arm hung at his side, useless for all intents and purposes. He'd caught a glimpse of the incision in the mirror and it wasn't pretty. Still, it was a basic surgical incision and he hadn't felt squeamish. The one on the left side of his abdomen was worse because every time he looked at it, he saw Kern's face as he plunged the knife in.

Mark had trouble grasping with his right hand, and wondered how he was going to get the shampoo out of the bottle. Luckily, it was a very small bottle, not much bigger than a travel size and he finally managed to squeeze some onto his left palm. Then he dropped the bottle, unable to keep a grip on it. He swiped the stuff out of his left hand onto the other and did his best to soap up his head.

It was a good thing that this was a hospital and presumably had huge hot water tanks. This was going to take awhile. Hoping he'd at least semi-washed everything, he closed his eyes, letting the hot spray rinse him. The sharp needles of water felt good. Cleansing. In here, he didn't smell the stink of antiseptic and other even less pleasant hospital odors. Just soap and shampoo. He could almost pretend he was home.

It was the first time he'd been alone since he'd gone to bed four nights ago. This was just what he needed, a few moments of privacy, moments to gather his thoughts and digest everything that had happened. Since waking up yesterday, he'd had doctors, nurses and, visitors parading in and out of his room in a constant stream.

Between the disruptions and the pain meds, he'd only briefly thought about the reason he was here in the first place. The grace period was over. The memories, the fear and horror he'd felt re-surfaced, bubbling up inside of him like a cauldron of boiling water.

Why? Why did it happen? Why him? Mark raised head, eyes closed. The water pelted his face and stung the abrasions on his neck. He swallowed hard in a futile attempt to suppress his feelings. He felt a wave of hot, intense anger sweep through him; anger at the things done to him and the aftermath that he'd have to deal with. Mark raised his hand, his fingers clenched in a loose fist. He wanted to hit something. Hard. But he couldn't. The pain and bandages stopped him and he leaned his forehead against the wall. He was completely helpless. Like he'd felt in the warehouse. He hung his head and couldn't stop the sob of pure frustration as it burst from within him. What if he had fought a little harder? Could he have done something differently?

He swiped at the water running into his eyes and then looked at his right hand. The bandage was beginning to come off in the water. Trembling, he raised his arm and tugged at the loose end with his teeth. The tape gave way and the dressing fell away from his palm, dangling by a single piece of adhesive.

The wound on his palm was a deep purplish fading to a dark angry red. The middle, the actual hole, was raw and puckered. He turned his hand over. This side had been against the wood and was scraped and ragged. The wound looked bigger on top, and as he studied the injury, he had a sickening thought. What if he could see right through his hand? His stomach began churning, and hand shaking, he held it up, but he didn't look. He couldn't look.

Staggering against the cold tiles, he leaned over and vomited what little breakfast he'd eaten. Gagging and retching, wave after wave ripped through him until finally his belly relented. Exhausted, he raised his head and caught the water in his mouth, not caring that it was hot. He rinsed and then spit. Completely drained, he reached out and shut the water off. His legs shook as he dried himself off and pulled on a clean hospital gown. He shuffled out to his bed, grateful when he eased down and lay back. Mark closed his eyes and blocked all thought from his mind.

* * *

A few minutes later, he awoke from a light doze when his nurse returned. Mark remembered with a pang of guilt that he had forgotten to call and say he was done with his shower.

"Okay, Mark. I'm just going to re-wrap your hands and feet now." She looked up at him with a bright smile.

Her name-tag caught his eye. "Okay, Brenda." He

tried to swallow down the sudden queasiness when she took his hand and ran her fingers lightly over the wound as she examined it.

"It looks pretty good. No drainage and the swelling is down." Brenda spread some ointment on the wound and with practiced ease, wrapped it and repeated the procedure on his other hand and his feet.

Mark averted his eyes, choosing instead to watch the wall clock's second hand sweep across the numbers. The procedure didn't hurt, but that didn't prevent him from breaking out in a sweat at the mere thought of seeing the wounds. Would he ever be able to look at his own hands again?

After finishing with the bandages, she helped him ease his arm into the sling once more. He gave a groan of relief, not realizing how much discomfort he'd been in until the sling once again supported his shoulder.

Brenda fiddled with his I.V, chattering away about the weather as Mark's eyes slid closed.

* * *

"This is his room. He's sleeping now, but we have to wake him to check his vitals soon if you want to wait."

Lily nodded. "I'll do that. Thank you." She cringed when the chair scraped against the tile as she sat down, hoping it wouldn't awaken Mark. He stirred on the bed and she held her breath, hoping he'd settle back to sleep.

"Lily?" His voice was less hoarse than yesterday, but she thought it still sounded painful.

"Hey, Mark." She stood, giving the chair a dirty look when it screeched again. Not that it mattered anymore.

His hand rested on the sheet, and she reached for it, mindful of the bandages and I.V. "How are you feeling?" His skin was warm, almost hot. He pulled out of her grasp, but only to raise the head of the bed.

"I'm okay. Still sore, but better than I was." Although he said the right things, his demeanor said something else. He looked exhausted. Dark circles stood out on his pale skin. There was something else in his tone too. It hadn't been there yesterday. Then he'd still been groggy and his throat had been so sore that he'd said very little in the brief periods of time that he'd been awake.

She smoothed a hand against his cheek. "You feel a little warm."

Mark turned his head away from her hand.

"How's your shoulder? Are you due for some pain meds?" She tried to take his hand again, but he pulled it away.

He sighed. "It's okay, Lily. I'm fine."

She could sense him closing down.

"Talk to me, Mark." She rested her hand on the bedrail."I know you're hurting."

He shifted in the bed, wincing, and tugged the sheet up higher on his lap. Their dry rustle sounded loud in the room.

He looked down and mumbled, "I…I…should have fought harder, Lily."

"Fought harder? Mark, you're covered in bruises from head to toe and the police tested some blood they found in your loft and it wasn't yours. I'd say you fought pretty damn hard." She wondered if she should be less stern, but she knew Mark and his tendency to blame himself for everything.

"I bit someone." He gave a short laugh.

"What?"

"They were all around me and someone got too close to my mouth and I bit down as hard as I could. That must be what the blood was from."

"See? What else could you have done? The police also found almost a dozen different footprints in the alley outside your building. There's no way you could have fought your way past all of them."

"So, that means they haven't actually caught anybody yet?" His eyes were flat and his voice guarded. She knew he was trying not to let any fear leak through. Tears sprang to her eyes and she blinked them back as she shook her head. "Not yet, but they have a lot of leads. They think that the girl, Judy Medea, might have had something to do with it. They found the missing keys in a pile of snow behind the studio and she was the last person besides you or me to be in the office that day."

"Oh, she was there all right. I know exactly who's behind it all." His voice was hard. Angry. "Kern and about a dozen other people." He went silent then and Lily didn't push for more details. She rubbed his arm and he didn't pull away, accepting that small comfort.

Lily pulled a chair right up beside the bed as close as she could and continued the gentle stroking. She finally saw him relax and his breathing settled into a soft rhythm as he fell asleep. The tears she'd fought to hold back trickled out and she swiped at them with her free hand. She didn't believe in vengeance, but right at that moment, if Kern had been standing before her, she didn't think she'd have any qualms about hurting him.

CHAPTER FOURTEEN

Adrian supervised the unloading of the small truck by his followers. Most of the furniture from the Oak Park house had been abandoned, but it couldn't be helped. His desk and leather chair were the exception. He scowled at the necessity of moving and glanced at the rundown apartment building that was to be their temporary home. How it hadn't yet been condemned by the city was anyone's guess, but a few phone calls and the exchange of cash had made it available. He surveyed the neighborhood, batting away a tattered newspaper that blew towards his face. The area looked like a war zone. Half the windows were missing from the buildings and grass was a luxury the street couldn't afford. Front stoops crumbled onto muddy patches of bare ground littered with broken bottles, pop cans, and paper. The few trees and bushes were decorated with twisted plastic shopping bags that snapped in the stiff wind.

At least it was only temporary. His followers had balked, but at least they wouldn't have to worry about nosy neighbors. In this area, nobody paid any attention to what happened to others. It was just what Adrian needed right now.

How the police had found them at the warehouse so quickly still mystified him. The most dangerous part, the actual abduction, had gone without a hitch. Once at the warehouse, they should have had all the night to complete the ceremony. Taylor shouldn't have been reported missing until morning, but when the police scanner started buzzing with activity at Taylor's loft, Adrian had set lookouts with instructions to report back any suspicious vehicles. It was the only thing that saved them.

Taylor had been in bad shape when they'd left, and Adrian had held out hope he would die from his wounds, but it wasn't to be. He shrugged it off, it wasn't worth second guessing his restraint when he'd stabbed the man. At the time, it had added necessary drama. He hadn't missed the morbid fascination of many in the guild, and had overheard several talking about that moment.

Besides, he could never let his doubts show in front of his followers. Instead, he took credit for the media frenzy. He had put the Guild of the Rose on the radar. Every news outlet in the country had run a story on them. Adrian chuckled, loving the comparisons to Jim Baker's cult. What he wouldn't give to have the number of followers Baker had, but as usual, the press had stretched and exaggerated the truth. While the attention increased the risk, it also catapulted Kern to the front pages of the news and he basked in the notoriety.

As the last of the boxes were carted into the building, Adrian followed his members inside. He strode into the lobby of the apartment complex. He'd instructed everything to be unloaded there first so that it could later be distributed among the four apartments in the building.

"Everyone, please find a place to sit."

Some of the women glanced at the floor with their noses wrinkled and remarked about sitting on mouse droppings and cockroaches. Adrian narrowed his eyes.

"Sit!"

Startled, all of the members sat without another word of protest. He pinned each one with a look until they squirmed and glanced away. "I will not hear another word about the condition of this building. Even as you all are bitching about bugs and rodents, I am making plans. Plans like you have never imagined. The Guild of the Rose will become known throughout the world."

He surveyed them, relishing how their shock turned to curiosity as he allowed the tension to build.

"We did not fail with Mark Taylor. Instead, he is even more famous than he was before, and that was *our* doing. We have that kind of power. When we bring him down for the final time, our power will be immeasurable. People will flock to our guild hoping to become members." He pointed at them. "As senior members, you will all be bishops when that happens. My inner circle. Think of the power you will have."

He swept an arm out, and said, "All of this is but a minor inconvenience, a small price to pay. Soon, we will have a complex to rival any on earth. It will have fountains and statues. There will be private apartments for all of you, and all of your needs will be taken care of. You will want for nothing."

Their eyes lit up and he let it sink in for a few moments. "These things take time. For now, we sit tight while I lay some groundwork. I'll have to leave the country for a short time to make some arrangements. In the meantime, Judy Medea will be in charge. She's proven herself worthy. You will obey her as you would me."

Judy's head came up in surprise as she gave a tentative smile. He still wasn't sure of her loyalty, but he was positive of her fear. She would do whatever he told her to do.

* * *

Mark awoke and his eyes went to the chair beside the bed. It was empty and he felt a pang of disappointment. He hadn't been very pleasant to Lily and it was no wonder she had left. He looked at the big clock on the wall, surprised to see that it was late afternoon.

Brenda entered carrying a dinner tray. "How about some real food? Feel up to it?" She set the tray on his table and removed the lid from the plate. "You were sleeping so I ordered for you. I figured a hamburger would be a safe bet. Is that okay?"

Mark nodded. "Sure. That looks good."

A nurse appeared at the door and spoke to Brenda about a patient in another room. "Okay, Mark. I have to go, but if you need anything, put on your light."

"Thanks. I should be fine." Mark sat up on the edge of the bed and pulled the table closer, scanning the tray for ketchup packets. He spotted several next to the ever-present green Jell-O and reached for one. Realizing he couldn't open it with his hands, he put the edge between his teeth and pulled. The packet ripped open but flew out of his hand and slid across the floor towards the door. "Dammit!"

"Lose something, Mark?"

He looked up from the smear of red on the floor to see Jessie step into the room and bend to pick up the errant packet.

"Whoa!" Jim sidestepped to avoid running into her

169

backside. "Maybe you shouldn't do that, Jessica." A wide grin split his face.

Jessie straightened and raised an eyebrow at Jim. Mark almost felt sorry for the other man being on the receiving end of the look. Jim's grin dissolved. Jessie tossed the packet in the garbage can then approached the bed, her expression softening.

"How are you feeling?"

Mark put the lid back on his dinner. "Okay." He looked between the two. Was this a social call or did they have news for him? What little appetite he'd had dwindled to nothing.

"You're looking a lot better than you did the last time we saw you." Jim leaned against the wall, his hands in his pockets as he appraised Mark.

Mark couldn't remember them visiting, but maybe he'd been out of it when they had come by. "I was probably pretty sedated then. I don't remember much about the first few days I was here." He reached for his juice. His appetite was gone but his mouth was dry as a sandbox.

Jessie looked confused and glanced at Jim then back to Mark. "I think Jim meant at the warehouse."

Jim nodded, his expression grim. "Yeah, Taylor, that was pretty...bizarre."

The bottom dropped out of Mark's belly and his ears began to buzz. In some part of his mind, he was aware that someone had rescued him but he hadn't thought that part through yet. They had been there? Jim and Jessie had seen him like that? He couldn't look at them as he imagined how he must have appeared to them. He swallowed bile. He'd been hanging there in the warehouse like a side of beef.

For the second time that day, he felt like vomiting. It was bad enough knowing that others knew of his humiliation, but to have someone he knew witness it firsthand was like a kick to the gut. Mark closed his eyes and leaned his head on his hand, his elbow propped on the table. He wished Kern would have just finished him off. It would have been a lot more merciful than letting him die of humiliation.

"Damn, Taylor! What's wrong?" Jim was beside him, his hand on Mark's right shoulder. "You just looked like someone drained what little color you had right out of you."

Jim moved the table out of the way and tried to urge Mark back in the bed. "Lie down before you pass out."

Jessie pushed the nurse call light and when it was answered, barked out, "We need some help in here!"

Mark, cradled his head in his hand, his eyes shut, while he mustered the last shred of dignity he had left. "Get out. Just leave me alone."

* * *

Mark's body shuddered as he hunched over and after a few seconds, he brought his feet up and lay curled on his side. Jessica leaned over him, pulling the covers up, but Mark ignored her presence, his mouth clamped into a tight line and his eyes still closed.

Jim stepped away from the bed and reached out, grasping Jessica's elbow and giving a little tug. When she looked at him with an eyebrow raised in question, he angled his head towards the door. He wasn't sure what had set Taylor off, but it was obvious that the man was barely keeping it together.

"But--" Jessica tried to shake off Jim's hand, shooting a worried glance at Mark.

"Let's go." Without waiting, Jim turned and headed towards the hall and after a moment, he heard the tap of Jessica's boots on the tile behind him.

He strode down the hall until he found a little sitting area and she followed him.

"Jim! He needs some help in there. We should get the nurse."

"What he needs is a little time to get himself together." Jim crossed his arms and leaned one hip against a window ledge, half-sitting. "Couldn't you tell that Mark was about to lose it in there?"

She wore a puzzled expression and tucked her hair behind her ear and glanced back down the hallway towards Mark's door. "I thought he was in pain…"

Jim gazed down at his foot resting on the floor, tapping it against the tiles as he tried to think of a way to explain his theory to Jessica without causing further embarrassment to Taylor. At first, Jim had been as mystified as Jessica at Mark's sudden change in demeanor, but he thought back over the conversation and realized what had hit Mark so hard.

Jim had done enough interrogations and had seen subjects display similar reactions, especially if the interrogator threatened to show videos of the questioning to the subject's family. They were often terrified of loved ones seeing them like that. The feeling of helplessness and of being a victim was almost as hard for some to handle as the actual attack. It didn't matter that Taylor wasn't new to...interrogations, this was different. Jim refused to think of his own past questioning of Taylor as torture, it wasn't even close to what these animals had done. Taylor had been the victim of a brutal beating, torture and attempted murder, that went beyond anything the government had done to him.

"Jessica, you've worked as a cop long enough to recognize that Mark is acting like most other victims. He doesn't want people he cares about to see him as vulnerable or helpless."

At first she looked confused, but then her face colored as she understood Jim's implication. "He doesn't want me to see him like this, but, I'm investigating the case. How am I going to find out anything if he won't speak to me?"

"Dan is investigating the case --you're off it, from what I understand."

"Well, technically, sure, I know that." She shrugged one shoulder and crossed her arms, turning away. "I wanted to see how he was doing and I thought he would welcome a friendly face asking him the questions instead of--"

"My mean ugly mug?" Jim teased gently and stepped around Jessie, making her face him. He looked her in the eye. "I'm going to go back and talk to him, if he'll let me. As crazy as it sounds, he's familiar with me seeing him like this. I might not be as threatening. Why don't you wait here for now?"

"Yeah, I guess, " she said and sank down onto one of the easy chairs.

* * *

"Taylor? Can I come in for a minute?"

Mark thought about ignoring the request, but he already felt like a fool for the way he had behaved. He cracked his eyes and saw it was only Jim and he wondered where Jessie was and if she was out in the hall.

Jim must have seen the question in Mark's eyes and shook his head. "It's just me."

Still not quite able to meet Jim's eyes, Mark nodded and said, "Yeah, come on in." He raised the head of the bed and straightened the covers. "Sorry about tossing you out...I...I just--"

"It's okay, don't worry about it," Jim said, cutting Mark's apology short. "I'm the one who should be apologizing." He ambled into the room, stopped and crossed his arms.

Mark took a sip of water, not quite sure what Jim was getting at. He set the cup down and flexed his right hand several times. It was still painful, but he was beginning to have more strength in it. Fidgeting, he adjusted the strap on his sling.

"I had hoped to get some information from you, but I can see this probably isn't a good time. That's okay though. One more day isn't going to make a whole lot of difference." Jim pulled up a chair and sat down with a sigh.

Mark looked out the window. It was almost dark and the orange sunset slashed across the horizon. Neither man spoke, and the silence hung in the air like a thick heavy fog. Mark felt Jim's gaze boring into him. Unable to resist any longer, he turned to look at him. What he saw in the other man's eyes surprised him. He expected to see pity but what he saw instead was anger.

Jim leaned forward, his arms resting across his knees. "Mark, you know that what happened to you wasn't your fault, don't you?"

Mark looked away, his eyes on the wall beyond the foot of the bed, but his focus was inward. It was his choice to respond to the first assault on Judy Medea. Then, he had invited her to the studio for an interview. He was sure she had taken the keys then. How could he have been so gullible? Why hadn't he checked his loft for the keys after Lily had reported them missing? *Stupid!* His biggest regret was in not getting away. Lily had a point about how many people had been there, but still, he should have thought of a way of getting free.

"It doesn't really matter what I think, does it, Jim? The fact is, I let them do that to me. Things I did or...or...didn't do, contributed to what happened." Mark clenched his fist, ignoring the pain. Narrowing his eyes, he turned to Jim. "I could have made them end it sooner." His voice was low and harsh as he continued, "I begged him to shoot me, but I should have forced him to do it." Mark's breathing became ragged as he thought back and tried to think of ways he could have prevented the crucifixion.

"Maybe he didn't have a gun...but he had a knife. I should have attacked Kern. Either I would have succeeded in getting away, or I'd have died trying." He almost forgot Jim sitting beside him as he imagined different plans of action. "Anything would have been better than what happened."

"Whoa, Mark, hold up. Are you saying you wanted to die in there?"

Mark clamped his mouth shut, his jaw muscles

twitching. The thought had crossed his mind. He looked down at the fingers of his left hand poking out of the sling and picked at the bandage circling his palm.

When he spoke, his voice was barely above a whisper, "It's not that I *wanted* to die. I thought I was going to die anyway and I just didn't want to die--" He broke off; that wasn't quite right. His face burned as he dropped his gaze, his eyes roaming the hills and valleys of the bedspread covering his lap. "I didn't want to be found...like...like that."

Jim sighed and stood. Mark risked a glance at him. The CIA officer had his hands in his pockets and wandered to the window. He glanced at a few of the cards lined up on the ledge like soldiers at attention and picked up a couple. He was quiet for a minute or so then turned, his eyes drilling through Mark with their intensity. "You know, there's no shame in surviving."

CHAPTER FIFTEEN

"So, I take it he spoke to you?" Jessica stood as Jim approached. He could tell she was trying to keep her expression professional, but he could feel the anxiety thrumming just beneath her calm exterior.

Stopping a few paces in front of her, he sighed and said, "Yes, he did." How much should he reveal? That Mark thought it was his fault? That he had wanted to die fighting rather than be found like he was? Before he could decide, he spotted Taylor's doctor walking towards the nurses' station. Mark's frame of mind was precarious enough that Jim felt the doctor should be made aware of it. His own experience with Mark in the brig had given him some insight into the other man's psyche, and right now, Taylor was as low as he'd ever seen him.

"Dr. Jenkins!" Jim walked briskly, catching up to the man. "Could I speak with you a moment?"

The doctor set a chart down and stepped around the desk. He nodded to Jessica then turned his gaze to Jim. "Sure. Is there something I can do for you?"

"Yes, perhaps. I was just in talking to Mark Taylor." Jim paused, wanting to word this carefully. "He seems rather depressed. I just wondered if you were aware of how he's handling things. Mentally, that is."

The doctor leaned back, resting one elbow on the high desktop, his expression thoughtful. "What did he say?"

Jim felt like he might be treading on shaky ground and that maybe he was invading Mark's privacy, but he also knew he had to tell the doctor. Mark's demeanor worried him that much. "Somehow, he feels like he's partly to blame. Like if he would have done something differently or fought harder he could have prevented what happened."

"That's not too uncommon for victims of violence."

Nodding, Jim added, "And more than that, he even said that he wished he would have died rather than be found like he was."

Jessica sucked in a deep breath, and at the sound, Jim glanced at her. Her eyes were wide as she looked at him, seeking confirmation. "Are you sure, Jim?"

He gave a short nod and turned his attention to the doctor who sighed and crossed his arms. "The other day, Mark made a remark and I asked him if he'd like to speak to someone; a chaplain or a psychiatrist--someone like that. He declined, but I'll suggest it again. Unless he's a risk to himself or others, it's the best I can do."

Jim nodded. It was a start. He held out his hand. "I appreciate it, doc."

Jenkins shook Jim's hand, his expression grim. "He seems like a good guy who's been dealt a bad hand lately."

Jim and Jessica exchanged looks, and Jim turned to the doctor and said, "You don't know the half of it."

* * *

Matthew Jenkins watched the two leave. He had a feeling that their concern for his patient was more than just professional. Over the last few days, Matthew had encountered many people who had asked questions about Mark; people who usually had a story to tell about how they knew his patient. Some of the tales were mundane, some funny, but a few were incredible. He couldn't answer their inquiries due to confidentiality issues, but he felt the compassion and concern of the people and saw the outpouring of cards and well wishes sent to his patient.

Matthew circled behind the desk and grabbed Taylor's chart, flipping it open to the progress notes. Though staring down at the form in the chart, his mind remained mired in the non-medical issues facing his patient. The problem was that Mark was isolated from this show of support.

First, he had been in ICU, and now, although in a regular room, security was tight. Only a select few people were allowed in to see him, otherwise, the hospital would have been overwhelmed with people. Even knowing they couldn't get in, the crowd outside the front entrance hadn't diminished. Instead, it seemed to grow larger each day. Crosses and candles had begun to dot the parkway and security had their hands full removing the items when they were left on the hospital grounds. Between over-seeing the crowd and watching the many entrances, Matthew had heard that the security department was stretched thin and had mandatory overtime shifts running. A Chicago police cruiser was a permanent fixture in front of the hospital, and more units patrolled the nearby streets. Matthew had never seen anything like it.

Shaking his head, he read through the surgeon's note, glad to see that Taylor's minor post-op infection had cleared up. Tests of Taylor's kidney function had also come back within normal limits. The profound shock Mark had been in when he'd first arrived in the emergency room could have done permanent damage. Physically, the man was healing and Matthew would probably discharge him tomorrow. He hoped Taylor was ready to face the media.

Matthew snapped the chart closed, and strode to Mark's room. He needed to have a real talk with the guy.

He found his patient picking listlessly at his meal. From the large quantity of food remaining on the tray, it didn't appear he'd consumed very much. "You know, it works better if you actually eat it," Matthew advised as he halted beside the bed. Looking down at the burger and limp fries, he had to concede that the food hardly looked appetizing.

Mark glanced up at him, before covering his plate with the domed lid. "Yeah, I had some company a little while ago and the food got cold."

"Would you like to get another tray? I'm sure the nurse could call down for another one for you."

Shaking his head, Mark said, "No, that's okay. I'm not hungry."

"Hmm…well, I was thinking about sending you home tomorrow, but if you don't have an appetite, maybe we'll need to keep you another day or so and investigate that." Matthew was only half-bluffing. Mark had just been advanced to a general diet. He would have to eat some regular food before he left so that they would know he could tolerate it.

Mark's eyes, wide with alarm, shot to his. "I have an appetite! Just…not right this minute." He rubbed the heel of his hand against his forehead, and then let it drop.

"Doc, you gotta let me out of here tomorrow."

"What's so important about tomorrow?"

Mark sighed. "I just...I feel like I need to go home. That once I'm there, I'll be able to..." His voice had become quiet before trailing off, and his gaze shifted to the window, staring at the black rectangle.

"You'll be able to forget what happened to you?"

Mark took a deep breath and swallowed before nodding. He kept his face averted.

Matthew looked around and pulled the nearest chair over and sat down. He leaned forward and touched Mark's right arm, noting the slight flinch of the other man. "Listen, Mark. I really think you should talk to someone. Someone like a mental health professional who can help you deal with all of this."

The ticking of the clock was loud in the room and Matthew began to wonder if Mark was going to ignore his suggestion when his patient finally leaned back against the bed. His head angled up as he focused on the ceiling, and Matthew was glad to see that the bruising on Mark's neck was beginning to fade slightly.

"Okay."

Mark's voice was so quiet, Matthew almost missed the reply. "What?"

"I said okay. I'll talk to someone." There was a trace of bitterness to his tone, and he still focused on the ceiling where it met the far wall, avoiding Matthew's eyes.

"There's nothing to feel ashamed about, Mark."

"Why does everyone keep *saying* that?" Mark finally looked at him. His eyes narrowed. "How would you or Jim know what it felt like to be dragged out of bed and be led around like a dog on a leash? Huh? *How?* Did you

181

ever watch as someone pounded a nail through your hand, Doc? *Well?* Did you?"

Matthew stood and closed the door, bracing against it with one hand for a few seconds as he organized his thoughts. How could he answer those questions? Obviously, he had never been in that situation and now he felt ashamed of the advice he had given Mark. It was trite and sounded like a platitude. Feeling completely inadequate, he returned to his seat and gave a heavy sigh.

Mark's face was a stony mask, and he stared straight ahead now, but his good hand clenched around a can of pop. The sound of the metal snapping as it slowly crumpled punctuated Mark's harsh breathing.

"You're right, Mark. I have no idea what you're feeling now. I'm sorry for my comment."

The can popped as it collapsed completely, and the remains of the drink bubbled out onto the table. Matthew worried about the wound on Mark's hand, but before he could warn him, Mark released the can and gave the table a shove.

His body sagged back and he flopped his forearm over his eyes. "Damn. I did it again." Mark gave a choked laugh. "At this rate, I won't have to worry about being embarrassed in front of anyone because there won't be anyone who'll want to be in the same room with me." The arm fell back to the bed and Mark turned to Matthew. "I'm sorry, Doc."

Matthew swallowed a lump in his throat and shook his head. "Not necessary. No more apologies, Mark. You feel what you feel and who am I to say it's wrong?" Matthew stood and passed a hand over his eyes, rubbing them. He felt completely drained. "Do you have a preference for a psychiatrist? If not, I can recommend some good names."

Mark shook his head.

"Okay, well there's a couple that would be good. There's John Newsome. He's excellent, or Scott Palmer. You can't go wrong with either of those guys."

Mark's eyes widened and he sat up straight in the bed. "Scott Palmer?"

Matthew nodded. "Yeah. He's a great guy. I think you'd like him."

A wry smile twisted Mark's mouth and he shook his head. "Yeah, I think I will. He's the one I need to talk to."

Matthew was surprised at Mark's change in attitude. "Okay. I'll give him a call and write the consult request. I know you want to go home, but I think we'll give it one more day so you can get your appetite back and talk to Dr. Palmer."

* * *

Adrian handed over his identification to the border patrol guard at the checkpoint into Ciudad Juarez, Mexico and tried to curb his impatience as it was studied. The flight from Chicago to El Paso had been the riskiest part of the trip. His photo had flashed so many times on the TV, even he was getting tired of looking at it. His blond dye job, scruffy whiskers and blue contacts had altered his appearance significantly, but just to make sure, he'd added a slouch to his walk that he hoped made him seem shorter and heavier.

Of course, the ID was fake, but it was the best money could buy. He had a passport, driver's license, credit cards and even mock up photos of him in his alternate identity with his 'family'. That had been a stroke of genius. He'd kept all of it hidden in a safe deposit box using yet a third identity. Not only did he keep the fail-safe identity, he stored most of the Guild's assets there as well, converting it to easily portable jewelry, precious gems and cash. If he had to, he could disappear at a moment's notice, and live out his life on a tropical island as Lee Bigham. Adrian scowled at the idea. There was no fun in that.

The Mexican soldier glanced from the ID in his hand to Adrian's face then asked the purpose of Adrian's visit.

"Tourist." Adrian beamed and then added, "I'm heading to Cabo to do a little snorkeling. Can you give me directions?" He pulled out the map of Mexico he'd purchased, and took his time unfolding it until it was a large unwieldy square. He didn't miss the soldier's sigh of annoyance. It was just the response he was looking for. The soldier waved him on.

Adrian flung the map onto the floor of the car. His only worry had been being identified leaving the country, but he'd felt confident his disguise and passport would let him sail through. So far, everything had gone without a hitch. Years of saving every penny and living in fleabag buildings was about to pay off.

The colorful buildings didn't hide the poverty of the area. Graffiti stained buildings squatted close together, their bright colors giving a falsely festive look to the neighborhoods. Cruising the streets, he was glad he'd memorized the route to his meeting location. Every street looked the same. He raised an eyebrow at a particularly garish purple building next to the panaderia that was his goal. His contact had insisted that a bakery would cause less suspicion than meeting at a bar although Kern felt exposed in the bright sunlight. It was only mid-morning, so his cover of buying some pastries and eating them at the third table from the door wouldn't look out of the ordinary.

Javier Mendez sauntered into the bakery, glanced at Adrian, but showed no signs of recognition as he made his way to the counter and ordered.

Adrian sipped his coffee. A few minutes later, Mendez joined him and pulled out the opposite chair. He took a bite of some large pastry and spoke around the food, "Buenos dias."

Adrian ignored the pleasantry. "Have the arrangements been made?"

Mendez set his pastry down and dusted the powdered sugar from his fingers as he said in lightly accented English, "Si, the house will be ready in a month. I think you will be happy with it. Much space and no close neighbors."

"Excellent. Is it on the ocean?" It would be much easier to come and go by boat and access had been one of Adrian's stipulations. As a foreigner, he wasn't allowed to buy oceanfront property, but there were ways around the law.

"It's set back in a small bay."

"Sounds perfect." Adrian smiled. "Now, about the other thing." As distasteful as Adrian found it, the only way to raise sizable amounts of cash quickly was in the drug trade, and his members had become adept at dealing to the rich North Shore kids who were afraid to go into the ghetto areas of Chicago.

"Shipments will begin as soon as payment is

received."

"I have it right here." Adrian scanned the small bakery and made sure nobody was paying any attention as he passed an English to Spanish dictionary across the table. The center had been hollowed out and contained a small package of gemstones.

Mendez slipped the package out, and with a quizzical expression, peered into the small velvet bag. Afterward, he tugged the drawstrings tight and tossed the bag onto the table. "We agreed on cash, not a bunch of rocks."

Leaning forward, he struggled to keep his voice calm as he covered the bag with his hand. "We agreed on a price, not a method of payment. I couldn't very well cross the border with a suitcase full of cash. What would I have done if I'd been searched? Besides, these jewels are worth twice what you demanded."

Taking another bite of the pastry, Mendez shrugged. "Maybe. Maybe not. Do I look like a jeweler to you?"

"I can go elsewhere for what I want."

"You think so?" Mendez dabbed a spot of sugar from the corner of his mouth with a paper napkin. "I think that I'm the only one willing to deal with you now, after that repulsive stunt you pulled off in Chicago."

"What repulsive stunt?"

Mendez glanced sideways and his lip curled. "You crucified that man."

"It was part of a sacred ritual. We're not just some street gang like you're used to dealing with. We're a holy guild. Our foundation is based on sacred rituals and spiritual growth."

"Spiritual growth. Of course." Mendez rolled his eyes. "You've managed to accomplish what I thought was impossible. You have offended even the heads of the most violent cartels in Mexico. I had a difficult time setting up a supply line because nobody wanted to do business with you."

"You mean the same people that murder women and children? I didn't know they had standards." Adrian shook his head in disgust and continued, "Besides, Taylor didn't die, he's perfectly fine."

"They're saying he really is some kind of saint, and all the churches have been praying for him. You might want to re-think moving your headquarters down here."

"It'll blow over."

Mendez shrugged. "We are a Catholic country, senor. Surely you realize that your 'ritual' could stir up some passion in my countrymen." With that comment, he stood and casually took the bag of gems, tucking them into his pocket. "These had better be twice the worth or I'll be in contact. Otherwise, this will be our last meeting in person."

CHAPTER SIXTEEN

"…yeah, Lily, pretty much everything including shoes. I think my sneakers should be okay to wear." Mark pinched the bridge of his nose as he tried to remember where he had removed his shoes last. Probably right inside the door, but with everything that went on that night the sneakers could be anywhere in the loft by now.

He supposed he could wear slippers home if he had to. "I'll see ya later. Bye."

Walking was easier today than the day before and Mark quickly showered, blocking out all thought and just letting the water pour over him. Afterwards, he even managed to shave and only nicked himself a couple of times. As he blotted the tiny cuts with tissue, he grimaced at the hideous purple and yellow bruises on his throat. Maybe he should have asked Lily to bring him a turtleneck. Other than his throat, he looked okay, which surprised him somewhat. He felt so different inside and was sure it would reflect in his outward appearance.

He wished the doctor would discharge him today. When breakfast had come, Mark had eaten as much of it as he could and even managed to choke down a few bites of the oatmeal. Physically, he felt pretty good. His knife wound bothered him the most along with the ever-present headache. He was almost used to it by now, only really noticing it when it would flare up in response to sudden movement.

Mark sat in the chair and turned the television off. The last thing he wanted to see was more coverage of what had happened to him. When he had woken up this morning, the local news had been filming from right outside the hospital, and Mark had been amazed at all the people gathered out there. He hadn't had a chance to watch any coverage before, and it hadn't occurred to him that he was the main topic in the news.

There was so much else on his mind that the events prior to the assault seemed distant. Apparently, what had happened to him had fired up the public's interest. He took a deep breath and rubbed his forehead. As if he didn't have enough to deal with already.

There was a light knock on his door and Mark looked over to see Scott Palmer standing in the threshold. Warring emotions battled in his mind. Dread that he would have to talk—yet again—about what had happened. Already, he could feel his heart speed up. A glimmer of hope tried to balance the dread. Hope that this man would be able to help him sort out all his turbulent feelings so that they would finally quiet down and he would feel like himself again. He hated the way he felt right now. It was like riding a never-ending roller coaster.

"Mark?" Scott stepped into the room and approached him. "I'm Dr. Scott Palmer. We met last week, remember?" There was an awkward moment when Scott stuck out his hand and Mark reached to shake it, then remembered the bandages around his palm. He hesitated and Scott cleared his throat and let his own hand drop to his side. "Ah, sorry about that. I guess it's not a good idea to shake hands just yet."

Mark nodded and tried to smooth over the moment. "Of course I remember you. How is little Thomas?" It surprised Mark that Scott didn't have a pad of paper or anything.

Scott smiled. "Thomas is great. Keeping us busy and on our toes as usual. Every night, we say a prayer thanking God for sending you to catch him." He sat on the edge of the bed, facing Mark and held his hands loosely clasped in front of him.

Swallowing, Mark looked away. Did God have something to do with sending him to save Thomas? He had asked himself similar questions ever since he'd realized the camera delivered photos of things that hadn't yet happened. How did it work and why did it allow him to save some people but not others? Mark felt resentment well up. Why wasn't he able to save himself? If God had given him the camera and inspired the dreams, why would he would put Mark through all that? Was it a punishment? Had he done something wrong?

"Are you okay, Mark?"

"Yeah…sorry about that. I kind of zoned out there," Mark mumbled, feeling his face flame. "I was just thinking about some things. I'm glad I was there too. I got lucky and was just in the right place at the right time for once." He scratched the back of his head and tried to smile. It felt stiff and phony but he attempted to keep it pasted on even as Scott gave him a skeptical look.

"Right time, right place?" Scott stood and ambled to the window.

Mark watched him glance down towards the front of the building. The psychiatrist was quiet for a moment, but his expression was alert and Mark could see him watching the media down below. Finally, he nodded towards the crowd and not taking his eyes from them said, "You know that you've been big news this last week."

Mark took that as a statement and not a question so he kept silent and wondered where Scott was going with this.

"I've heard dozens of stories where you've been in the right place at the right time." Scott finally turned from the window and leaned a hip on the ledge. He gave Mark a grin, his eyes crinkling in the corners. "You must have impeccable timing, Mark Taylor."

Mark had to laugh at that comment, he couldn't help it. "Yeah. I guess I do…sometimes." He sobered at the last word.

"Sometimes?"

Mark picked at a bit of bandage adhesive on the back of his left hand and gave a half shrug. "I'm not always where I need to be at the time I need to be there. Or I am, but something changes and I…I fail at what I was there to do." He knew what he said wouldn't make much sense but couldn't think how to explain it without telling about the camera.

"How did you feel when you failed?" Scott regarded him, his brown eyes reminding Mark of a serious, adult version of little Thomas's.

A spark of anger ignited in him. He leaned forward and said, "How did I *feel*? How do you think I'd feel after allowing people to die? I felt like--" Biting back a curse, he sat back hard and avoided Scott's gaze by focusing on the trees outside his window. Tiny green buds dotted the branches.

"Allowing? That's kind of an odd choice of words."

Mark heard a rustle of clothing then the tap of footsteps and he glanced at the psychiatrist. Scott was pulling a chair from the other side of the room towards the windows and Mark winced when one of the legs scraped the floor with a harsh sound. Scott didn't set it directly in front of Mark; instead he angled it facing the windows.

"I hope you don't mind if I sit?"

Motioning towards the chair, Mark nodded. "Be my guest."

"You didn't answer my question, Mark. Did you intend for anyone to die? Did you stand by and do nothing?"

Mark's eyes narrowed. "Of course not. I couldn't stand by and watch someone die and not try to help. But I should have tried harder. Maybe what happened to me was…" He scrubbed a hand down his face and pinched the bridge of his nose before letting his hand drop. "…was payback. For not doing what I was supposed to do." He slumped in the chair, his elbow propped on the arm and his hand supporting his head. It was all becoming clear to him now. Not only had he failed at making some saves over the years, but he had let the secret of the camera out when he'd been interrogated.

"What were you were supposed to do? Why do you think it was up to you to do anything?"

Mark sighed. "Because it's what I do." He had turned his face so that his mouth was half- covered by his hand and the statement came out muffled. "I have to change things."

"I don't follow you, Mark." Scott's voice held a questioning note and when Mark glanced at him, he saw the doctor's brow furrowed in confusion.

Dropping his hand, Mark straightened in the chair. What the hell...he might as well tell Scott about the camera. What more could it do to punish him? And he was just so tired of pretending. "You're here officially, right?" Mark swallowed hard and continued, "I mean, as my psychiatrist...not just dropping in to say hello or anything..."

Scott held his gaze, steady and unwavering. "Yes, Mark, that's correct."

"Well, you probably already suspect that I'm crazy, so what I'm about to tell you will just confirm it." Mark laughed, the sound sharp and bitter.

* * *

Scott winced at Mark's harsh laughter. He could hear the underlying pain and saw the way he held himself, as if bracing for an attack. "If you want to tell me something, it will be held in confidence, if that's what you're worried about. As far as crazy, well, I can tell you right now that after years of experience dealing with mentally unstable people, you don't seem to fit the bill."

Mark's eyes flickered with hope, but it was replaced almost immediately with a guarded look. Whatever he was about to tell Scott was causing him to put up a protective front.

"I...I have a special camera, and when I use it, I get photos of future events. Always tragedies, never any good stuff." Mark's mouth twisted into a wry grin. "It would be great if I got photos of winning lottery tickets, but so far, it's always bad stuff. Anyway, most days...well, except for while I've been here in the hospital, I take the photos, develop them, and that night, I dream the details."

Although brimming with questions, Scott decided to just sit back and listen without asking anything until Mark was done speaking. When the other man paused, he encouraged, "Go on, I'm listening."

At first, Mark had looked down while speaking, but now he met Scott's eyes. "I use the information to fix things... to save people. It's what I do."

Scott nodded. It was apparent that Mark completely believed what he was saying.

Surprise flashed on Mark's face. "Well, that's pretty much it. I don't know how it works or why I'm the only one it seems to work for, as far as the dreams go. Just lucky, I guess." A self-mocking grin faded. "I used to wonder but..." He took a deep breath and gave a small shrug, wincing slightly. "I gave up questioning it...until now."

Scott had more questions and while he wanted to believe Mark, it was an incredible tale. He'd treated many patients over the years who suffered from an altered sense of reality. Many thought they had special abilities. Some believed that they could fly; others claimed to read minds or to hear voices telling them the future. This was the first time that anyone had claimed to be able to foretell the future with the aid of a camera and dreams.

"Have you spoken to anyone else about this...gift...of yours?" Scott tried to phrase the question as neutrally as he possibly could, but his skepticism must have slipped through anyway. Mark faced him, his eyes boring into Scott while anger, hurt and then resignation slid through their depths.

Mark's voice was like cold, hard granite. "Yes, as a matter of fact I have. I was imprisoned for over a year. Those guys...the interrogators...they know how to get a man to confess to anything if it'll make the questioning stop."

Scott tried to keep his expression neutral, but this was news he hadn't expected. "So, these interrogators—they believed you?"

Mark looked out the window briefly before dropping his gaze to the floor. "No. Not at first. I tried proving it one time, when I predicted the questions and outcome of an interrogation session, but...months went by. I don't know if it helped, but eventually, I was released due to lack of evidence."

Scott had to ask. "Evidence of what?"

"Terrorism."

The comment was so matter of fact, Scott had to replay it in his mind to make sure he'd heard correctly. "*Terrorism?*"

Mark's skin took on a pink tinge that Scott detected even with the pallor from the man's recent blood loss.

He looked Scott straight in the eye and said, "I didn't do anything, so you can stop worrying. Since my release, I have a few people who believe me...but I can't go into details. I...I shouldn't even be telling you. I've been told the camera is now classified information."

"Ah." Scott couldn't believe how disappointed he felt. "I see." He was beginning to believe that this was a very unusual case because Mark didn't display any of the normal symptoms of being delusional. He didn't ramble, he made eye contact and he seemed perfectly sane, except for this one specific delusion. Classified information. The perfect excuse not to give information and paranoid schizophrenic people often claimed government conspiracies and connections.

"It's true. There was an incident at the Cubs game last summer that I helped the government prevent...but my part in it was kept under wraps." Mark's voice sounded defensive as he stood and hobbled a few steps to the window, leaning against the sill. He was quiet for a long moment while his eyes seemed to focus on something out in the park across the street. Scott noticed Mark's throat working as if he was going to say something, but he didn't, and after a moment, his shoulders slumped as though in defeat.

Scott sighed. He wanted to help this man so badly, but he was at a loss. He decided to change the focus from the camera to Mark's mood swings and possible depression. "I wonder if you could tell me about your outburst yesterday. What triggered it?"

Mark's mouth twisted into a humorless smile and he shook his head ruefully as he turned from the window. "You'll have to be more specific. Which outburst are you talking about?"

"Whichever one you want to talk about."

Mark gave him a long look and sat down again. "You're good at this psychiatric stuff, aren't you?"

Scott smiled. At least Mark looked calmer now, but Scott still kept a watchful eye on him. He'd learned long ago that patients tended to have mercurial mood swings and were unpredictable.

"I was talking to Jessie and Jim--"

"I'm sorry to interrupt, but who are they? Just so I can keep it all straight."

"That's okay. They're friends, sort of. I found out yesterday that--" Mark stopped and his gaze dropped to the floor again, or maybe his feet, Scott wasn't sure. " — they were the ones who found me. I guess I had a hard time with that."

"Why did it bother you, Mark?" Scott observed his patient and noted how his skin flushed.

"It bothered me because I can imagine how I looked up there. I feel so stupid!" Mark swallowed and kept his head lowered. "Of all the people to find me, it had to be them."

"Why is that a problem?"

"Because they'll think less of me."

"Why do you care what they think of you?"

Mark raised his head and sighed. but kept his face averted. "I guess because I really respect them a lot. Jim...well, he's a good guy." He paused and laughed. "If he heard me say that, he'd think for sure I'd gone off the deep end."

"Why is that?"

"Because he was one of my interrogators."

Either Mark was one of the most forgiving guys in the world, or as an interrogator, this Jim fellow had created a kind of Stockholm-type bond with his prisoner. Interesting concept.

"And you think that he'll think less of you now that he's seen you at what you perceive to be your lowest point?"

Mark nodded. He rubbed his eyes with his thumb and fingers for a few seconds and then cleared his throat. Scott thought he was going to say something more but he didn't, he just took a deep breath and let it out slowly...shakily.

"And the other person...Jessie? Will he think the same thing?"

Mark shook his head. "She."

"Excuse me?"

"Jessie...she's a woman. Jessica." Mark's face turned a deep red and things became a little clearer to Scott.

"Do you have feelings for her?"

"We tried to have a relationship, but it didn't work." Mark's voice was low and Scott had to lean forward to hear him.

"How come?"

"How come? I'll tell you how come." Mark lurched out of the chair and turned to face Scott. "Because she thought I was a kook as it was, before I went to prison." He waved his hand in front of himself to indicate the injuries, "And now there's all this. Life with me is a non-stop party. What's next? Burning at the stake? Beheading? I can't ask a woman I love to deal with all of this."

Scott held up a hand. "Hold on, let me ask you something. Why don't you just stop using this camera?" He spread his hands wide. "All your problems would be solved."

Mark shook his head. "I...I tried doing that several times, but I can't. It's like a drug." He tried to run a hand through his hair, but the tape got caught, and he glared at it before letting his hand drop to his side. "I can't sleep, I have crazy dreams, and it just won't let me alone. It's become worse since I started using it after I got out of prison. It's as though it's trying to make up for lost time. Almost every day, I have to use it, or I'd never get any sleep."

Despite his skepticism, Scott was intrigued with how detailed Mark's story about the camera had become. In what he felt was a stroke of genius, Scott decided to change tact and use Mark's delusion to actually try and help him get past this feeling of shame. "Hmmm...how do you view victims that you save? Do you feel like they should be embarrassed because of what has happened to them?"

Mark shot him a look. "I know what you're getting at, but it's not the same. I have all this baggage already." He fell silent for a moment and appeared to be watching the crowd out front. Pointing vaguely towards the gathering, Mark spoke, his tone bitter, "Look at them, Doc. They think I'm some kind of...of savior...or something." He shook his head. "And you think I'm a nut."

Sighing, he turned to face Scott. "But I'm neither of those things. I'm just a guy. Just a regular guy."

CHAPTER SEVENTEEN

"Hey, Jessie, I got a possible lead on Kern's whereabouts." Dan strode into their office, tossing his overcoat onto the coat tree as he passed.

Jessie glanced up from a report she had been skimming. "Really?" She closed the folder and leaned back in her chair, following Dan with her eyes as he settled at his desk. "Where is he and how did you get the info?"

"It's actually a lead on Medea, but I'm hoping where she is, he can't be far away. A CTA bus driver called in a tip. He saw her on his bus this morning, and he noted where she got off. It was the 5000 block of West Jackson Boulevard."

"That corresponds to something I discovered."

Dan tilted his head. "*You* discovered?"

Jessie felt her face heat. "Okay, I get it, I'm off the case, but that doesn't mean I can't analyze the information that's here already." She waved a hand over the pile of files in her out box. "All I have to keep me busy is some scut work on old cases."

She saw a softening of his expression and pressed on, "One thing in Mark's favor is the public interest in this. The phone's been ringing off the hook with tips. I know I'm not on the case officially, but there's a stack of tips received since last night sitting on your desk. I took about the last ten of them." Jessie pointed to the pile of notes. It was a small thing, but at least it helped her feel like she was doing something to help.

Dan leaned forward and sorted through the papers. "Hmmm…some of this looks worthless, but there's a few that might pan out."

"What's this about Mexico?"

"I'll get to that. I took some notes on some of the more promising ones and that one was the prime tip." Jessie opened her desk drawer and pulled out a large notepad.

"Whoa, hold on a second. You took notes on my case? What else did you do? Call up the tipsters?"

Jessie set the pad on the top of her desk and shot a look at Dan. "As a matter of fact, I did. Is that a problem?"

Sighing, Dan rubbed his eyes. "No. It's fine." He made a 'give me' motion with his hand. "Let me see what you have."

Jessie tapped her pencil on her desk as he read over her notes. She knew this should have been a case like any other, but she was sure she was only kidding herself. In her mind, she could picture going to tell Mark that they had caught the bastard.

He chuckled and shook his head. "I won't be able to keep you off this short of changing partners, will I?"

"Probably not." She scooted closer to the desk and pointed to some of her notes on the pad. "I may have traced a bank account to Kern."

"Really?"

"Yes. Medea put some information on her job application for the job that Mark had offered her. Not much, just an address that didn't show up in her school or driver's license records, but it matched the address on a check used to pay her last semester of school and one for her hospital bill. I thought it might have been the place the cult lived before moving to the current one--which now appears abandoned, by the way."

"What makes you say that?"

"I checked the patrol officer's notes. Nobody in or out for three days."

"They could have just gone to ground for a little while."

She shook her head. "I don't think so. Medea was spotted in a neighborhood that's not far from the bank I found and that's miles from that house. There are only three branches in the city, and one is right on West Jackson. The address on the check is for a home in Oak Park."

"And they aren't at that address? "

She shook her head. "I wish, but no, they aren't. The tenants of the house have been there six months and they all checked out. However, I found out the landlord owns properties all over the city. One is the abandoned house, and he has more buildings in the area of the 5000 block of West Jackson. There's more, but with your tip that Medea was spotted in that area, I'd be willing to bet Kern stuck to his pattern of using this landlord. Less red tape."

"That makes sense." Dan flipped the pencil in his fingers, letting the eraser end repeatedly hit the desk top, his expression distant. He was processing the information. Jessie wanted to sigh with relief. He was allowing her to share. She'd been afraid he wouldn't listen since she wasn't supposed to be investigating.

"In addition, the account had a major withdrawal two days ago."

"How much?"

Jessie sank back into her seat. "Enough to live like royalty south of the border."

Dan nodded. "Good work, Jess. If we can get a confirmed sighting of him in Mexico, we can start the paperwork for extradition. I'll rest easier when this guy's locked up for a very long time." His phone rang and he grabbed it, tucking it against his shoulder and ear. "Detective Dan Miller."

"Thanks." Jessie felt some satisfaction, but until the guy was safely behind bars, she wouldn't be completely happy. She thought of how Mark had reacted to her hospital visit and how traumatized he had been. She could hardly contain her anger at Kern.

Nobody should have to go through what Mark had gone through. Especially not after all he'd already endured. But he was incredibly strong, she reminded herself. He'd already proven that. He would work this out on his own.

The thought of Mark going back to the loft alone sent a shiver through her. The last thing Mark would want is pity, especially from her.

She pushed the thought from her mind and tried to focus on her paperwork. Now was not the time to be wondering about Mark Taylor.

"Damn."

Jessie looked up at Dan's sharp tone. She had a feeling that something was up from the set of his mouth and the anger in his eyes. He looked at her and she just knew it had something to do with Mark.

"I'll be right there. In the meantime, call in all your off-duty security guards if you haven't already." He hung up and cursed again, then rose and grabbed his coat, shooting a look at Jessie as he shrugged into it. "You want to help me do some crowd control?"

* * *

Mark finished buttoning his shirt, fumbling with the top button. With one arm in a sling and the other with only a partially working hand made routine tasks frustrating. Still, wearing something other than a hospital gown felt wonderful. He had read somewhere that patients only absorbed about twenty percent of what a doctor told them. Mark shook his head ruefully. Now he believed it. It was hard to focus on what a fully-dressed doctor was saying while he, the patient, sat in a silly looking gown that left his backside bare.

Lily had dropped off his clothes last night and had stayed to chat a few minutes. Mark just wished the conversation hadn't been so stilted. Lily had called this morning and told him that more reporters than ever were gathered outside the studio, and that she was going to stay there to keep things under control. She said that the police wanted to know when he was discharged so they could escort him home. Mark wasn't thrilled with the thought of a police escort, but it beat trying to fight past the crowds. After making sure he had what he needed, Lily said she'd call the police and alert them that Mark had been released. He made a mental note to do something special for her when this was all over. She handled all the details and had gone beyond what a mere business partner would do.

Mark figured Dan would be the one to pick him up, since he was handling the case. He just hoped their conversation would be back to the normal stuff. To that end, he flipped on the television, intending to watch the sports scores. Baseball season was just about to begin and he wanted to arm himself with some of the latest opinions on how the Chicago teams stacked up this year. Dan was a huge baseball fan and even though he was a Sox fan, Mark tried not to hold that against him--at least, not too much.

The morning news was on, but it was all the national stories. While waiting for the local news, he slipped his shoes on. The light bandages around his feet felt constricting within the shoes. Tying the sneakers was out of the question, so he put his call light on and asked for some help when someone got a chance. It was embarrassing to have to ask, but it was just one more indignity and relatively minor so he just smiled and thanked the aide when she quickly tied the shoes for him.

Mark couldn't wait to get out of the hospital. He was tired of being cooped up in the same room for days on end with nothing to do but sleep. Sighing, he sat back in the chair and looked at the television. Still national stuff. He reached over and clicked it off. He would just have to wing it with Dan. In fact, that would give him something to ask the detective to help get the conversation off to a safe topic.

There came a soft knock on the open door. "Mark?"

Mark glanced over in surprise. He knew that voice and it definitely wasn't Dan's. "Jessie?" His heart thumped against his ribs. He hadn't seen her since he'd had his little breakdown. He felt his cheeks grow warm. "Wh--what are you doing here?"

"I guess you're getting sprung?" She approached Mark, her eyes roving the room. "I see you must have sent some of the stuff home already?" She nodded towards the empty windowsill.

Mark nodded. "Yeah. Lily took some of it last night. The other stuff I gave to the nurses to do with what they wanted." He scratched his head. "How'd you know I was going home? The doc only left about thirty minutes ago."

"News travels fast."

"Did Lily tell you? She's the only one I told so far."

"Sounds like Lily has been helping you quite a bit. I didn't realize you two were so close."

She hadn't looked at him while she spoke and he had to direct his reply to her back as she focused on something outside.

"She's been there for me. I owe her big time."

"I guess that's what friends are for." She faced him, a big smile plastered on her face.

Mark wondered at the emphasis on the word 'friend'. Was she implying that there was more between him and Lily? What difference would it make to her?

Jim strode through the doorway. "This is not going to be easy." He passed right by Mark and parted the blinds, peering through.

"Hi, Jim." Mark was a bit confused by his abrupt appearance and his declaration. He stood, noticing that his feet felt a little better with the shoes on. Maybe it was the extra support. He took a couple of steps towards Jim. "What're you looking at?" Sticking his fingers between two slats, he took a quick peek and his stomach churned. The crowd, only a few dozen before, had swelled to close to a hundred, and more people milled around on the sidewalk opposite the hospital.

"I'm just wondering how we're going to get you out

of here past the crowd and the press." He grimaced and glanced at Mark. "Some idiot leaked that you're being discharged today and now it's a madhouse out there."

Mark stepped back and sank down onto the chair. Acid burned the back of his throat and he thought he might vomit.

* * *

"Make some room, people!" Jim shouldered his way through the throng and brought his radio to his mouth, thumbing the talk button. "We need some more security out here!"

It had taken some heavy convincing, but he had finally talked Taylor into holding a short press conference. Sometimes the easiest way to end a story was to simply talk with the reporters and take the mystery out of what had happened.

Jim just hoped Mark would make it through the conference without passing out. When the guy had seen the horde, he had turned white as a sheet.

Due to lack of space, a makeshift press area had been set up in the circle drive in front of the hospital. Traffic had been blocked off and a podium pulled from a meeting room and set up just in front of the doors facing the reporters.

He hated that Taylor would be a sitting duck, and he knew Jessica wouldn't be happy with the plan, but this was Jim's show. The money laundering and crossing state lines, not to mention fleeing the country and then returning, had turned this into an FBI case.

He ordered uniformed officers to check the

identification of every member of the press, but there wasn't much he could do about the crowd gathering behind the reporters. It was a hospital, after all, and some people had legitimate reasons for being there. Kern was at large and although Jim didn't think the bastard would be able to do anything on such short notice; it still made him nervous.

He took a final look around, making sure everything was in place. Some technicians were testing the microphones and some suits from the hospital stood several feet behind the podium. Jim rolled his eyes. He hated that they were using this to get publicity for the hospital.

He checked that everyone was in place. Getting an affirmative from the officers, he took a deep breath. It was show time.

* * *

Mark stood just inside the doors and eyed the crowd with dread. He tilted his head and gulped water from the bottle someone had handed him. His mouth was still dry and he licked his lips. Why had he agreed to this? He just hoped that Jim had emphasized the 'short' part in the term 'short press conference.'

First some hospital administration were going to speak, then Jim, and then he would be last. Mark had no idea what to say to them, but Jim had told him to just answer only those questions that he wanted and to keep the replies brief. That wouldn't be a problem.

He felt jumpy and nervous and wished he could expend some pent up energy. Pacing was his normal outlet, but his feet were too sore and there wasn't much room in here anyway. His knee twitched as his usual impulses were denied. Glancing around, he was relieved to see Jim speaking to some hospital security just a few feet away. The lobby was crowded, and he spotted a couple of nurses who had cared for him. They waved and smiled. He wasn't sure if the grimace he returned would pass for a smile, but it was the best he could offer.

There was a squeal of feedback from the microphone as the hospital president took the podium. Mark winced and returned his focus to the crowd. Behind the reporters, onlookers spread out in an arc and overflowed into the street. He could hear some calling his name randomly, as though he would be able to pick them out of the crowd.

Taking a closer look, he wondered what would make all these people come out to see him. Every age and race seemed to be represented. He did a double take when he saw more than one wheelchair in the throng. His eyes roamed the sea of people, picking out a small child perched on sturdy shoulders, a young couple holding hands, and a woman with a dog on a leash.

Mark squinted. Was that the same dog he saw from his window a few days ago? It could be. He smiled. The dog tangled the leash around the woman's legs and then wandered over to a man nearby. The man wore black sweatshirt and held a large poster board. His attire sent a shiver through Mark, and he glanced at the sign and staggered backwards, almost tripping in his haste.

The sign depicted a human figure on a cross. The figure's coloring matched Mark's. Even from here, he could make out red streaks on the hands and feet. The water bottle fell from his fingers. His vision narrowed and he heard a dull roar in his ears.

"Mark!"

Voices swirled around him and an arm went around his waist and several hands pushed down on his right shoulder.

"Sit down, Mark. There's a chair right behind you."

Mark complied and blinked a few times as his vision cleared. He looked around to find himself the center of a small group made up of the nurses, his doctor, Jim and Jessie. Everyone focused on him and he squirmed, not comfortable being the center of attention. Looking down, he realized he was sitting in a wheelchair. Embarrassment seized him and he dropped his gaze and rubbed his forehead with his thumb and fingers. Dr. Jenkins knelt in front of the chair, looking up into Mark's face, his expression full of concern.

"What happened, Mark?"

Mark shook his head and let his hand fall to the armrest. "I...I don't know. I was just looking at all...all the people and I saw a guy with a sign. I guess I got light-headed for a second." A nurse slid in beside the chair and wrapped a blood pressure cuff around Mark's arm.

"Light-headed? You almost went out on us," Jim said. "What sign are you talking about?"

Mark didn't want to look at it again and his arm was immobilized while the cuff squeezed it, so he just inclined his head towards the crowd in general. "Just a stupid sign. It's nothing." He evaded Jim's steady look and instead watched the needle on the cuff bounce its way down.

Jessie rested her hand lightly on his bad shoulder. "Mark, can you give us a description?"

Mark found her regarding him with an expression he

couldn't read. He didn't think it was pity, but it was close. "A guy in a black sweatshirt over towards the north end."

The nurse removed the cuff. "BP is 86 over 48. Pulse is 112, Dr. Jenkins."

Dr. Jenkins stood and sighed. "Well, the numbers are a little out of the normal range but not too bad. What do you want to do, Mark? You don't have to do-"

"I see it," Jim broke in. "*Bastard.*" He raised his radio to his mouth and hurried away, motioning at some other officers to follow him as he left.

Everyone but Mark turned to look at the sign. He didn't need to.

"Mark, I'll just go out there and tell them that you aren't up to this right now, okay?" Dr. Jenkins turned towards the front doors.

Mark almost let him go, but then the anger that had been simmering for days boiled over. He was tired of being the victim. Tired of being the object of pity. "Wait, Doc."

* * *

The doctor went first and gave a rundown of Mark's medical status. They had discussed it when he agreed to the conference. Dr. Jenkins explained that it might make it easier if Mark didn't have to answer too many medical questions, and Mark was only too glad to agree.

A nurse handed Mark another bottle of water, and he downed several gulps, but his mouth still felt parched. He nudged the footrests out of the way and stood, waving off the hands extended in offers of help. "Thanks, but I can do it."

The podium looked a mile away, and he felt the weight of hundreds of eyes hanging on his every move. He fumbled with the microphone, trying to adjust it to his height. As he raised his eyes to the crowd, dozens of cameras flashed, and he squinted against the dots in his vision. Was he shaking as badly on the outside as he was on the inside?

He took a deep breath. "Uh...good morning. My name's Mark Taylor and--"

The crowd erupted in laughter and Mark had to smile. "Yeah, I guess you guys know that already." He cleared his throat and continued, "I can answer a few questions if anyone has any." Even though he knew it was beyond unlikely, there was just the tiniest flicker of hope that nobody would ask anything.

Reporters began shouting and Mark shook his head in confusion. He wasn't able to understand any of them. He spotted George Ortega near the front and felt a little better. He pointed at him. "Hey, George. Do you have a question?"

The reporters quieted expectantly.

George grinned and shot a triumphant look at the woman beside him. His face sobered before he said, "Hey, Taylor. How are you doin'?"

Well, that was an easy enough question. "Pretty good and every day is better than the one before, so I'm...I'm doing okay. Thanks for asking." He didn't know if that was George's only question, but his friend just smiled, so maybe this was going to be easier than he thought.

Mark took another swallow of water, and before the questions could be shouted at him, he pointed at the woman beside George.

"Thank you for taking my question. Can you tell us what was going through your mind when you were taken from your home?"

"Nothing specific. I was just trying my hardest to get away."

After that, more questions were shouted and Mark did his best to understand them. "I had no idea what was happening at first."

"No, I've never had a relationship with Judy Medea." He shook his head wondering how that rumor ever took hold.

"Lily Martin had nothing to do with Medea and the missing keys. I'm sorry. I can't discuss that aspect of the case."

The questions were coming fast and furious, and he tried to answer as many as he could. "I guess I've just been lucky that I've been in the right place at the right time to help a few people."

"I'm afraid I've been advised not to answer that due to the continuing investigation." Mark was glad that Jim had given him a few good comments to say in reply to questions he either couldn't answer or didn't want to answer.

"Hell yeah, it hurt. *A lot*." Mark glared at the reporter. "What do you think?" *Idiot*.

"I've never claimed to be anything except a co-owner of a photography studio. All that other stuff, that's crap you guys said, not me." Out of the corner of his eye, he saw Jim move up on his left, just a little behind him as a reporter asked Mark if he was the second coming.

"No, dammit! I'm not the savior. I have no divine powers, and I am not the Son of God. I'm the son of *Gene*

Taylor!" Mark ran his hand through his hair and ignored the rest of the shouted questions.

Looking down, he circled his finger in a wet spot on the podium left by the water bottle and tried to find a way to make them leave him in peace. Finally, he looked up. His eyes roved the crowd, lingering on some, willing them to understand. *Needing* them to understand-- praying that they would. "I just want to go home and live my life."

CHAPTER EIGHTEEN

"Come on, Taylor."

Jim put a hand on Mark's back and guided him from the podium, making it easier for Mark to ignore the questions that were still being flung at him. He limped through the main entrance, dropped into the wheelchair, and propped his head on his hand. The chair began rolling, but Mark didn't bother to look where he was going; he just watched the white and gray flecked tiles slide beneath him. Vaguely, he heard Jim walking somewhere behind him, the rapid clip of his shoes matched by the squeak of the nurse's as she pushed the chair. On his other side came Jessie's quick familiar step.

Eventually, Mark raised his gaze as the hallways lengthened and dimmed and they encountered more turns. The mute posse passed noisy equipment rooms, empty boxes stacked in the hall, and large bins piled high with red trash bags. Finally, they exited through a door, and ended up on a loading dock. A plain blue sedan was parked beside it, and by the similarity with Jim's vehicle, Mark recognized the car as government issue.

The chair stilled. The nurse set the brakes and said, "Here we are. You take care now, Mark."

Mark turned to her and forced his best to smile. "Thanks so much for everything. Everybody was great."

"Come on, we don't have too much time." Jim moved

up to Mark's side ushered him into the backseat while he took the driver's seat. Jessie climbed into the back from the other side.

Mark had pictured the police getting him to a cab safely, not a true police escort. "What's the deal? Why can't I just take a cab?"

"Look, Taylor, every reporter in the city -- hell-half of the ones in the country -- want to corner you. We're doing this to make sure you get home in one piece."

"But--"

"Just shut the door, we'll discuss the rest en route."

Mark sighed. He wasn't up to arguing, and Jim had a point. "Fine."

"Here's the deal. Kern is still at large, and going by what happened to witnesses in the past, it's a good bet that he's making more plans for you."

Mark shivered as if someone had doused him with a bucket of cold water, and looked from Jim to Jessie in disbelief. He had thought everything was over; that he would be able to get on with his life. His jaw tightened, and he turned away from them, staring out the window, but not seeing the pedestrians crowding the walkways, instead he saw Kern's pale face and dark, reptilian eyes.

"Mark? Are you okay?" Jim asked quietly.

The tone was a far cry from his normal no-nonsense all-business tone, and Mark was mildly surprised. He found he couldn't trust his own voice at the moment though, so he kept quiet, just giving a short nod in response. In effort to rid his mind of the image of Kern, at the next stoplight, he focused on a young couple who appeared to be window-shopping. The woman pointed at a set of bright yellow kitchenware in the display case. She smiled up at the guy, who just grinned and shook his head. All Mark could think about was how lucky they were.

Jim cleared his throat and Mark glanced at him. More good news was on the way. He could tell from Jim's posture. "What else?"

"Well, we aren't sure it's safe for you to go back to your loft."

Truthfully, Mark's stomach twisted into knots at the thought of sleeping in his bed. He wanted to go home, but his sense of security felt completely violated there. Still, he knew it was important to get back to his routine as soon as possible. He couldn't avoid going back forever, so the sooner the better. "But we're almost there now."

"Yeah, we assumed you might need to get some of your clothes and things, and then we can take you to another location."

"I don't want to go anywhere else." The thought of being forced to leave his home against his will-- yet again -- sent a surge of panic through him.

Jessie shook her head. "Look, Mark, we've arranged for you to stay with a friend of a friend for a few days until we get more figured out. He lives in Indiana."

"Uh-uh." Mark crossed his arms. "I have to stay here. It's not an option." He was being stubborn and he knew it, but so far, all except one of the camera's tragedies had occurred within the city limits. Besides, he had photo-shoots scheduled. They had canceled too many already.

"We know this isn't easy, but we don't have many choices."

"Listen you guys, I appreciate all the trouble that you've gone to, but I need to stay in my loft." Mark glanced at them, then dropped his gaze as he tightened the strap on his sling. "I...I guess it's like climbing back in the saddle, you know? The sooner I do it, the better." He swallowed and heat climbed his face. In all his recent encounters with these two, it seemed like he always ended up looking like a basket case. "Besides, all my equipment is there."

The car pulled up in front of the studio, and Mark saw that Lily hadn't been kidding. The sidewalk out front was a zoo. Cameras began flashing before he even opened the door. Mark sighed and turned to Jim. "I hate this. Will it ever end?"

Jim's mouth set in a firm line and he took a deep breath, his gaze fastened on Mark's eyes. "I know you do. We're doing our best to catch Kern but I'm afraid we don't have any control over the press."

Jessie pointed towards the front of the car. "Dan came here ahead of us, trying to keep things quiet. I'll go find him to come help us get you inside safely." She exited the vehicle and began ordering reporters to back up and give them some room. Jim watched for a second then turned his attention back to Mark. "Hang in there."

"Hanging is not my strong suit," he responded with a tired grin, trying to lighten the mood. It might have worked, except the door suddenly opened.

Dan stuck his head in Mark's door. "Are you ready? I'll do my best to clear the way."

Mark nodded, his gaze darting over Dan's shoulder, thankful that at least the sound of the crowd covered the hammering of his heart. Trying to ignore the shouted questions along with the screams and squeals from the people gathered behind the reporters, he took a deep breath and climbed out of the car.

* * *

Jim pushed the door against the people who crowded it, and boomed, "Back off, people! Let the man out!" He searched for Jessica. She was tough, but her slim frame proved a disadvantage in this situation. Jim spotted her urging the crowd from the entrance.

Jim maneuvered with his back to the car door, but he didn't need to be looking to know exactly when Taylor came out. The screams and shouts became deafening, and the camera flashes had him seeing spots. *Damn it!*

He checked to see how Dan and Mark were faring, and felt a jolt of disbelief when hands reached over the detective's shoulders and grabbed at Mark. The poor guy stumbled back, almost falling into the still open car door. Jim took a quick step towards him even as Dan swatted the arms away.

"Hands off!" Dan shoved the offenders back and blocked further access, allowing Mark to stand and move towards the door of the studio. Jim added his voice and felt like a football player trying to crash through a goal line stand. He went ahead of the other two to aid Jessica as she stood with her arms out, attempting to block as many people as she could. A few steps behind Jim, the crowd closed in like tsunami of people, pushing those in front right into Mark. Jim looked over his shoulder just as Mark staggered.

What were these people *thinking*? The crowd seemed to worship Taylor, and yet, they were terrifying the man.

Pissed, he pulled his cell-phone out of his pocket and

called the Chicago P.D. dispatch and identified himself before saying, "We're at the corner of Hubbard and Wells, and need back up immediately. There's a mob situation going on right now!"

Jim shouldered his way through the crowd, trying to be mindful of the many small children he saw mingling in the throng. Not only was Mark at risk here, so were those children. It wouldn't take much for one to fall under the feet of the mass of people and get trampled before anyone even noticed. "Please, folks! Someone's going to get hurt here. Back up!"

Jessica left her place near the door and returned to help Dan as the two of them tried to clear the way for Mark while Jim was forced to push back against the crowd on his side.

Jim cast a glance over his shoulder when he didn't feel the press of Jessica, Dan and Mark behind him. Their progress was stymied and Mark appeared rooted to the sidewalk. He turned towards Jim, his face drained of color, his eyes, huge and fixed on the mob. Jim saw him shudder when a sea of hands reached for him. He was teetering on the edge of panic. Jim had seen the signs before in other situations. It went beyond the deer in the headlights look. It was akin to a deer surrounded by a pack of salivating wolves. He swore when he noticed that Taylor kept his weight off his right foot. That was probably part of the problem. Not only was the guy surrounded, but he was hobbled too. Just like a deer with his tendons slashed. Easy prey.

Jim fought his way back to the trio, wondering when the hell the cops would arrive. At that instant, a child darted between legs and touched Taylor's hand, then

March Into Hell

dashed back with a squeal of triumph. Like a switch being thrown, people swarmed forward, their mass too much for four people to fend off.

Even the reporters started looking frightened and now many turned to face the crowd, adding their own shouts to those of Jim's. Taylor's shirt sleeve was torn by some seeking hand, and he tottered as he lost his balance for a second. If it hadn't been for a reporter steadying him, he would have gone down. Jim hated to think what the outcome would be if that happened.

Several babies were shoved towards Mark and he limped backwards, holding his hand up. Over the din, Jim could barely hear him as he pleaded, "I'm not what you guys think. Please…just let me go inside."

In response, another baby was pushed towards him. At the same time, the crowd surged forward, knocking the infant from the mother's hands. Mark dipped his shoulder and caught the baby between his right arm and his chest, using his left hand to steady the infant.

The mother screeched, "He saved my baby! Did you all see that?" Instead of taking her baby back, she lifted her arms heavenward and closed her eyes, swaying back and forth, chanting, "Praise the Lord."

Jim reached Mark and took the child and returned her to the mother, startling her into opening her eyes. With a snort of disgust, Jim put one arm across Taylor's shoulders, and shoved people with the other as he forced their way through the crowd. Taylor let out a strangled groan as Jim dragged him along. He hated having to pull Mark , knowing the guy was hardly in the best shape to be rushed through a crowd, but there was no other option.

Sirens announced the arrival of the police—finally—

and also caused the people to turn their attention away for a moment. It was all they needed the door open, Dan blocked the crowd from entering, and Jim and Mark stumbled into the building.

The dim interior, so quiet after the screams and shouts, seemed almost unnatural.

Lily was waiting inside and took Mark's arm, letting him lean on her as he hobbled towards the back of the studio. It took the combined strength of the other three to shut the door and lock it against the push of people. The trio leaned back against the door, gasping for breath. Nobody spoke.

Mark limped to his desk and collapsed onto his chair, his head hanging as his chest heaved.

Jim staggered over, surprised at how drained he felt. He sat on the edge of the desk. His heart still raced, and he couldn't imagine what Mark was feeling. Hearing pounding, he looked to the door, glad to see Dan remained against it, standing guard. Jessica had crossed to the back corner of the office and was filling a paper cup from a standing water cooler. He glanced back at Mark. "You okay?"

Mark nodded but didn't look up. His right elbow rested on his knee and his hand reached under his sling to rub his abdomen. Jim remembered the stab wound he'd suffered and he noted a long scratch on Mark's exposed shoulder. Jim grimaced. It was his fault. It was his job to see that Taylor made it through the crowd, and he should have anticipated something like this. Instead, he had failed miserably.

Mark took the cup from Jessica and guzzled the water. Jim pushed off the desk to grab a drink too. After he downed the first cup and re-filled it, he finally felt his heart slow down. He tried to take stock of the situation. "How's it looking out there?"

Dan peered out the front window then threw over his shoulder, "I think it would be best if you got out of sight, Mark."

Jessica edged towards the windows. "I wouldn't put it past them to break out the glass."

Jim followed her gaze, his mouth dropping open at the faces pressed against the window. "I guess this didn't go quite how we planned." Uniformed officers began moving people back from the windows, but Jim could see it wasn't an easy task.

Mark raised his head at that, a hint of smile turning up the corners of his mouth. "No?" He straightened, wincing as he did, his eyes going to Jessica. "Thanks for the drink, but about now, a shot of whiskey might be more appropriate."

Jessica smiled. "I hear you. I think I could use one myself."

Jim wanted to join in the conversation, and knew that after the harrowing encounter, a little light-hearted banter was exactly what Mark needed, but he had to stay focused. Just because they hadn't seen Kern, didn't mean he or one of his followers wasn't lurking in the crowd.

"Hey! I can fill that request!" Lily practically leaped across the room and flung open a cabinet against the back wall.

Mark took a deep breath, then raised his hand in a stop gesture as Lily reached behind some folders and lenses, and pulled a bottle of liquor out of the cabinet. "That's okay. I was only kidding, Lily. I'm still on antibiotics and I don't know how they would react to alcohol. I appreciate the thought, though. I'm sure it would have taken the edge off."

Dan grimaced and said, "Sorry about how this went down, Mark. I should have called back-up before you guys even got here. I just didn't think the crowd would be so aggressive. I mean, they were out there singing hymns a little while ago."

Mark waved him off. "It's not your fault. I shouldn't have stopped moving. I just kind of…froze, I guess." He raked his good hand through his hair and Jim didn't miss the slight trembling.

For all his lighthearted talk about shots of whiskey, Jim could see how shaken up he was inside. He crossed to stand in front of Mark. "Seriously, I need to know if there was any damage done."

Mark looked at his foot, hesitating. "Not really, but my foot got stepped on pretty good."

It took a moment for Jim to realize Mark was probably afraid to look—not that he could blame him.

Jim's own stomach churned at what they might find, and didn't know if he could look either. "Should I call paramedics?"

Mark pushed back in the chair. "No! It's fine. Last thing I want to do is add to the circus."

Jessica strode over from the windows. "Let me see." She took her jacket off and threw it over the back of a chair before bending on one knee reaching for Mark's foot.

Jim made a mental note to thank her.

Mark withdrew his foot from her grasp, and turned so that it was under the table. He wore an expression of horror. "It's fine!"

"Christ, Mark, it's just a foot. It's not like she asked you to drop your pants." Jim shook his head in mock annoyance.

Jessica's face turned pink and matched the color of Mark's ears. She, at least, overcame her embarrassment. "Come on. It's either that or we take you back to the hospital for them to look."

Mark's eyes narrowed and he looked from Dan to Jim and over to Lily. When no one offered any refuge, his shoulders slumped. He leaned over and tried to reach his laces to untie them, but stopped short and grabbed his stomach, his eyes screwed shut in a grimace. It was few seconds before he opened them again. Lily closed in on his side, her hand going to his back.

"You okay?" Jim stepped closer, but if Mark wasn't okay, he didn't know what he could do about it.

Mark nodded as he blew out a breath. "I just moved wrong."

Jessica bent and took his foot. "It's not a big deal. You think cops don't get hurt and need help sometimes? What would happen if we refused to let our fellow officers help us?"

He scowled, but extended his foot for Jessica to reach, then grabbed onto the side of the desk, wincing when she pulled the shoe off.

"Sorry, Mark."

Jessica glanced up, her expression sincere and it dawned on Jim that her tone had changed. Gone was the no nonsense professional tone he was used to hearing. In its place, was an intimate, soft inflection. That was forgotten when he got a look at a large blood-stain on Mark's sock. He swallowed and was glad he wasn't the one doing the examining.

Lily made a face and turned away. Apparently she wasn't a natural born medic either.

"You ready?" Jessica's hand hovered over Mark's foot.

"Okay." Mark's knuckles blanched as he gripped the arm of the chair, but Jim credited him with being braver than he would have been in the same situation as Mark leaned forward for a better look. Jessica eased his sock off and began unwinding the bandage.

Jim scrunched his eyes up in sympathy and tried to look away, but it was like a car wreck, he had to see. Lily looked like she was turning a bit green, so Jim said, "Lily, why don't you see if you have some clean cloth or bandages around?"

Obviously relieved for an excuse to get away, Lily stepped away from Mark. "Sure, I'll be right back."

Jessica turned his foot carefully, running her fingers lightly under it. Mark squirmed and her head shot up. "Does that hurt?"

"No...it...tickles." Now Mark's whole face turned a deep red, but he grinned.

Jessica laughed. "Sorry. I think just the scab came off and maybe some bruising on top." She took the towel Lily handed her and dabbed at the blood. Once it was clean, it didn't look so bad. Jessica rolled his sock back on, and Mark put his foot back in the shoe, his movements slow and careful. Jessica tied the shoe loosely before standing. She tucked her hair behind her ear. "There. Good as new."

"Thanks, Jessie." Mark stood and took a step, his grimace easing after a few test steps. He stopped in front of Jim, Dan and Jessica and extended his hand to Jim. "Well, thanks for the ride."

Jim stared at him in confusion. "What do you mean? Aren't you just going to get a few things?" He shot a glance at Jessica, wondering what she thought of this.

She frowned and put her hands on her hips. "What's the deal, Mark? What about the safe house?"

"Sorry, but I'm staying here. I told you guys that in the car. I can't live my life looking over my shoulder forever. If Kern is coming after me, I want to be on my own territory. At least now, my guard is up."

Jessie shook her head and Jim's mouth set in a firm line, but he finally scrubbed a hand down his face and sighed. "Fine, Taylor. We can't force you to go to a safe house." He crossed his arms and added, "About the best I can do is ask the Chicago PD put a few extra patrols around and check in with you daily." Jim glanced at Jessica to confirm the suggestion. It wasn't his call, officially.

She nodded and turned to Dan. "That should be possible, right?"

"I think we can manage to get the okay, but we can't promise more than a few days. The lieutenant won't approve more than that. Budget crunch and all."

Jim understood budgets only too well. He jabbed a finger in Mark's direction. "Keep your phone handy. If you see anything, hear anything, or hell, have one of your dreams, give us a call. Got it?"

"Got it. I'm just going to head upstairs and relax. I'll be fine. I doubt even Kern would try anything with all the witnesses around."

Jim decided he'd come by in the morning to check in on Mark. He didn't quite trust the phone arrangement any more.

Jessica sighed. "I'm not comfortable with you staying alone. I can stop by in the morning and check in with you. You might need help with your bandages."

"Lily, do you have the keys for the new locks? I'd like to give one to Jessie so she can come up in the morning." Mark kept his gaze locked on Jessica as he spoke and Jim had a feeling that Jessica had nothing to worry about when it came to Lily.

Jim shook off the surge of pleasure that revelation gave him. He didn't have time to entertain thoughts of romance. Besides, while Lily was cute, she was ten years younger than him, and he'd only met her a few times before the night of Mark's abduction.

Lily rummaged in her desk and pulled out a key ring. "Here you go. I got three sets. I wasn't sure how many you'd need. The locksmith assured me the place is more secure than Fort Knox now."

"That's great, Lil. Thanks." He took a set and handed it to Jessica, his eyes more alive than Jim had seen in a long time.

Jim changed his mind about checking in. He had a feeling Jessica would get a much better reception. He hid a smile as she flushed and nodded.

Lily laughed, obviously not the least upset that Jessica would have the nursing duties. "Great! It's settled then."

CHAPTER NINETEEN

The minute Jessie, Dan and Jim left, Mark took a deep breath and let it out slowly. The adrenaline rush from the day's events had completely dissipated, and now he felt drained.

Lily locked the door after the trio had left and closed all the blinds. Mark turned towards the door at the back of the office that led up to his loft. Something smelled great and his mouth watered. After bland hospital food, he was ready for something good. "Did you cook something, Lily?"

She grinned and caught up to him. "Yeah. Kind of a welcome home lunch. It's nothing fancy, just my sloppy joes and hash browns. I turned it off when I came downstairs when I heard the commotion outside. I just hope it's not too cold by now."

It was the perfect choice. He loved how she made them. The sauce was a blend of sweet and tangy and went great with salty hash browns. "That was really nice of you. Thanks. I can't wait."

"Good, because it's been ready for over an hour. I didn't know about the press conference until I saw it on the news at noon."

"Yeah. It was sprung on me last minute. It wasn't my idea."

"I didn't think it was, but you did great."

"Liar." He expected her to laugh, and when she was silent, he looked at her. "What's wrong?"

She stopped and rubbed her eyes.

Confused, Mark stepped in front of her and lifted her chin with one finger. "Lil? What is it?"

"I'm just angry at what is happening to you. It's not fair."

Mark smiled and pulled her into a one-armed hug. "Aren't you the one who's always saying God has a plan?"

Her shoulders shook as she chuckled against him. Pulling back, she wiped her eyes. "Yes, you're right. And I believe it. That doesn't mean I don't think that sometimes God's plans royally suck."

He laughed. "Come on. Let's go eat lunch."

Hobbling a bit, Mark made his way towards the steps, not relishing the thought of climbing them, but he found that going slowly helped and it wasn't bad. Entering, he felt a wave of both relief and dread wash over him. He was relieved to be home. There was no doubt about that, but this was where the cult had first attacked him, and he wasn't sure he'd ever feel completely secure here again.

Lily turned to him when he stopped just inside the door. "Mark? Are you okay?"

"Yeah, I'm fine, just a little creeped out." He tried to laugh, but it died in his throat. To forget about his fears, he looked around, noticing that the loft was immaculate. A lot cleaner even than it had been before the attack. He had to smile at that. He wasn't a slob, but when things got crazy with the camera, housekeeping chores fell by the wayside. "The place looks fantastic."

She smiled. "Thank you. I only organized the clean-up crew. Jessie helped and got her sister to pitch in as well. Did you know you had something green and fuzzy growing in your fruit bin in the fridge?"

Mark laughed. "No, I did not know that—not sure I wanted to either." He plopped down on the sofa with a sigh. "Sit down, Lily. We haven't had much chance to talk lately."

Lily settled in her usual chair. "We haven't, have we?"

Mark sagged against the back of the sofa; his arms limp. Closing his eyes, he relaxed for a few moments then the smell of his lunch made his stomach growl and he stood and followed his nose to the stove. The pan was still hot.

"I can get that, Mark."

"No, I'm good. You stay there. I'm tired of being waited on. I'm not entirely crippled."

Lily had already set out a couple of plates, so he just ladled the mixture onto the buns and saw that the hash browns were staying warm in the oven. In a few minutes he had plates ready. He pushed them to the side of the breakfast bar closest to Lily and called her to eat. He turned back and grabbed them each a can of pop out of his newly-stocked fridge.

"Who do I owe for all the food?"

Lily took a bite then wiped her mouth on a napkin. "It came from the petty cash."

Mark grinned. "I had a feeling."

They ate in silence, and he thought about the night of his abduction. He couldn't help it. There were so many unanswered questions. "Hey, Lily, how did anyone find me that night? If you told me already, I don't remember."

Lily set her fork down. "No, I didn't get a chance to

tell you. You had so much going on at the hospital, with nurses coming in and out so often, the moment was never right." She paused, dabbed her mouth with a paper napkin, and said, "Jim had a dream. In his dream, he saw what was happening to you. He tried to ignore it, but when you didn't answer your phone, he came here in the middle of the night."

Mark almost choked on his hash browns. He grabbed his drink and gulped down a large mouthful. "Jim had a dream? Like what I have?"

"Sort of, but it wasn't a future dream. It was in real time, as close as we can figure. We didn't know that then. We hoped we'd get to you before what he saw, and what was in the pictures, could actually occur."

"Pictures?"

Lily nodded. "Yes. From your camera."

A dozen questions flew to the tip of his tongue, but he bit them back to allow Lily to finish. "So, then what happened?"

"Well, as soon as Jim got here, he realized something had happened. The place was a mess. The door was wide open, and he called Jessie. It was the middle of the night, of course, but she came right over. After calling the police, they found the camera, and I developed the film at Gary's camera shop. The pictures led us to the warehouse."

"If I had developed my film that night..." The implications hit him. If only he had followed his usual routine.

Lily's eyes welled. "Yes. That thought has plagued me since I developed the film and we saw the pictures of you." She picked at her meal, her head bent. A tear splashed onto the countertop.

"Whoa. Wait a second. You don't think this is your fault, do you?"

She shrugged. "What am I supposed to think? If I hadn't talked you out of developing the film, you'd have seen what would happen, and at least had a chance of preventing it."

"You don't know that." Mark tried to think it through. The timing was all wrong. It was always harder to change the outcome when things happened at night or early morning. If 9/11 had happened at five in the evening instead of early in the day, he might have been able to make a difference there too, but it had been out of his control. "Besides, even if I developed the film, I wouldn't have had time to dream about it. They came for me in the middle of the night."

His heart pounded. Even just thinking about it brought back the terror of that night. He rubbed his temples. "What I want to know is how Jim factored into all of this? It doesn't make sense. How and why would Jim dream about what had happened--"

"No, it wasn't 'had happened', it's what was happening right then, possibly while he was there. At least, that's the way I understood it. It was the prayers he heard first."

"Prayers?"

"Yes. Bits and pieces of prayers." Lily's gaze dropped to the top of the breakfast bar for an instant before she took a deep breath and nodded. "Your praying woke him up. It wasn't until after he was awake that he had the dream or vision of you in the "How is that possible?" It wasn't at all what happened when he had his future dreams. While they often felt real, he always had the sensation of waking at the end. It never was the other way around.

Lily's lips compressed warehouse."

as she slowly shook her head and reached for his hand. "I have a theory." She bit her lip and closed her other hand over the top of Mark's, sandwiching his between hers. "I think you reached out to him."

Mark started, caught by surprise at her comment. "Reached out? What do you mean?"

"I think," she cocked her head to the side, "that your abilities expanded. You prayed for help, and God, as He does so often, didn't answer directly, but allowed your plea to be heard by someone. Someone who could then come to your aid." She gave his hand a gentle squeeze and smiled, "You reached out to Jim with your mind."

He yanked his hand out of her grasp. "No way. You're saying that I somehow sent a message to... Jim?" Shaking his head, he slid off the stool. "That's like…like mental telepathy. Nope. No way." He laughed sarcastically. "Lily, I think you're right about a lot of things, but not this. I'm not some kind of freak."

She shrugged. "I never said you were a freak. You have a gift. You should embrace it."

"Some gift. This is more like a curse." He raked his hand through his hair. "A new sweater is a gift, Lily. A necktie is a gift, but mental telepathy and seeing the future, that's something else completely. I don't know what it is, but it sure as hell is not a gift."

Lily nodded. "Yes, it is. And Mark, I hope someday you'll realize how truly amazing it is. Whatever or whomever controls how the camera and dreams work, did not want you to die that night. You have someone watching out for you."

Mark backed away from the breakfast bar, shaken by the thought. He was used to the magic that was the camera, but thinking about its origins and why it worked through him was something he tried not to think about. The idea that there could be more magic heading his way terrified him.

* * *

Lily insisted on washing the dishes and put the leftovers away for him to eat later. "Mark, why don't you rest a bit?"

His bed sported a new navy blue comforter and it looked soft and inviting, but he didn't feel like lying in bed. It felt weird to do so while Lily still puttered in the kitchen. He noted the new deadbolt on his door and felt a little more secure. After a while, bored, he put an old Jimmy Stewart movie in the DVD player, and stretched out on the couch. Even though it was one of his favorite movies, he couldn't concentrate. The commotion outside showed no signs of letting up and he rolled to a sitting position with a sigh, rubbing his stab wound absently.

Shouts and some kind of singing filtered up to his living room, even over the sound of the movie, and he stood and made his way to the window overlooking the street. Down below, in addition to the reporters, a large crowd like the one outside the hospital had formed. A police car was parked out front and its presence instilled a measure of comfort in him. He didn't know where Kern was or even if he was still after him, but he was at a loss as to why Kern had come after him to begin with.

Mark stepped back when someone below looked up and pointed. The noise intensified and cameras began flashing. Sighing, he turned away and almost bumped into Lily.

"I take it they saw you?" Her lips pursed into a frown.

Glancing over his shoulder at the window, he took a deep breath and said, "Yeah. Lily...how am I gonna do anything with them hanging around?"

She shook her head. "I guess after a while they'll get tired of waiting for some kind of 'sign' from you and leave. Besides, until you're healed enough to use the camera, you don't have to worry about it."

He looked at his bedside table on the far end of the loft. It was empty except for the light and clock radio. "Speaking of the camera, do you know where it is?"

Lily slapped her forehead, her eyes wide. "Shoot. I forgot. It's in the trunk of my car. I can run out to get it if you want."

Mark considered telling her no. He wasn't sure he'd be up to it, but while he hated to admit it, he missed the dreams already. "If you think you can make it past the crowd that would be great."

"No problem. I'm getting good at ignoring them, plus they think I'm boring. As long as they quit interfering with clients coming to the studio--"

"Wait. What do you mean by 'quit interfering? Has that happened?"

Her face colored as though she had let a secret slip. "It's not a big deal, Mark. Just a few clients called to cancel. They were a little freaked out by the crowd."

"Shit. I'm sorry, Lily. I'll make up the losses. I have some money saved and--"

She put her hands on her hips and interrupted, "You will not! You were upfront with me when we forged this partnership, and I was straight with you when I said I could handle it." Her eyes twinkled as she said, "Besides, for every person who has canceled, about three more have called to make appointments. We're swamped, partner." She grinned at him. "I'll be right back."

A few minutes later, she returned, the camera in hand. "I only had to fend off a dozen of your groupies."

Mark limped from the window where he'd been anxiously watching. "Seriously?" The crowd had stirred about the time Lily would have been outside, but he hadn't been able to see her car from his vantage point.

"No, I'm teasing. What I really wanted to do was give them the finger, but my mother might have seen it on the news."

Mark chuckled as he took the camera from her. He held his breath in anticipation of receiving the jolt of energy that he always got from the device. He waited. After thirty seconds, he frowned. Nothing. The camera didn't thrum or vibrate. It sat cold and lifeless in the palm of his hand.

"What's wrong?"

Mark turned the camera over, making sure it was the right one. Not that he had any that looked like it, but someone might have switched it out if they suspected. He squinted at it, sure it was his camera, but there was no connection. "It doesn't feel right."

"I didn't put any film in it, maybe that's what's wrong."

"I always keep some film in the closet, on the shelf." He tilted his head towards the closet next to the bathroom.

Lily found it and brought it over. Mark fumbled with the latch to get the door open to load the film, balancing the camera on his knees and holding it steady with the fingers of his left hand that poked out of his sling.

"You want me to do it?"

Mark shook his head. "No, I can manage." It took longer than normal, but he loaded the film and then headed towards the window. It was tricky holding the camera in one hand, but he lifted it and started snapping pictures of the crowd below. The photos would come out crappy, since he was taking them through dusty windows, but he wasn't worried about quality or composition of the photos. What did worry him was the lack of energy flowing from the camera.

Lily followed him, but stopped and leaned against the back of the couch. "Can you ever tell when it's working? Does it feel different when you press the shutter?"

He would have shrugged, but remembered in the nick of time not to. "Usually I can feel something even when I'm only holding it, and maybe it's because of the damage to my hands, but right now, it feels dead."

She made a noise that sounded sympathetic, but he concentrated on trying to get a few shots and didn't respond. He would have preferred to go outside and take photos randomly around town, like he normally did, but it was out of the question today.

When he finished off the roll, he let Lily take it downstairs to develop. There was no need for him to do that part. An hour later, she returned, her expression grim.

He knew the answer before she even told him. "It didn't work, did it?"

She shook her head and held up the photos. They

appeared exactly as he'd photographed them. "Look at it this way, Mark. Whomever controls the camera and your dreams probably also realizes that you aren't able to correct anything at the moment."

"I can do stuff now, Lily." Mark scrubbed a hand down his face, cursing softly when the corner of the dressing scratched his cheek a little. "Maybe not big saves, but I could do something."

"I'm sure you probably can, but maybe the camera genie feels like you shouldn't have to."

"Maybe." He didn't know why he considered the camera's lack of future photo production as personally directed at him, but he did. How often did he complain about the camera? Daily. Instead of worrying, he should be whooping for joy. What if he was finally done with it? The thought was unsettling. Mark leaned his right elbow on the arm of the couch and rested his head against his hand.

Lily made her way to the door. "Mark, why don't you at least try to sleep? I'm sure in a few days, things will get back to normal." She paused with her hand on the knob. "Will you be okay up here?"

Mark lifted his head, feeling his face burn. He was grateful for her tact, knowing what she really meant was if he afraid to stay alone? He cleared his throat. "Yes. I'll be fine. Thanks, Lily. For everything."

She smiled. "You're welcome. I'm glad you're home, Mark."

* * *

Mark watched a movie the rest of the afternoon and

as the sun began setting, he roused himself from the couch. This was normally his favorite time of day. Dusk dimmed the room while infusing it with a rosy glow from the setting sun as it reflected off the windows on the building opposite. Squares of light checkered the walls. He ate a bowl of cereal, not feeling like making anything big for dinner.

Afterwards, he washed up and came out of the bathroom to a loft that was almost completely dark. A chill raised the hair on his arms at the silence and darkness, and he hurried to turn on the light on the end table.

Later, in bed, he told himself that he just wasn't used to sleeping in complete darkness after the hospital, but after tossing and turning for an hour, he sat up. Every fiber of his being cried out in weariness, but as soon he'd relax, he'd hear a squeak or rattle. He rationalized it was probably just the sounds of the old building as it settled, but it still set him on edge. The fact that the cult had entered the loft so quietly, and he hadn't even known until they were pulling him from his bed, continued to haunt his memories.

If only he could know for sure that he would hear someone trying to get in the room. His mind flashed to the cans of soup in the cupboard. Feeling both stupid and relieved at the idea, he gathered the cans. It took a few tries, but he was finally able to balance one on the doorknob, and stacked a few more in front of the door. It wouldn't stop anyone from entering, but at least he'd hear them if they tried.

He sank back on the bed and fell into a dreamless sleep.

CHAPTER TWENTY

Mark awoke to the sound of pounding on the door followed by a thud as the soup can fell, knocking over the two beneath it. One can rolled noisily across the floor. His heart crashed against his ribs like a wild animal trying to escape its cage. He bolted up in bed.

"Mark?"

Jessie. He sagged back against the pillows and then flung the covers back and sat up again, slowly this time. He bit back a groan at a sharp twinge from his wound in his stomach. "Hold on." His voice sounded scratchy and he cleared his throat. "I'm coming." Standing, he raked his hand through his hair and tottered to the door. The first steps in the morning were always the hardest.

As soon as he opened the door, Jessie pushed past him, and looked around, her face alert. "What was that noise I heard? I thought you fell or something."

Mark stole a guilty glance at the cans. He debated ignoring them or picking them up, but chose to ignore them as well as her question. "Did you need something?"

Jessie turned from her inspection of the loft, her stance relaxing. "I was just stopping by, like I said I would."

Her gaze dropped, and Mark wanted to disappear into the floor when her eyes widened and focused on the soup cans. She took a step and grabbed one, her brow furrowing. Holding it, she looked at the other two and arched an eyebrow at him. "Is this your alarm system, or are the Boy Scouts coming by to collect for a food drive?"

Mark took the can from her, wanting to snatch it out of her hand, but refraining only because he didn't trust his grip yet. "Something like that." He motioned to the open door. "Well, now you've done your job. If you'll excuse me, I have things to do."

Embarrassment made him more abrupt than he intended. He'd looked forward to Jessie stopping by, and now he'd ruined it with his stupid fears and soup cans.

Ignoring the hint, Jessie strolled to the couch and sat. "Hmmm...soup cans. That was actually a pretty good idea, Mark. I like it."

Sighing, Mark shut the door. "Listen, I know you probably think it's crazy, but at least I knew I'd be able to hear if...if someone came back."

The amusement melted off Jessie's face and her eyes grew serious. "I know. I meant what I said. It is a good idea." She bit her lip, her focus shifting away from him before coming back a moment later. "It's hard learning to feel safe again. I know that."

Mark felt his throat constrict and he swallowed, unable to respond. Jessie surprised him with her perceptiveness, but then she had been a cop a long time. He guessed she knew a thing or two about these kinds of things. He took a deep breath and inclined his head towards the bathroom. "Excuse me...I gotta...I'll be back in a sec."

Her amused expression returned. "Take your time. I have all day."

He almost stopped and went back for a clarification,

but decided he'd find out soon enough. Quickly, he grabbed his clean clothes from his dresser and went to shower.

Toweling off, he realized he'd need some help getting his sling back on. He'd tugged his jeans on, even managing to button and zip them. The shirt was easy as he had chosen a button down and after pulling it on, eased his arm into the sling. Mark couldn't wait to be rid of the thing, but he still had awhile before the surgically repaired shoulder would be strong enough to support his arm.

He was becoming adept at doing most things one-handed, especially as his hand healed, but he couldn't wrap the belt around his back and hook it onto the front of the sling. It wasn't strictly necessary, but it eased the pressure on his neck. Opening the door, he stepped into the living area. "Uh, Jessie? Can you give me a hand--"

A half-eaten granola bar dangled from her fingers as she perched on a stool at the breakfast bar. A glass of orange juice sat beside her. She looked at him and nodded, setting the bar down. "Sure." She hopped off the stool and strode towards him.

Brushing her hands together, ignoring the few crumbs that fell from them, she said, "I noticed the camera on the counter. Don't you think you should take a little break from it?"

Mark felt a surge of anger. It was misdirected, and he knew it even as he snapped, "What is it with everyone wanting me to give up the camera?"

She held her hands up as though warding him off. "Hey, it was just a suggestion."

Mark forgot about the camera as she moved closer

and reached around him to retrieve the dangling belt. The familiar light floral scent of her hair wafted up to him, and he wanted to bury his nose in the shiny strands.

"I just thought you might do more harm than good with the camera right now. I never intended to make it sound like you should give it up completely." She stepped back, hooked the clip onto the ring and tightened the strap. "I should warn you that the news is still overrun with Mark Taylor stories. One camp thinks you're the second coming, the other thinks you're a total fraud."

Mark grunted as his shoulder pulled back with her tugging. The pain drew him from his thoughts of her hair and made him wonder if she was right. A rock settled in his stomach. He had an inkling what could be the problem with the camera. It had tested him and found him wanting.

Finished, Jessie looked up at him. "Are you okay? You look a little green around the gills."

Trying to walk lightly, he made his way to the bed and sat on the edge. "Yeah. I'm fine," he answered, his voice flat.

Finding his shoes, he eased his feet into them; not that he was going anywhere, but it was easier on his feet to walk with the support of the sneakers.

Jessie followed him and sat on the bed too. "You don't sound fine." Her eyes tried to lock with his, but he averted his gaze.

"I just thought of something, but it's not a big deal." He took a deep breath and stared at the soup can across the room. It had bumped into the wall and lay as evidence of his flawed character.

"Care to share?" Jessie asked quietly, her voice laden

with concern.

Swallowing, he closed his eyes for a second. "I think the news is partly right about me."

She crossed her arms. "What part would that be? Do I need to start going to the Church of Taylor?"

He laughed and shook his head. "No, nothing like that...but...but what if it was some kind of...test?" Mark glanced at her quickly then shifted his focus to the floor, finding a fascinating scratch on the wooden surface.

"You think God was testing you?"

Nodding, he risked raising his head. "Maybe."

"What makes you think God had anything to do with it? It was just a sicko cult leader who was trying to make a name for himself with his members."

"But why did he pick me? Other than that brief encounter, he didn't know me from Adam." Mark cringed at his poor choice of words. "And he got away with that, so why come back and risk getting caught? I mean, he knew that I could identify him."

Jessie shrugged. "Your name was in the news and it would have a bigger impact than just anyone off the street."

"Exactly. But why was I in the news to begin with?"

"Because of all that crap that the reporter said about you. Kern bought her story."

Mark took a deep breath and let it out slowly. "Yeah. She's the one who mentioned the second coming. We both know it's a crazy notion, but I can't get around the fact that the photos and dreams are true. Which begs the question of how does it work, and why am I the one who gets the dreams?"

"You're not starting to believe your own press, are

you?" she asked, punctuating the question with a chuckle.

"No, that's not what I'm getting at. I don't believe that I'm special, but I am beginning to wonder if I'm just an instrument, a puppet. A way for God--or whoever--to fix mistakes or hand out second chances."

"Kind of like a mob hit man in reverse." Jessie smirked.

Mark rolled his eyes. "You know what? Just forget it." He stood and crossed the room and slumped onto the sofa.

* * *

Jessie closed her eyes and shook her head, cursing her smart-ass mouth. It had been her armor from her teen years, her defense mechanism against classmates who'd teased her for being too skinny, with big eyes, buck teeth and scraggly blond hair. Her only defense had been her sharp tongue. After she filled out and had her braces off, boys stopped teasing her, but she'd found that in times of stress, the old habit of striking out with sarcasm kicked into high gear.

Hesitantly, she approached Mark and sank onto the chair beside the couch. He sat on the edge of the cushion, his head resting on his hand and elbow propped on his knee. His hair, still wet, stood on end from when he'd run a hand through it. The strands slowly settled into place, except for two stubborn spikes. She reached out of habit, intending to pat them into place, but he blocked her hand and leaned away from her. Her throat tightened, the feeling working its way down to settle in her chest. It hurt more than she expected, but no more than she deserved.

"I'm sorry, Mark. This is why I left. I'm no good for you. You need someone like Lily who never dives into the sarcasm pool head first."

"Lily? What the hell are you talking about?"

"You guys would be perfect for each other. She's cute. She believes in you with all her heart and you're both photographers--"

"So does that mean Jim would be perfect for you? Or your partner, Dan?" He looked away and stabbed his hand through his hair.

Jessie sighed. "No, that's not what I mean. I meant that I think you *are* special, even if I try to pretend that you aren't."

Mark turned, his eyes questioning.

She nodded. "I know. I don't act like it, but that's because it scares the crap out of me, Mark. I don't measure up. I'm not good enough for you."

Confusion crossed his face, and then he laughed. "Now you're the one falling for the stories." He shook his head, chuckling.

Taking a deep breath, Jessie stood and paced behind the couch. She stopped at the brick support beam, remembering entering the loft the night when Mark had been taken. The sight of blood on the bricks had sent terror shooting through her heart. Since then, she had tried repairing the cracks in her armor.

She trailed her fingers over the rough brick. Someone had cleaned it, but she could still spot a dark stain about six feet off the ground. Behind her, she heard Mark stand and limp towards her. His gait was better than it had been the day before, but she knew his feet still caused him pain. She turned and found him beside her. Lately, she had seen him sitting or lying down, but now, he towered over her and her eyes were level with his chin. He was looking over her head at the bricks and a muscle tightened in his jaw.

"They held me there first, and I thought they were going to kill me right then."

Jessie looked back at the pillar. "There was blood on it when I came up here that night." Mark glanced at her, but she wasn't sure if what she said registered because his eyes were distant.

"Kern told me that what they were doing was a test-- to see if I was like Jesus...because I had saved a lot of people." His voice cracked and he cleared it before continuing, "and Jesus saved people too."

Jessie hadn't heard this part. Mark had told what had happened physically, but hadn't offered many details. Dread curled her toes. What else had they said to him?

"He told me he could do a different ritual instead. An...an Aztec one where they would rip my heart out and show it to me before I died." He made a motion with his hand in front of his chest. His eyes were wide and focused somewhere beyond the pillar.

She felt like she might vomit. No wonder he was so worried about Kern coming back.

"Then he put the knife against me and he...he stabbed me and I thought he was going to do it--that he would pull my heart right out of my chest." His hand went to his stab wound and he rubbed it absently, his eyes a million miles away. "He said I was lucky because he didn't put it all the way in."

Jessie shuddered and closed her eyes. Now she fully understood why Mark had begged Kern to shoot him.

"I'm sorry."

He blinked and focused on her, his brows drawing together in confusion. "What do you have to be sorry about? You didn't have anything to do with it."

"I know, but I wish I could have prevented it from happening. Between the camera and Jim's dream, it seems like we should have been able to stop it."

Mark shook his head. "That's why I think it was a test. I had the photos right there on my camera, but I didn't bother to develop them. This was all my fault, nobody else's."

Now he wasn't making sense. "Who do you think is testing you?"

"I don't know." Mark sighed and circled the sofa, sitting heavily and rubbed his hand down his face. "The camera...it's part of all of this. I don't know how or why, but for some reason, the camera uses me to show certain images that I can change. If I could figure out who controls the camera, I could figure out how it works."

It was obvious to her who was in control, and she didn't believe God was testing Mark. Wasn't fifteen months as an enemy combatant test enough? "I have no doubt where the images on the camera come from and who plants them in your dreams. What I do doubt is that it was some kind of macabre test. What happened was a glitch. A mistake. Nothing more. You were meant to see the film, but you were tired and didn't. It just means you're human. "

"You think I don't know that? Every time I screw up--and I've done it plenty of times, Jess--I look in the mirror and know that I'm just some idiot who's in over his head. God finally figured it out too. It doesn't surprise me that he's given up on me."

"Fine. Keep thinking that, Mark, and you'll never get your gift back."

He rose from the couch and crossed to the door. "I have some things to do in my office."

* * *

Mark took a sip of coffee. Lily hadn't yet arrived and he was glad for a few moments of quiet as he sat at his desk. He looked through the drawers, noting that things had been moved around, but Lily had told him of the police's initial efforts to find out where he was. As far as he could tell, Jessie was still upstairs. That was fine with him. He'd already embarrassed himself enough around her.

Taking out a pencil, he opened the account books, intending to do some bookwork, but after glancing through them, his mind wandered. His brain was too full of questions to continue working on the books. Was Jessie right? Had it all just been a colossal mistake? He could handle that. It wouldn't be the first time he'd failed to stop something, and he doubted it would be his last. The difference was he'd always tried before. He hadn't ignored the camera like he had the night of his kidnapping. He drummed his fingers on the desk. The urge to talk to someone was strong and he pulled out his wallet and retrieved Scott Palmer's card.

As he lifted the phone to dial, Jessie knocked on the door and opened it. "Mark?" She tucked her hair behind her ear in the nervous habit that she had. "Can I come in?"

Mark dropped the phone and palmed the card. He

slid it into the top drawer. Jessie's eyes followed his movement, but she didn't question him. "Since you're here already. You might as well come on in."

She took a deep breath and let it out, her gaze darting to the left before settling on him. "I'm sorry if I sounded patronizing. I was trying not to upset you and I guess I failed at that."

Mark didn't let his face soften and he didn't speak. Did she think he was so fragile that she couldn't be straight with him?

Stepping into the room, she crossed her arms and her eyes dropped to the floor. "Look, I'm a cop. I'm trained to be skeptical."

"And you're very good at your job," Mark said, his voice hard.

Jessie bit her lip then said, "I thought I was good at it, but I guess I'm not as good as I believed. If I was good, I'd have found Kern already, and, well, anyway, I wanted to tell you that I called Dan and he's going to send over a uniformed cop to keep an eye on the place."

Mark relented. He couldn't help it. Her distress and sincerity was plain as day in the expression on her face. Jessie was never this humble and he couldn't stand it. He sighed and motioned to the chair on the other side of the desk. Propping one elbow on the desk, he swiveled to be parallel to the desk and tilted back in the chair. "Don't leave. If I have to have a babysitter, I'd rather have you than some other cop."

"Are you sure?"

"Yeah, I am."

She sat and took a deep breath, and her shoulders visibly relaxed. After a moment, she glanced at the phone.

"Were you getting ready to call someone?"

Mark felt the blood rush to his face. "Uh, yeah, actually I was going to make a personal call."

Nodding, she stood and crossed to the door. "I'll take a look around the place. Are you doing photo-shoots today?"

"I'm not shooting, but Lily has a couple. I have a ton of paperwork I can do." At least one little piece of his life could get back to normal. He picked up the phone, and instead of calling Scott Palmer, he called Lily to ask her if she needed him to switch out backdrops. After clearing the air with Jessie, he didn't feel the need to call the psychiatrist anymore.

CHAPTER TWENTY-ONE

Mark ventured outside for the first time a few days later. He was so weary of being cooped up, and the weather was unseasonably warm. Cops patrolled often enough that the crowd had thinned, and a fender bender down the street claimed the crowds' attention for the moment.

He stood in the doorway and closed his eyes for an instant. The sun heated his face and a soft breeze tickled through his hair. It felt wonderful.

The snow had completely melted, even the dirty piles in the corners of parking lots. The sky dazzled an endless deep blue. Mark decided to head towards the lake front. He always liked watching the first sailboats of the season sail out on trial runs.

The second he stepped foot onto the sidewalk, someone spotted him, and before he knew it, he was surrounded. Mark held his arm out, trying to keep people away from his injured shoulder. "Hey!"

The hands touched him and his skin crawled. The sensation was so much like the night of his abduction that it was all he could do to keep from striking out. His breathing quickened. "Get back!" He reflexively swung his arm when someone touched his head.

Mark tried to duck away from the people, but a woman had a determined grip on his collar. The material pulled on his still tender neck, and he reached up to pry his shirt from her fingers. With a loud rip, the material gave way.

It was like a feeding frenzy in a shark tank. More hands reached in, tearing bits from his shirt and even his pleas that they were hurting him didn't stop them. If they were so in awe of him, why would they do this? Only the whoop of a police siren, and the screech of tires as an unmarked sedan came to halt at the curb beside him kept Mark from hitting someone or being torn apart.

"Step away from the man!"

Mark had never been so happy to hear Jim's sharp commanding tone. He sagged as the crowd fell back.

"You okay, Mark?" Jim's eyes bore into him, his mouth set in an angry line.

Mark nodded. Jim ordered the people to leave or they'd be arrested for assault. The threat of arrest did the trick and the crowd dispersed, some waving scraps of Mark's shirt as trophies.

Without a word, Mark turned and headed back into the studio and up to his loft. Anger filled him and he yanked a new shirt from his drawer. It took some effort to untangle the tattered remains of his old shirt from the belt of the sling and the longer it took, the angrier he became. Footsteps sounded on the stairs. Finally, he reached behind his neck and pulled the support band over his head and tore the whole contraption off and flung it to the floor.

"You're sure you're okay?"

"Yeah. I'm fine, Jim." He knew the other man wasn't to blame, but Jim was the one that was there. "Those people are *crazy*!" Mark pulled his shirt over his head. He

2

was so mad he was shaking and his next statement came out low and harsh, "I can't live my life like this."

"You won't have to. It might not seem like it after that experience, but the crowds are down to about half of what they were a few days ago." Jim shoved his hands in his pockets and said, "Unfortunately, the ones who are still hanging around are the real zealots."

Mark shook his torn shirt in Jim's direction. "Ya think?" He threw the shirt on the sofa.

"Where were you going?"

"What difference does it make?"

Jim's eyes narrowed. "Look, Taylor, I don't give a damn, but since Kern's still out there as well as Medea, it might be a good idea to at least tell me when and where you're going so if you come up missing, we'll know where to start looking!"

Mark's anger evaporated and he dropped onto the couch and leaned forward. Cradling his head in his hands, he closed his eyes in embarrassment. "I'm sorry. I know it's not your fault."

"Forget it. Anyway, I was coming by to tell you that there was a possible sighting of Kern in the city. It hasn't been confirmed, but I wanted to keep you up to date. You have your phone, right?"

Mark raised his head, his stomach knotted up tighter than a strand of old Christmas lights. "Yeah. I've been carrying it."

"Good. Listen, I don't care if you're going to see your bookie, I want to know about it, understand?"

With a snort of laughter, Mark let a smile crack his face. "Yeah. Got it. Loud and clear."

"Good. I spoke with Jessie this morning and she's

going to come by and stay here later today and until then, the CPD will increase patrols around the neighborhood. Tonight, Dan said he'd send over a uniformed officer to park in front of the building."

Mark stood and held out his hand. "Thanks for saving my butt out there."

Jim smiled and shook the outstretched hand. "No problem."

* * *

Mark spent the rest of the morning cooped up in his office going over paperwork. It was a chore he hated and never seemed to find the time to do thoroughly. Now, he had nothing *but* time. He looked at the clock and wondered when Jessie was going to show up. He took a sip from a bottle of water and bent over the books again. After an hour, he tossed his pencil down and rubbed his eyes. The numbers had begun to dance and blur and he knew he was done. He stretched and winced when he forgot about his shoulder for a moment. He needed a break and decided to head to O'Leary's Pub. It had been his and Jessie's favorite place to grab a burger and beer, and right now, he craved something familiar and comforting. After a quick call to Jim that left him feeling like a teenager calling his dad for permission, Mark called a cab and made it out the door without incident.

The lunch crowd had left and happy hour hadn't yet begun as Mark ventured into the bar, relieved at the change of scenery. He was glad he hadn't hidden away at home. He saw some patrons point and whisper, but nobody approached him and he was grateful for that.

"Hey, Bob. How're you doing?" Mark approached the bar.

"Great. How 'bout you?" Bob wasn't a chatty bartender, and not much fazed him. If he knew about Mark's recent troubles, he kept it to himself.

"Good. Can I get a tapper?"

Bob nodded. "Sure thing." He filled a tall glass and slid it in front of Mark. "I heard you had a bit of trouble."

Mark sipped the cold brew. "Yeah, but it's all good now."

"Glad to hear." After a pause, he added, "The Cubs are coming on in a few minutes. You want me to put them on?"

"Sure." He smiled and took another swig then rounded the bar and settled on a stool closer to the TV to watch the game. It felt good to do normal things.

Jessie showed up during the fourth inning. "Hey, Mark. This isn't exactly staying out of sight."

Mark finished off his second beer and set the glass down with a thump. The leash was beginning to strangle him. "Look, Jess, I can't hide forever."

"Nobody's asking for forever, just a few more days."

"How did you know I was here?"

"I got to the loft, and you were nowhere to be found. I called Jim. He said you were here. He also mentioned the fiasco this morning. What were you thinking to leave without someone around? You were just damn lucky Jim showed up when he did." She stood in front of him, arms crossed and her eyes flashing as she cast a dubious glance at the empty glass. "I thought you were on medications?"

"I finished them, not that it's any of your business."

Bob turned to look at Jessie and then gave Mark an

amused look. Feeling like a scolded schoolboy, Mark slid off the stool and headed for the door. She could follow or not, but he wasn't going to invite her. The rapid click of her shoes behind him let him know that she followed.

Her car was parked out front, and he debated passing it and walking home or catching a cab, but decided it would just make him look silly, so he climbed into the passenger seat when she unlocked the door. Neither spoke on the drive back to Mark's loft, and the feeling of being a teen caught out after curfew settled over him. He had a feeling it was going to be a long evening.

* * *

"Where's your sling?"

Mark ignored her while he found the remote between the sofa cushions and turned the game on. If he was lucky, he'd get to see the last few innings. He flopped onto the couch and brought his legs up, crossing them at the ankles. He heard her sigh as she moved behind him and then a thump as she set her purse on the counter top. The refrigerator door creaked and he found it somewhat amusing that she still felt comfortable enough to help herself. It even felt right.

He tilted his head towards her when she sat on the chair, a bottle of water in one hand and a bag of cookies in her lap. He didn't even know he had cookies. Chocolate chip. His favorite. It must have been one of the items that Lily had stocked him with.

She bit into one then spoke a few seconds later. "I guess I should have kept my mouth shut at O'Leary's. I didn't mean to embarrass you. I think it's low blood sugar.

I'm starving."

Mark returned his focus on the game, but he felt tension ease out of his muscles.

"Who's winning?"

"Cubs. Three to two." Without looking, he held his hand out and Jessie placed three cookies in it. He smiled.

They crunched cookies and Jessie poured them each a tall glass of milk to go with them. By the bottom of the seventh inning, Mark felt his eyes grow heavy.

* * *

Mark awoke by degrees as he heard the game still droning on—something about extra innings. A distant car horn sounded. He was so comfortable that he was loathe to move. With nowhere important to go, he allowed himself the luxury of relaxing. It was so quiet, he wondered if Jessie had left.

He cracked his eyes open. The light outside filtered pink and gold through the windows. Jessie sat slumped in the chair, her legs stretched out, and he assumed she was dozing. Then he saw her eyes were open and focused on him. Her face wore a soft look he hadn't seen in ages, and curious, he kept his eyes only slivered, watching her through his eyelashes.

While she freely watched him, Mark took the opportunity to return the observation. Her skin glowed in the soft light. He always thought she had beautiful eyes when they weren't shooting daggers at him. The long lashes and delicately arched brows framed eyes that didn't miss a thing. Her white blouse fit her well and he admired the smooth skin of her neck and followed it down to where it disappeared.

She continued to observe him, her gaze roaming his body, lingering at times. For the first time since she'd left him, she looked at him not with anger, pity, or exasperation but with something else. His body recognized the look and his face warmed. Would she see his breathing quicken? Mark shifted, and knew that his face must be flaming red now.

Her eyes widened and flew to his. Jessie's cheeks stained as she met his gaze. Mark couldn't look away and surprise shot through him when she held the look. Her tongue darted out, touching the corner of her mouth for an instant and it was all he could do not to groan. He sat up, his eyes dropping to her lips. And then lower. He couldn't help himself. The fabric made a slim V to the buttons and seemed to draw his eyes down like an arrow point. The visible skin turned a dull red.

"H-have a good nap?" Jessie dipped her head, looking anywhere but at him.

Mark nodded. "Yep. A great nap."

He scooted over on the sofa, his knee brushing her thigh and he felt a jolt of heat where their bodies touched.

Jessie flinched, but left her leg resting against his. His heart raced when he saw the wild beating of the pulse in her neck. Without thinking, he reached out to touch it. Her eyes followed his hand, and her breath fluttered across his knuckles. He touched the pulse point, feeling the strong beat of her heart. Jessie's skin felt like warm satin under his fingertips, and he couldn't get enough of it. Her hair fell forward as she leaned into his hand.

Mark slid his hand farther back, burying his fingers in the silky strands, and her head lolled back as she let out a soft sigh.

"Jessie."

She opened her eyes and his breath caught at the simmering passion. Leaning in, he captured her lips, tasting them and felt a thrill when he met no resistance. He groaned when her mouth opened, welcoming him. Her arms circled his neck, her fingers skimming through his hair. He'd missed this.

He needed more and pressed closer, lengthening the kiss, savoring it. It wasn't enough. Mark trailed kisses down her neck. She tilted her head, allowing him access. God, she tasted wonderful. Following the curve of her throat down, he felt her shudder beneath his lips. His body trembled as her hands dove down the back of his shirt.

His exploration of her throat continued as he pushed the material aside. Her scent enveloped him, intoxicating his senses. Mark trailed his hand down, his fingers working the first button, popping it free. She leaned back into the chair and Mark followed as he stood, his body almost lying atop hers. Her hands undid several of his shirt buttons and he moaned against the swell of her breast when her hands roamed his shoulders. He freed another button and opened her blouse, absorbing the sight of her. He dipped his head, kissing the valley between her breasts and reached his hands beneath her to unclasp her bra, but his hand tangled in the strap from her shoulder holster. With a muffled curse, he tugged on it.

"Wait!" Jessie went rigid and sat up, almost bashing Mark's nose with her knee as she scrambled backwards.

Bewildered and panting, Mark stumbled back, half falling on the sofa behind him. "W-what?"

Jessie swung her legs over the arm of the chair and clutched the edges of her shirt, pulling them together. "We...we can't do this."

Mark licked his lips, still tasting the hint of salty tang from her skin. "Why not?"

"Because I'm working and you're...you're a victim I'm supposed to be protecting, that's why not!"

His eyes snapped to hers and his stomach clenched. "A *victim*? That's how you think of me?"

Her head was down as she straightened her clothing. "Look, Mark. You've been under a lot of stress and..." Her face flushed a deep red. "...and it's natural to look for relief and we have a history, so I understand why you thought—."

"Stop!" Mark dropped his head and closed his eyes. After a moment, he was able to get his breathing under control, but he glanced at the zipper of his jeans and felt his skin burn all the way to the tips of his ears. He stood and turned his back to her, not knowing what to do. It was a one-room loft and no way was he going to flee to the bathroom. His voice was hoarse when he spoke again. "Could you just...just give me a minute?"

"Sure."

He heard her footsteps head towards the kitchen and the water turned on. Mark ran a hand through his hair and tried to push the image of Jessie lying beneath him out of his mind. Getting his body back under control should have been easy after she splashed the victim label all over him like a pail of ice water, but his mind and body had opposite ideas.

"You okay?"

Mark groaned. Why couldn't she just leave him be?

"I'm fine." Even to his own ears, his voice sounded tight. He took a few more deep breaths, then strode to the kitchen and opened the fridge, grabbing a beer. He dared her to say anything as he shot her a look.

"Look, Mark, I didn't mean that I think of you as *just* a victim. You know I think you're more than that." She stood in the doorway between the kitchen and the living area.

He slugged back several gulps of the beer and swiped his mouth with the back of his hand. Raising an eyebrow, he said, "Oh no? Well, what exactly do you think of me, Jessie?" Mark pushed past her and tried to ignore the sizzle he felt when his arm brushed against hers.

He didn't expect a reply and her silence didn't surprise him. He stood behind the couch, tipped the bottle and stared blankly at the ballgame. He felt shame at how far he had carried the kiss. This was Jessie. She'd made her feelings about him known when she'd left him.

Even without looking, he sensed her presence behind him, but he couldn't bring himself to turn around. He dreaded seeing her opinion of him scrawled all over her face. Instead, he wandered to the window.

Dusk had deepened, casting the street below in dark purple shadows. The light of a couple dozen candles bobbed and weaved as a small crowd mingled on the walk. Could they see him up in the window? The loft was dim, but the television cast a glow. Just in case, Mark raised his beer in a mocking toast. "Bottoms up!" The brew was cold and he savored the taste.

"Feel better?"

"No." Mark didn't look at her.

She sighed. "Look, I'm working. What if something

happened while we were...you know?"

Mark tried to keep his anger flowing, but she had a point.

"If Kern comes, and I can't get to my gun or cell phone, what good am I up here?"

Mark glanced at her. Her eyes scanned the crowd below and he knew she wasn't seeing them as religious zealots, but as possible Kern followers. He regarded them as a nuisance, she viewed them as impending criminals. "My timing stinks."

Jessie laughed. "Correction. *Our* timing stinks. Someday maybe we'll have a chance to discuss things when there's not some major catastrophe or crisis looming on the horizon."

Mark moved away from the window. He didn't want to wait for someday. One thing he had learned from all he endured, is that someday might never come.

* * *

Mark and Jessie settled in for the evening. Mark ordered Chinese food and they talked about their childhoods. She laughed at his all-American upbringing in a small town. He tried to understand her city savvy, knowing that even as long as he'd lived in Chicago, he didn't have the same attitude as born city-dwellers. Mostly, he grinned so much, the curve of his mouth felt permanent. Now that the sexual tension was acknowledged, he could relax in her presence for the first time in months.

"Your turn." Jessie sat on the chair, her legs drawn up and crossed. A big bowl of popcorn rested in her lap.

Mark shook his head. "Oh no. It was your idea to bring up our most embarrassing moments. You have to go first."

Jessie tilted her head, gazed at the ceiling and then laughed. "Okay, I got one. I had a fancy dinner to attend at some hoity-toity restaurant. I don't normally get invited to those kinds of things and I was so excited!" She reached into the bowl and tossed a few kernels in her mouth. "It was snowing and I didn't want to ruin my new shoes. I had splurged and bought a pair of designer pumps and you know how hard those heels are to walk in."

Mark had no idea but nodded to encourage her to continue.

"I grabbed my boots, and reached in my closet and snagged the shoes out, thinking about how clever I was to wear the boots in the car and then switch to the heels when I arrived.

"Uh-huh." He didn't care a whit about the shoes, but the sparkle in her eyes as she told her tale had him hooked. "Smart thinking."

"Well, it would have been if I hadn't grabbed two different style pumps, both for the left foot!

Snorting with laughter, Mark leaned over and helped himself to the popcorn. He held it with his hand shelved against his belly. There would probably be a big grease stain from the ton of butter she had doused it with, but he didn't care. "So what did you do?"

"I did what any lowly cop would do in that situation. I drove around looking for a Cheap Feet shoe store. Unfortunately, the whole town was filthy rich and didn't have one, so I did the next best thing." She ate some more popcorn.

"And what would that be?"

"I jammed my right foot into the left shoe. That wasn't even the hard part." Her eyes danced. "The hard part came when I realized that the heels were different heights."

Mark laughed, picturing Jessie hobbling around in the shoes. He continued to snicker as he stretched back on the couch. His shoulder was beginning to ache from being unsupported all day, but he didn't want to break the spell.

"Okay."

"Okay...what?" He rubbed the sore joint and hoped he could distract her from what he knew she wanted.

She tossed a few kernels of popcorn at him. "You gotta tell your most embarrassing moment."

Mark scratched his head. "I'm not sure I can narrow it down to just one." He slanted a look at her. "Well, actually, I think my most embarrassing moment occurred just a few hours ago."

Jessie blushed. She opened her mouth, but before she could speak, someone knocked on the door. She jumped up, popcorn flying as the bowl toppled to the floor.

Mark swung around to a sitting position, cursing his lack of sling as his arm felt like a heavy dead weight. If someone burst in, he'd be at an even greater disadvantage with his arm unsupported.

Jessie had her gun in hand as she crossed to the door. "Who is it?"

"Chicago P.D, ma'am."

She cracked the door and then holstered her weapon. She stepped halfway into the hall and said something to the cop. A minute later, she came back in and shut the door.

Disappointment washed over Mark. He could see by her look that she was leaving. There was no reason for her stay with the patrol outside his building all night.

As though reading his mind, she turned to face him. "Guess I can get home now."

At least she sounded a little disappointed too. He nodded.

CHAPTER TWENTY-ONE

Jim pushed the off button of his cell phone, feeling the pressure of Mark's scrutiny from the other side of the breakfast bar. He wished he had better news to tell him, but at least they'd located Kern's group. "That was Jessica. There's good news and bad news. Good news is, they found where the cult is staying."

Mark's eyes widened. "Where are they?"

"An apartment building on the southwest side. 5000 block of West Jackson. Not a nice neighborhood, apparently."

"So, they can arrest them and this nightmare will be over?" The hope in his voice was palpable.

Jim sighed. "I wish they could, but by your own admission, you couldn't see the faces of anyone but Judy Medea and Adrian Kern. Neither were on the premises when CPD investigated. All they were able to do was some questioning as to their whereabouts."

"You're kidding." Mark wandered out of the kitchen and over to the sofa. As if his legs had turned to water, he sank onto it.

Jim picked up his mug of coffee and moved out to the living room area. "Listen, Mark. We'll find him. Plenty of people are working on this. Not only because of what happened to you, but because of the similarities between what happened to Judy Medea and the other young woman who was killed before she could testify. He's created a pattern, and now we can get him."

"Here's the good news. A tip came in from an informant in Mexico who says he talked to Kern, or at least a guy claiming credit for what happened to you. He reported that Kern was trying to arrange a shipping pipeline of drugs to finance his cult's activities. He thinks everything is arranged, but the informant says that his bosses want nothing to do with him. It seems that despite their violence, they are religious folks."

Mark raised an eyebrow and gave a snort of disbelief.

Jim chuckled. "Yes, I realize the irony of that. Despite their violent ways, they go to church on Sundays."

He set his mug on the coffee table, sat on the chair, and began ticking off the rest of the information. "From Mexico, we know he stayed with a woman in El Paso. Her name turned up in an old file. We sent a man to the house, but it turns out we just missed him. We are getting closer, Mark. Not only that, but Medea might still be around here and just wasn't home. CPD will be keeping an eye on the apartment and if she shows up, she'll be arrested."

"And in the meantime? What if they don't show up for months? Do I live my life watching over my shoulder?"

Jim had no answer as he sat in the chair beside the couch. Kern's history had shown that he was never in a hurry to exact revenge. He'd never even been tied to any of the deaths of witnesses. It was only now that everything was being scrutinized that the grand puzzle of Kern's scheme was coming into focus. He sipped the coffee, trying to delay the worst part, that he hadn't even passed on the bad news yet. "There's more. According to the police, the cult has swelled to triple its previous size."

That got Mark's attention. His eyes snapped to Jim's.

"Because of all the media?"

Jim nodded. "I'm afraid so. The publicity has flushed all the weirdos, zealots and sickos out from under the rocks they live under when they aren't acting like crazy fools."

Mark's mouth set in a hard line. He stood and for a few seconds, he remained motionless. Finally, he turned to Jim and said, "You know what? I'm not going to spend my life hiding in here." He swept his arm in an arc to encompass the loft. "If Kern's going to get me, I might as well meet him halfway." With that he crossed to the other end of the loft and grabbed his camera off his night table. He opened the drawer and pulled out a roll of film.

Jim rose and stepped in front of Mark as the other man approached the door. It was going to be hell trying to protect a moving target, but he couldn't officially keep Mark confined to his home. "Hold up. Where are you going?"

Mark slung the camera's strap over his neck, wincing as it settled, but the hard resolve in his eyes didn't waver. "I'm going out to take some photos. You have a problem with that?" He brushed past Jim and grabbed his jacket off the stand beside the door. With his left arm in a sling, he had to fumble with the coat to get it over his confined arm and slide his good arm into the sleeve.

Jim watched, keeping his urge to help under tight control as Mark managed to get his left hand out far enough to hang onto the edge of the coat to hold it steady so he could zip it. "I thought that camera didn't work?"

Mark tugged on the zipper and then arranged the camera strap on the outside of his coat collar. "It works just fine." He paused and the muscle in his jaw jumped. "It just doesn't give me future photos."

"You knew that's what I meant."

Eyes narrowed, Mark glanced at him. "Yeah, but I thought you wanted confirmation. You want the truth? Here it is. I screwed up and I lost my ability. I'm not even sure why you're still hanging out around here. What value am I to you now?"

Mark's question hit him like a brick to the face. As much as he hated to admit it, without the possibility of foretelling of a future terrorist attack, Mark Taylor had no value as an asset. "First of all, whether you get the ability back or not, no way do I believe that you screwed up. What you've already done as part of the Wrigley Field plot cements your place as an American hero-"

Mark scoffed before Jim could finish. "Cut the crap, Jim. I'm just a regular guy, which is *exactly* what I wished for." He opened the door and motioned with his chin for Jim to proceed him.

Jim shrugged and said with mild sarcasm, "Despite your amazing abilities, you were only able to change the future, Mark, not the past. You saved a bunch of people, and in my book, that's a hero. You can't change that no matter what happens from here on out."

The door clicked shut behind him and Jim measured his pace to allow Mark to keep up. Steps seemed to be harder for him to navigate than flat ground, and Jim slowed even more.

"I'm glad I'm done with it." Mark released the handrail long enough to point towards the door at the bottom of the steps. "Now if you could just tell all those folks hanging out by my door that the freak show is over, I'll be eternally grateful."

Despite Mark's attempt to act like he didn't care, Jim could hear the pain in his voice. The guy was torn and Jim suspected that Mark didn't want to stop saving people, he just wanted to do it completely anonymously. He was at home behind the camera, not in front of the lens. Being a hero brought the risk of too much attention and that went against Mark's natural inclination to make others look good and just record history, not make it.

Jim nodded. "I'll be glad to clear the way for you."

* * *

Mark tried to ignore the crowd as he followed closely behind Jim, but when a woman thrust her baby at him, he reacted on instinct, cradling the baby girl with his good hand an instant before pushing her gently back into her mother's arms. "Ma'am. Please take her. I don't want her to get hurt."

The woman took her back, tears pouring down her face as she turned to others behind her and shouted, "Did you hear that? He said he didn't want her to get hurt! That means my baby's heart will be fixed!"

Mark stopped, intending to correct the woman's assumption, but Jim turned and edged between the woman and Mark and with a hand to Mark's back urged him forward and said, "Don't bother. Let her believe what she wants."

"But she thinks I fixed the baby's heart. I can't let her believe that."

"You have no control over it, unfortunately. What you can control is getting your ass into my car so I can get you the hell out of here."

Mark hesitated. "I was going to take the "L" or maybe a cab." The doctor hadn't cleared him to drive yet, but he hoped he'd get the okay in a week when he went back for a follow-up.

"Impossible. You'll be mobbed before you reach it. Just get in the damn car, Taylor." Jim opened the door for him.

As the crowd surged towards him after the woman's pronouncement, Mark didn't need any more urging. He flinched when a hand reached for his head, but the fingers only brushed his hair before he ducked into the car.

Feeling like a fish in bowl, Mark kept his eyes forward as people pushed against his window. Jim slipped in his side and started the car, pulling away fast enough that the people had to jump back.

"Shit, Jim! You almost ran a few of them over." Mark turned to look behind them to make sure no bodies lay in the road.

"I didn't come close, but it would serve them right, the imbeciles." Jim looked in the rear view mirror, his brow furrowed in concern, and Mark wasn't fooled. It had been close. Damn close.

Mark settled into the seat and asked, "Where are we going?"

Jim suddenly laughed. "I have no idea. Away from there is all I had in mind." He glanced at Mark. "Where did you want to go? You're calling the shots, I'm just the chauffeur."

"I didn't have a set destination. I was just going to go take photos." His intention had been to take the bull by the horns and regain control of his life without worrying about the cult and Kern. An inkling of an idea took root.

Instead of waiting around, he'd go to them-show them he wasn't afraid. "I want to see the apartment."

"The cult's apartment?"

Mark nodded, then realized Jim was driving and not looking at him, so he said, "Yeah. I want to take some photos of it."

The side of Jim's mouth quirked as he shrugged. "If you say so."

"What? You don't think I should?"

"I like the idea of taking it to Kern and the cult, but I don't think we should tip our hand. I think it would be better to draw them out."

Drumming his fingers on the armrest, Mark tried to shake off the idea that popped into his head. No way. It was crazy. "You said that Kern has a history of getting rid of witnesses, right?"

"Yes, that's correct."

Jim stopped at a light and turned to Mark, but Mark ignored the other man for a moment as a crystal clear scene formed in his mind. It was so powerful, it made him shiver in response. It was almost like a future dream, only different, because he wasn't dreaming.

"Taylor? I don't think I like that look on your face. What are you thinking?"

The car jumped forward, and Mark was grateful to feel Jim's gaze leave him and turn to the road. The concept was crazy. It wouldn't work. Still...what if it did? "What if we bait a trap for Kern?"

"I knew I wouldn't like what you were thinking." Jim sent Mark a sidelong glance. "What kind of trap?"

"I could hold a meeting."

"What kind of meeting? I'm not sure I get it."

"I was thinking some kind of religious meeting...like a revival or something." His face burned and he knew he shouldn't have brought it up. What did he know about revivals? "It's just that all these people are hanging around anyway. If I held some kind of ceremony, they would come, I know it. I just have a feeling that Kern and his group would come too."

"Huh." Jim didn't look at Mark as he turned right on to Jackson. "He'd probably know it was a trap. Especially since you told everyone in the press conference that you wanted to be left alone."

Mark's hopes sank. Jim was right. He couldn't just have a meeting without arousing suspicion. "Yeah, I guess so."

They drove in silence for several minutes, before Jim cleared his throat. "You might not be able to pull it off without looking suspicious, but I could."

"What could you pull off?" Mark was totally confused.

"I could hold a revival as a sort of disciple of yours." A flush crept up Jim's neck from his collar.

Mark grinned. "A disciple? Seriously?"

Jim shrugged, but didn't look at Mark. Instead his eyes appeared to be locked on the road ahead of them. "Listen, we never spoke about what happened the night of your kidnapping."

Mark felt his own face heat up. "So?"

The car swerved suddenly and Mark had to grip the door handle to keep from sliding into the door as Jim parked the car along the curb. The action sent a shard of pain through his still tender palm. "Jeez, give a warning next time you do that, would you?" He flexed his fingers a few times until the pain eased.

The car lurched as Jim slammed it in to park. "Taylor, this isn't something I'm comfortable talking about either."

"Lily already told me what happened. I admit it's kind of weird, but I don't think it was what she was saying, like I called out to you or anything." Even voicing the possibility embarrassed him. "I think it was just a freaky coincidence. Probably the scene was planted in your subconscious by what you knew of Judy Medea's incident."

Jim laughed, but it lacked humor. Instead, he seemed to be laughing at himself.

"What's so funny?"

"I finally realized how you must feel every time you try to tell someone about your dreams."

That statement caught Mark off-guard. Was he acting condescending to Jim? "Sorry. I'll shut-up and listen."

"I'll keep it brief. I heard you praying. It was so loud, it woke me up in the middle of the night. I know it was real, not some figment of my imagination, but that's not important for my plan. I'll have to take on a different identity to pull this off, but I have some resources at my disposal who can give me a new identity, history and experiences so authentic, my own mother would start to doubt who I am."

Jim finally faced Mark, his mouth curved into a rueful smile. "What I propose is passing out flyers to your fans, that I'm going to hold a revival of sorts. I'll tell all about my dream, but I'll keep the photo part out of it. "

Mark nodded, but his thoughts had snagged on the part about Jim waking up because of the praying. "Do you think I reached out to you?"

Jim was silent for a long moment. "Hell if I know. I'm not a praying kind of guy, but if you can get future photos and dreams, I guess anything is possible."

"Yeah. I suppose. I'm not much for religion either," Mark admitted.

Jim laughed and this time there was no doubt who it was directed at. "Yes, that was obvious as even I realized you mangled every prayer you uttered during your ordeal."

"Hey, in my defense, I was under just a little bit of stress." Mark smiled.

Tilting his head in acknowledgment, the smile faded from Jim's face. "True. Sorry for joking about it."

"No, it's all good." Mark took a deep breath and discovered it was the truth. Joking about the horror eased some of the awkwardness.

"I wonder if you could do it again?"

"Do what?"

"What if you reached out again? Would it only be to me, or could you do it to others?"

Mark shrugged. "I could try, but how would I know for sure? If I told someone beforehand, like Lily or someone, they might 'hear' me because they expect to. If I don't tell someone, they might just think it was some bizarre hallucination."

"What if you sent out a message and Kern received it?"

"First of all, that would be beyond creepy, but secondly, how would I direct it? How did I send it to you?" Mark closed his eyes. The last thing he wanted to do was revisit that scene, but how could he know how he'd done it if he didn't look back and see if there was

277

something he'd done? "I remember the smell of the smoke, and the crackle of the fire. I was...beyond terror. I was going to die." He paused, all humor gone from his mind now.

"Never mind, Mark. Forget about it." The car jerked as Jim put it into drive. The sound of the blinker was loud in the silence.

"I kind of zoned out while it was happening. Just before the hammer and nails part. I thought of my family, friends, events in my life. Not like my life passing in front of my eyes, exactly. It was more like I just wanted my last thoughts to be something other than the fear. They were tying me down, I guess, but at some point, my mind went back to all those prayers I half-learned in Sunday school." Mark gave a wry chuckle. "Maybe if I'd have memorized them like I was supposed to, they'd have worked a little better for me."

He glanced at Jim to find the other man watching him, his face inscrutable. "Anyway, that was pretty much it. There was nothing special I did that I can recall."

Jim took a deep breath and turned to look out his side window before facing Mark again. "I felt it again, just now when you were talking. I saw a flash of something. Your Sunday school teacher—she had strawberry blond hair, right? A little on the plump side? And I also saw some little kid stuffing his mouth with cookies."

The confusion on Jim's face would have been comical in other circumstances.

A chill washed over Mark. "Yeah, she did have reddish hair. You saw it?" As he'd thought about Sunday school, he'd had a quick mental image of Mrs. Perry standing in the dim living room, her own son polishing off the cookies that were supposed to be for all of them. "Maybe you're the one with the magic?'

"No, I don't think so, but we may never know for sure if you don't know how you do it."

"Honestly, if I have to feel that fear every time I send out some kind of mental image, I'd rather not have the power."

"I don't blame you, but if you could try and focus it just enough to draw Kern to a meeting, afterward, you can forget all of this and go back to your semi-normal life."

"I thought flyers were going to draw him to the meeting?"

"They might, but he might not risk it, despite the temptation, but if he can be enticed by a little mental summons, that would make it a sure thing."

Mark shook his head. "Okay, so assuming Kern is there, however he gets word of the revival, what are you going to do? My idea was just to get him there so he could be arrested. I didn't plan to hold an actual revival."

"It has to look real, or Kern will get spooked and may not show his face. I'm going to talk about your miracles a little bit and then, I hate to say it, but you're going to have to make an appearance. Nobody will come out to see me."

"But I thought that would look suspicious?"

Jim drummed his fingers on the steering wheel, his eyes distant. "We might have to make it look like we'd 'captured' you—like Kern did."

Mark turned and leaned back against the car door, holding his hand up. "No way."

"It's the only way I can think of to draw out Kern and his followers. In fact, we can approach Kern's group ahead of time, tell them personally about the revival. It'll be a secret meeting, but we'll make sure to invite his followers, possibly make a pact to join his guild."

"You want to hold a revival with me as the unwilling guest, and invite Kern's group to attend?"

"Yes, and mixed in with the worshipers will be police and FBI."

Jim stopped the car in front of a derelict building, and Mark leaned forward to see past him. So this was it. It certainly wasn't impressive. The crumbling cement steps led up to a building that looked like it should have been demolished about the time of the Vietnam War. The yard was nothing but a narrow strip of mud split by a cracked sidewalk. At least three of the windows were boarded over with plywood, and the brick had graffiti decorating the lower third of the building.

Mark looked around. "I'm going to get some shots. Keep an eye out for me." He slipped his left arm out of the sling. He could manage without the support for a few minutes. He stepped out of the car and took a half dozen snapshots of the building and the neighborhood.

If nothing else, there could be something useful in the photos that might not jump out at them now. As he raised the camera to squeeze in a few more, a jolt of energy shot through his hands.

CHAPTER TWENTY-TWO

Adrian exited Union Station, shouldering his way through the throngs of commuters. He was tired and stiff from the long train ride, and the bus ride from El Paso to San Antonio had been even worse. His neck felt stiff and he rolled his head to ease the pain. If only the border police hadn't taken him aside to question him. He couldn't believe they'd searched his rental car. Good thing he'd made other provisions to send the goods north. Did he look like a drug mule? Hell no. Even in his disguise, it should have been apparent to the cops that he was above that kind of thing.

Now there would be a detailed record of him crossing the border, even if it was under an alias, he hated to leave a loose end dangling. He glared at a woman clutching a toddler's hand as they impeded his way on the sidewalk. He skirted around them, his irritation adding to his foul mood. It still angered him that he'd been forced to use his last established alias.

He'd already burned through three for this trip. Not only did it cost him money to create a new one to replace the used ones, but it took time to build a legitimate history for each one. Sure, Tom Peterson, his newest identity, had a paper history, but a good detective would be able to cut through it if he was looking. Adrian hated to use it to buy his bus and train tickets, it was a potential paper trail, but there was no way around it. At least he'd had the foresight to keep this complete identity package at Sonya's home in El Paso.

Despite the cold drizzle, the memory of Sonya's welcome embrace warmed him. She was the only woman who understood him. When he achieved the power due him, he would bring her to the new compound, when he established it.

As a cab drove by and splashed him with dirty water, he vowed it was going to be sooner rather than later and definitely not in Chicago. Sonya's pitiful begging to come with him to Chicago had almost swayed him, but he'd placated her by telling her of his need for a place to hideout, a bolt hole, if needed.

He'd contemplated buying a plane ticket, but security at airports was too tight. The chances were slim that anyone would recognize him with his blond hair, but he wasn't taking any chances.

Taking the 'L' was the last thing he wanted to do, but it was the last train he'd have to take for a while. As he settled onto the hard plastic seat, he froze. On the floor of the train was a bright yellow flyer with Mark Taylor's photo. He ignored the dirty look from the woman on the opposite seat as he lunged from his seat and snatched the paper off the floor.

* * *

Mark swished the developer over the prints, wondering if this time, the magic would return. It had been a week since he'd taken pictures of the cult's building. Those photos hadn't developed into anything special, but the energy had returned to the device. It had been a week since then and even without the future photos, Mark had been busy. Jim and Jessie had been busy doing their own parts, putting word on the street about the revival. With their connections, they could plant information.

Meanwhile, Mark arranged the use of a warehouse, folding chairs and a sound system. It was almost a good thing he didn't have any future photos to worry about. Tomorrow was the big day, and his stomach was tied up in knots. Even though his 'capture' would be faked, just the thought of having to re-enact something like that made him shiver. He forced the thought out of his head as he noted the images emerging on the prints.

Damn. Deja-vu.

Lily and Jessie looked up from where they were hunched over a floor plan of the warehouse as Mark approached with the still damp photos, and held up the prints, his feelings mixed as he announced, "I have pictures."

Jessie held a red pen poised over the paper. "You mean, you have *pictures?* Future ones?"

"Yep."

Lily beamed at him. "I told you. The camera was waiting for you to be healed before putting you back to work."

He gingerly rotated his shoulder. It was far from completely healed, but he didn't need the sling anymore, and that was a relief. "Maybe, except while I have pictures, it would have been nice to start out with something easy. Instead, it looks like a repeat of my kidnapping."

Jessie tossed the pen on to the desk and stepped over

to him, her hand out to see the photos. "Well, it's not like you weren't aware of the kidnapping, and it's not real, so it shouldn't be all that shocking."

"Yeah, well, even if the photo depicts a staged scene, it's still a little disconcerting to see a photo of myself lying in a puddle of blood."

Lily rubbed her hand up his arm, her expression concerned, before turning her attention to the pictures. She tilted her head to look at the images as Jessie flipped through them.

Mark crossed his arms as he watched them examine the shots. Jim's idea had been okay in theory, but now that he could see the outcome, it wasn't looking so promising.

Jessie held one up. "I'm not positive, but the tall guy in the background could be Kern."

He shook his head. "I suppose it's possible, but he's out of focus so it's impossible to tell."

Lily pointed to another shadowy figure. "Is that Medea?"

Mark shrugged, and instantly regretted it as the muscles, unused for so long, protested the sudden movement. "It's a woman with her build, but the hair color is wrong. That's all I can tell." He waved a hand at the stack of photos. "Truthfully, I barely looked at those pictures. The other one I mentioned sort of took priority in my mind."

Jessie moved that photo to the top of the pile. "I can see how it might." Her eyes met his, and he was sure the fear in hers mirrored his own.

Lily squeezed his arm and said, "Mark, I know it looks bad, but you can change this like you do your other photos—don't forget that."

He tore his gaze from Jessie and took a deep breath before focusing on Lily. "Yeah, I'm trying to keep that in mind. Guess I should let Jim know about this new development." He tried to smile at his bad pun, but if it looked as sickly as it felt, it wouldn't fool either of the women.

* * *

Jim exited the car, and slammed the door of the old beater. He tugged on the ragged Army surplus jacket, and ran a hand over his unshaven face. As soon as he'd begun contemplating the ruse, he'd forgone shaving, and in just a few days, he had a nice bristly shadow. The amount of gray whiskers mixed with the dark ones had been an unwelcome surprise, but he had to concede it lent him a scraggly look that he couldn't have acquired any other way. To finish the transformation to Reverend Jim, he'd obtained a hair piece of long, stringy gray hair. Undercover operations had plenty of people who'd been able to help him change his appearance completely.

With a slow look around the seedy neighborhood, Jim sauntered up to the front door of the house believed to be the headquarters of the Guild of the Rose.

The house had been under surveillance since it had been discovered, and word had come that Kern might be in the residence. Nobody had seen him enter, but someone matching his height and build had been seen silhouetted against a shade.

Jim knocked.

After about thirty seconds a woman's voice came through the intercom. "Who is it?"

Jim smiled. "Hi, ma'am. My name's Reverend Jim, and I'm here to talk to y'all about a meetin' I'm planning."

"You must have the wrong building. Nobody here is interested in a 'meetin'.'"

Rubbing a hand against his whiskers, Jim shook his head. "Well, see, that's not how we heard it. We heard that the Rose had a big interest in Mark Taylor. I just thought y'all might want to take a gander at him in a few nights. He's the guest of honor at a revival I'm planning. We was wonderin' if y'all might want to help out"

Muffled voices came over the intercom, and a minute later, a young woman opened the door. "Come in. We'd like to hear more."

"Yes, ma'am. I thought you would." He grinned and followed her down a flight of steps into a large dimly lit room that probably was a laundry room at one time. Chairs lined up six rows deep and about ten chairs per row. This confirmed the estimate that the Guild had expanded. A podium anchored one end of the room, but the woman led Jim to the far end.

"Have a seat, please. Someone will be with you in a moment.'

Jim obliged and relaxed against the back of the metal folding chair, his hands intertwined behind his head, and his ankles crossed. He expected the wait to be relatively long. They would be looking up his name on the Internet. That's what Jim would have done, and Kern seemed like a bright man too.

They'd get plenty of hits, at least. Reverend Jim was a flashy preacher. Of course, they wouldn't be able to tell that all the search engine hits had been planted by some of the FBIs best computer geeks. A few even had photos of

Jim preaching to groups. He smirked. Gotta love Photoshop. A couple of pictures of Jim against a green screen with different attire, and his team had created an evangelical empire.

After almost thirty minutes, a door behind the podium opened and a tall man entered. Jim recognized him from his photos, although he'd changed his hair to a darker color and had a touch of gray at the temple, presumably to lend distinction. Instinct pressed him to stand and be on guard, but he fought it, holding onto his relaxed pose for several long seconds after Kern had stopped a short distance beyond Jim's crossed feet. Damned if he was going to show any fear or concede any power to this man.

Kern's presence filled the room, making the six men who flanked him insignificant. His cold, dark eyes fixed on Jim. "You have succeeded in piquing our curiosity. A revival, you say? What do you plan to do at this meeting?"

Jim planted his feet on the floor and straightened in the chair. "Are you the one who runs this Guild?"

Kern smiled and clasped his hands loosely in front of him. "Who I am isn't important. I have been given the authority in this matter. "

Jim pretended to think the matter over as he stood and began pacing. "I don't know. I was kind of hoping to talk to the man in charge—the one who tested Taylor the first time. That was a stroke of pure genius."

The only reaction from Kern was a lift of his eyebrow.

"See, here's the thing. I don't know how y'all did it. How you were able to draw me to the ceremony that night?

Real confusion flashed across Kern's face before he

was able to mask it, but Jim pushed his advantage. "It was incredible! There I was, just mindin' my own business, sleeping, and next thing I know, I'm sucked into the warehouse like a spirit or something."

"Excuse me?"

Jim nodded, hoping his enthusiastic reaction wouldn't displace the hairpiece. "I was right there, man! All those prayers and the Hail Mary right at the end—it was inspiring, let me tell you."

Shock and disbelief warred on Kern's features, replaced an instant later with anger. He grabbed Jim by the front of his shirt. "Who have you been speaking to? If one of the members of the Guild has leaked anything, they'll have to be dealt with."

It was all Jim could to do not to shrug off Kern's hands and lay him out, but he stayed in his role. "I'm tellin' ya, I *saw* it with my own two eyes. I think Mark Taylor pulled me there with his prayers."

Eyes narrowed, Kern released him. "Prove it."

"Satanus, non sum dignus... sed tantum dic verbo." Jim plucked Kern's hands from his shirt. "Yer followers, they couldn't hear you whisper it over the fire, but I could. I was right there and I saw your doubt." Jim used his fingertips to push Kern away as he said in a low, mocking voice, "*Satan, I am not worthy, but only say the word.*"

Kern stepped back, his arms dropping to his sides in surprise.

Jim smirked. "Yep. I'm the only one who heard you voice your fears, and it just so happens I know just enough Latin to understand the phrase." He'd kept Kern's utterance a secret, not even telling Taylor, holding it back as an ace in the hole if he ever needed it.

He rubbed his hands together and paced in front of Kern. "So, at the little shindig I'm holding, I am planning on recounting the whole thing, but of course," he paused his pacing, and held a hand on his chest, "I can omit that last bit...if you co-operate."

With a stiff nod, Kern said, "I'll pass along my recommendation to our leader, but I can't promise anything."

"Here's the deal. I want lots of folks at the meeting so I need your help to spread the word. I plan to collect boatloads of money from the people who turn up. I've already printed up hundreds of flyers, t-shirts and even — get this — we have small crosses that we can sell for a fortune after Taylor blesses them." Jim grinned.

"Where does the Guild of the Rose come into this picture?"

"I want your people at the revival. They are experienced at this sort of thing. They are disciplined. My people, well, they get to shouting and feeling the spirit. They aren't much good for what I have in mind."

Kern regarded him with hooded eyes, having regained control of his emotions and giving nothing away. "And what do you have in mind?"

"I thought the crucifixion was outstanding. Just outsanding, and wish I could re-enact it, but I don't think we'd get away with it. So, what I want is to force Taylor to reveal his magic. There must be a way to persuade him. I'm not any good at that kind of thing. Hell, look at me? I can't carry it off like you could." Jim chuckled.

CHAPTER TWENTY-THREE

Adrian studied the flyer. Tomorrow night. It wasn't much time to plan something, but he couldn't let a golden opportunity like this pass. Taylor could identify him and despite the aliases, he didn't intend to spend the time in prison, or worse, hiding. With Taylor dead, there would be no witness. No one in his guild would dare point a finger at him, he was sure of that.

He sat on the edge of his desk and stared out the window, absently missing the inspiring view from his previous office. Why did things have to be so difficult? So messy. Why did it take so much effort to achieve what he deserved? Half way down the street was a shabby church that had seen better days. It reminded him of the one where his father used to preach. When he was a child, he'd watch his father give his sermon to his small congregation. Part of him had been awed how the church members had hung on every word his father said. Like his father was God. The other part of him would look around at the hundred or so people and wonder why they wasted their time with a loser like his dad.

Couldn't they see that his father had nothing? The house provided for the pastor and his family was one step up from a shack. Adrian once asked why they didn't get a nice house. Didn't he deserve it for running around town helping all the church members every time one of them had a problem? Why did they have to bring meals every time someone was sick, died or had a baby? Nobody brought meals to them when his mom had yet another child. Adrian never understood the answer his father had given him— that the reward wasn't money or a fine house. It was the satisfaction of helping someone.

As far as Adrian could tell, there was no satisfaction to be had in helping anyone. All helping ever achieved was the helper got burned. Adrian remembered the time his dad had made him shovel snow for old Mr. Timmons. It wasn't Adrian's fault if the guy had later slipped on the ice coating the sidewalk. Timmon's could have tossed salt on the pavement as easily as he after the shoveling was done.

His father saw it differently, and had grounded him for a month and made him help Timmons after the old man had come home from the hospital. His dad said it would teach Adrian compassion.

Adrian scowled at the photo of Taylor on the flyer. He was a sucker just like Adrian's father. A do-gooder who probably thought he would be rewarded. Ha! Only a fool believed that nonsense. In fact, wasn't it said that God helped those who helped themselves?

He clenched the flyer, wanting to crumple Taylor's face in his fist and watch him burn in the garbage can, but he took a deep breath and flattened the flyer on his desk. As much as he wanted to crush the man, he could wait one more day and then do it in person.

What would be the best way? Another crucifixion would have sent a powerful message, but there wasn't time for something so elaborate. Still, it should be memorable. An assassination might be fitting. It would be quick and clean. Adrian stood and paced the small room.

He wanted some time to talk to Taylor first though - to see the fear in the other man's eyes again. This time, he would discover Taylor's secret. Then he would kill the man.

Taylor cared about other people. That was his weakness. Adrian circled his desk and settled into the chair. How could he take advantage of this weakness? He closed his eyes in concentration. Medea might be the key.

He tilted the chair back, sinking into the fragrant leather.

Four men dragged Mark Taylor through a doorway. He looked frightened, but also angry, his hands were bound behind him. Three of the men physically pushed him to a podium on the makeshift stage. The fourth man stood in front of the microphone. His long greasy hair and scraggly beard were flecked with gray while his robe looked like it had once been white. Reverend Jim. He gripped Taylor's arm, his fingers digging into Taylor's flesh.

"Welcome to our gathering, gentle people. I'm Reverend Jim, and as I promised we have Mark Taylor here as our special guest." He yanked at the struggling prisoner. "He was feeling a little shy, so we had to persuade him to come." Reverend Jim smiled. "Don't worry though, we didn't have to use extreme measures, not like what happened to him last time."

Adrian shifted in the chair. A part of his mind was still lodged in the dream, while the other part realized he was sitting in his office. An uncomfortable feeling pulled at him as he tried to awaken. The pull was too strong and he sank back into the dream.

Reverend Jim spoke about his dream. How Taylor had called out to him. "One minute, I was sleeping in my recliner, the next, I was awake and listening to Mark's prayers. I don't know how he did it, but he drew me there with his mind."

Taylor shook his head, but any protests he might have uttered were lost in the swell of noise from the audience.

Reverend Jim grabbed the microphone. "Folks, quiet down. We're gonna hear from the man himself in just a few minutes, but let me tell ya about a special treat we have planned. We have a representative of the Guild of the Rose here with us tonight. He has promised to show us how he was able to entice Taylor to use his incredible powers to reach out to me. In fact, he reached out to Mr. Kern as well, didn't he?" Reverend Jim grinned at Adrian. "He contacted you through a dream too, didn't he?"

Adrian woke up with a start and almost fell out of his leather chair. He blinked as a ray of sunlight stabbed into the office. He rubbed his hand down his face. It had been just a dream, but so real. He recalled every bit of it, more like he'd been there and walked through a door from the revival to his office -one minute he was there, the next, here. Even as he thought of it, it began to dim. Something about the dream was important. Could it finally be that he'd been given power by Satan?

Although he'd always preached about how powerful he was, he knew his gift was in persuasion, not anything truly otherworldly. This had felt different. While he'd been in the dream, he had felt like he'd been directed by someone else. He yanked open his desk drawer and grabbed a yellow legal pad. He needed to write it before he forgot. Perhaps Satan had shown him the way to seize Mark Taylor's power. It was a better plan than he had, and he just knew it would work. It was as if Satan had planted the scene in his head, it was so vivid. What was even better was that it had worked.

* * *

Mark jolted awake and rolled over on to his side, wincing as phantom pain jabbed his chest, a holdover from the dream. He glanced down, half-expecting to find himself covered in blood. Relief coursed through him as the reality sank in that it really had been one of his dreams. He'd expected the dream after viewing the photos, but this one had felt different. It seemed filtered, as though he wasn't quite part of it, but merely watching from the sidelines. It didn't make sense.

The warmth of the sun bathed him in a warm circle of light, and Mark settled into the comforter, loathe to get out of bed until he made sense of the dream. Had it been one of his prophetic dreams? Kern had been so prominent in it, which wasn't surprising, but Mark had the sense of seeing the dream from two perspectives--his own and Kern's. It was crazy. Like he'd had parallel trains of thought going at the same time.

Jim had said Mark should try reaching out to Kern to get him to the revival, and maybe viewing the photos had been enough. Stretching, Mark wondered if it had worked. His head even ached, as though Kern had left a trace of his evilness behind.

Mark shuddered, hoping like hell that nothing like that could happen. He sat up and swung his legs over the side of the bed. He needed to call Jim. He glanced at the clock. Seven a.m. Well, maybe he'd shower first. The stale smell of fear still clung to him.

* * *

Clouds had taken control of the sky and cast the loft

in shadows. Mark drummed his fingers on the breakfast bar, glancing around at Jim, Jessie and Lily. His dream had matched the photos, but only to a degree. He had only sketchy details. When he'd first awakened, he'd had the sense of knowing what Kern had been thinking in the dream, but the longer he was awake, Kern's thoughts slipped away. It was like trying to hold onto a handful of slime. The harder he tried to hang onto the details, the more they squirted out of his mind.

"That's it? All you remember is that Kern is wearing a dark suit, has gray hair at his temples, and you didn't see him until just before you were shot?" Jim glared at Mark as though he'd done something wrong.

"I told you reaching out to Kern wouldn't work. All it did was give me a muddled dream." Mark spun off the stool and yanked open the fridge. After staring inside for a few seconds, not sure what he was looking for, he snatched a bottle of water, then kicked the door shut hard enough to make the fridge contents rattle. He shouldered past Jim, and plopped onto the sofa.

The other three carried on a hushed conversation, but he tried to block them out, focusing on the scenes in his dream. He couldn't help if he wasn't shown everything. He got what he got and there was no way to edit in scenes he missed.

Lily sounded like she was scolding Jim and Mark almost smiled. She was the only one who seemed to get away with it. One of the stools clanked, followed by footsteps on the hardwood. Jessie stepped in front of him, blocking his view of the television as she sat on the coffee table.

He tried to ignore what she held, but she pushed the

Kevlar vest into his lap. "You have to wear it, Mark. If you refuse, we'll call the whole thing off."

"But now that we know what he's going to try, we can stop him before it gets to the point where he...he shoots me." His mouth suddenly devoid of moisture, he took a gulp of water.

"Just put the damn thing on, Taylor. I don't understand why you're arguing about it."

Mark swiped his arm over his mouth and craned his head to see Jim. "I just think the vest will show. If it does, it could alter what happens. If he sees the vest, he might do something differently than what he did in the dream."

Jim paced the loft, passing behind the sofa. It was making Mark nervous.

The pacing stopped. "Okay, so it's not the vest you object to, just that he might see it?"

Mark nodded. Jessie moved over to the chair beside the sofa, and he knew they both thought he was being pig-headed, but he couldn't shake the feeling that Kern was still there, still inside his head and privy to his thoughts. He tried to keep his uneasiness under wraps and pretend like this was a routine save.

"Be straight with us. Jessica and I get the feeling you're hiding something."

Mark sighed and massaged his forehead. "I'm not hiding anything. You saw the photos the same as me and Lily. I told you guys the whole dream, but I can't explain how I feel. It's like there's this..." He circled his hand in front of his face, "this feeling like Kern is here. I keep smelling rotten eggs and burnt popcorn, and for some reason, I think of him when I smell it. It's crazy, I know."

Lily perched on the other end of the sofa, her nose

wrinkled in disgust. "I bet Kern's soul smells more like shit than—"

The remark was so unexpected, Mark burst into laughter, cutting off whatever Lily said next. Jessie chuckled too, but then turned thoughtful. "Mark, what if you wore a robe like 'Reverend Jim' here plans on doing?"

Mark smiled at the hint of sarcasm in her Reverend Jim reference. When Jim had first told them his plan to be the Reverend and guide the revival, he and Jessie had almost laughed it off. Jim was the least religious person Mark knew. In fact, if the guy practiced a religion, Mark wasn't even sure what it was.

Lily had spoken in Jim's defense, saying it was perfect. Jim would be on the stage, or altar, as she'd called it, and would be able to see the crowd. As an added bonus, his robes would hide his gun.

A robe? Mark couldn't see himself in a robe. It would feel silly, but it could work. He didn't think that what he wore, as long as it wasn't a visible vest, would make much difference to Kern. "Can we find another robe on such short notice?"

"No problem." Jim had his cell phone out and began arranging it before the words were out of Mark's mouth.

Jessie moved from the chair to sit beside him on the sofa, resting her hand on his knee. "Listen, I know this whole thing has you spooked, but we won't let anything happen to you."

"I guess I'm not doing as good a job as I thought of hiding my fear." He chuckled as he twisted and untwisted the cap of his water bottle.

"Jeez, Mark, you have a good reason to be spooked. I know if I dreamed my own death by the hands of that monster, I'd be a basket-case."

Mark shrugged. "I just want it over."

"By tomorrow, it will be." Jim put his phone in his pocket, and grinned. "It's all arranged. Don't worry, Mark. I got my best guys on this. Kern is on a lot of wanted lists, and now we finally know when and where he'll be, thanks to you."

* * *

Mark paced the small office of the warehouse. He'd been sequestered since shortly after their meeting in his loft. Jim had wanted to beat the crowd so he wouldn't have to walk a gauntlet to enter the building. The office led out to the back of the altar, so he'd never have to go through the crowd. Mingling with the crowd was his second biggest fear. Kern, at least, was a known danger, but the crowd, even if they meant well, terrified him almost as much as Kern and his gun.

He'd been wired with a small ear piece. He wouldn't need a microphone hidden on him. With his cell, and a plain-clothed cop right outside the door, he was safe enough for now. Now, it was a matter of waiting. He padded from wall to wall, absently rubbing his shoulder. He'd worn the sling for most of the day, but had chosen to remove it for the revival. The tight quarters reminded him of his cell, and the fact that he couldn't leave, added to the impression of being a captive. Rationally, he knew he wasn't, but the feeling wasn't rational.

Sounds filtered to him from within the warehouse. Jim expected several hundred people to turn out, and had chairs set up for that many. His estimates came from what they could see of the crowd in the photos and from what Mark recalled from the dream, but they had mere snapshots of the event.

He paused his pacing long enough to cock his head and listen. It sounded like a lot more than a few hundred people out there. His stomach did a backflip. Why had he agreed to this? Mark pulled out the notes from his speech, but after staring at them, crumpled them and tossed them into a wastebasket. He was a terrible speechwriter. He'd be better off winging it.

There was a short, hard knock on the door, and Jim entered. "We have standing room only. In fact, we had to turn some folks away at the door, and they weren't too happy about it."

"How many is 'standing room only'?"

Jim shrugged. "Our permit allows for only a thousand people, so once the count hit that, we had turn folks away from getting inside, but a bunch decided that just being near the building would be better than nothing. They're hoping to hear your words of wisdom through the open doors."

Mark groaned. "I feel like such a fraud. I don't get why you can't just arrest him as soon as he shows up."

"You're not a fraud. Besides, remember the goal. Convicting the bastard. You can claim he was the one, but there's no physical evidence of Kern being present, and he'll get a dozen people from his group to put him somewhere else the evening you were abducted. Even if we arrest him, it'll get tossed out for lack of evidence. We need some kind of admission. As soon as Kern takes the bait and comes on stage. I'm hoping he'll slip about what happened before."

"Should I say anything about it? Try to incite him?" As much as he hated the idea of seeing the man again, getting a chance to confront Kern might be just what he needed to do.

Jim helped himself to a bottle of juice from a table full of refreshments Lily had sent over. She'd wanted to participate, but Jim didn't want any non-law enforcement, and with her red hair, she would be easy to recognize as Mark's business partner. She hadn't been thrilled with being regulated to providing the snacks.

Jim tilted the juice, draining the small bottle, then tossed in the trash. "It depends how you do it. I think if you outright accuse him, he's going to clam up. It might be better to play it quiet until we hear what he has to say." He glanced at his watch. "Okay, I guess it's time for us to hit the stage." He pulled a length of rope out from beneath his robe. "Sorry about this, but we have to make it look real."

"Yeah, I know." A wave of shivering overtook him. He tried to still it, but it was beyond his control.

Jim must have seen him shudder because he circled in front of him. "Mark, look at me."

Mark raised his gaze.

"We're not going to let anything bad happen to you. This is not going to be like before, understand? Do you trust me?"

Swallowing hard, Mark tried to quell the waves of shivering. Did he trust Jim? A year ago, he'd have laughed at the notion. Tonight, he nodded and put his hands behind his back. "Do what you have to do."

Jim tied the rope around Mark's wrists, and Mark took a deep breath.

"I didn't tie it too tight, did I? How about your

shoulder?"

The rope pinched, but Mark could live with it. "It's fine." The discomfort was the least of his worries.

As they entered the short hallway behind the stage, three of Jim's men flanked him. Mark wondered if they'd fool anyone. He thought they looked like FBI, but maybe it was just because he knew their real identities. Their clothing was thrift store bargain basket. One had a shaved head, the other two had long hair.

Bright lights bathed the stage and Mark didn't have to fake it too much as he instinctively balked as his guards pulled him in front of the crowd.

* * *

Kern fought the urge to push to the front of the crowd. The old guy had done it. He had Taylor.

"Welcome to our gathering, gentle people. I'm Reverend Jim, and as I promised we have Mark Taylor here as our special guest." He yanked at the struggling prisoner. "He was feeling a little shy, so we had to persuade him to come." Reverend Jim smiled. "Don't worry though, we didn't have to use extreme measures, not like what happened to him last time."

Kern scowled at the crowd around him, but no one seemed to notice. Their eyes were fixed on Taylor.

Reverend Jim pulled out a knife and Taylor's eyes grew huge, but all the reverend did was cut the binds. "There you go, Mark. I hope you don't have any hard feelings towards me. I just knew once you were here, you'd be eager to speak to my flock. Or your flock. They are all ready to do your bidding."

301

The crowd cheered their agreement. Taylor rubbed his wrists and glared at Reverend Jim as he was pushed closer to the podium.

"Come on, Mark. Share your wisdom with us. We are eager to learn from you." The reverend turned to the crowd, making motions for them to shout their agreement. They complied, and Adrian tried to shut out the screech from the woman on his right. The dream, so vivid upon waking, had faded throughout the day and he tried to hang onto bits and pieces. He'd been so sure that he'd seen the future in the dream, but now it was out of focus.

With a final dark look aimed at the reverend, Taylor tilted the microphone and tapped it, testing the sound. "I, uh, I don't know why I was brought here, and I doubt I have any wise words, but I'll tell you all this. I'm not some kind of savior, but then, I don't think any of you *need* a savior. Your savior is the person you see when you look in the mirror every morning. Every day is a new start. A day when you can choose to help someone or do nothing. What kind of choice will you make? Ask yourself that as you comb your hair or put on your make-up."

Taylor orated from a makeshift stage, and a hush settled over the crowd. The guy was so goddamn believable. Adrian bit back a scowl at the 'amens' shouted when Taylor finished speaking. Reverend Jim led the chorus of 'amens, a grin stretched from ear to ear.

Adrian eyed the old man, disgusted at his unkempt appearance. Why did fanaticism go hand-in-hand with bad personal hygiene? Adrian smoothed his hand down the front of his suit. For today's event, he had carefully chosen his best suit. It went well with the glasses and dark hair with just a touch of gray at the temples. He looked like a lawyer, banker or commodities trader - benign, but distinguished.

Adrian moved from his place at the back of the warehouse. He picked Medea out of the crowd by her jet black dye job. The goth makeup completed her transformation. She glanced over her shoulder at him. Kern nodded. Nobody noticed him. Things were progressing exactly as they had planned, despite the fading dream. He'd done it. He'd attained the power to see the future. Taylor wasn't the only one now. Adrian felt a wave of anticipation. In just a few minutes, he, Adrian Kern, would be the sole person alive with the power to dream of the future.

Reverend Jim nodded to Kern, their prearranged signal for Adrian to take over the show. Taylor stood awkwardly on the stage as Reverend Jim moved forward and gave him a hug. Adrian raised an eyebrow at the slight stiffening of Taylor's posture. The man was uncomfortable with the hug, but the crowd loved it. They surged towards the stage, as if they wanted to hug Taylor too. This was too perfect. As though watching a pre-recorded movie, Adrian glanced over at Medea, knowing what he would see before he'd even picked her out of the mob.

Medea moved with the crowd. Adrian saw the gun in her hand. She was going to go through with it. He'd been worried she would flake out, but now that everything was preceding exactly as he'd seen it, he merely smiled.

* * *

Mark blinked against the bright lights. The faces in

the audience appeared blurry, and he couldn't pick anyone out. His dream was hazy in his mind, and he felt a rush of panic. What would happen next? The photos of him on the floor only showed the end result, not exactly when it would occur. The dreams were supposed to fill in the blanks, only his dream had been watered down and faded with every passing second.

Within three feet of the stage, a woman lifted a pistol to her head and shouted, "Please, Mark, I need you to forgive me. After what I did to you, I don't deserve to live!"

He knew that voice and he squinted into the lights, finally picking her out of the crowd. She'd dyed her hair, but he recognized her. "Judy? Put the gun down. I don't have any powers to grant forgiveness. Besides, I have a feeling you were coerced. Please put the gun down, Judy." Mark glanced around, looking for Jim. What was he supposed to do now? If this had been in the dream, he had no recollection of it.

Medea shook her head. "I can't. I did an awful thing and I can't live with myself unless you forgive me."

Jim sidled closer to Mark. "Do as Mark says, and put the gun down, miss."

The agents who'd escorted Mark onstage closed ranks around him. The crowd had scattered, leaving empty chairs around Judy. Was that Jessie and Dan easing towards her?

Judy's gaze wavered, but Mark had the impression it was in response to something else, not him or the officers approaching from behind. The gun remained planted firmly against her temple. Where was Kern? Was he here? Jim must have had the same thought because he dipped his head and Mark caught Kern's name mentioned as Jim fired off orders into his hidden microphone.

Mark tried to recall if this had been part of his dream. There had been a photo with Judy in it. Lily had tentatively ID'd her, but with the dyed hair and not much left of her head, it had been hard to know for sure. Was he supposed to stop Judy from committing suicide?

He tried to push through the agents, but they didn't allow him through. Shoulder to shoulder, they pointed their guns at Medea, which made no sense to Mark. She already held a gun against her head. He was taller than they were, so he settled for looking between them, and re-establishing eye contact with Judy. Jim could deal with Kern if he was around.

"Judy, listen to me." Her eyes pulled from whatever she'd been focusing on and settled on Mark.

"That's it. You don't need to do this. Set the gun down. Just put it right there on the stage. Whatever role you played in my kidnapping, we can talk about later. I'm fine now. It's not too late for you to come forward and talk to the police. You have to understand—it's not up to me to forgive anyone. You go to the police and if you do, I bet you can work a deal. I'll do whatever I can to help, okay?"

Judy bit her lip and tears welled in her eyes. "Why?"

"Why what?" Mark pushed the agents from behind, urging them a little closer to Medea, but they held their ground and he couldn't blame them for not wanting to get too close to the gun.

"Why would you help me, after what I did?"

Mark wished he had time to think of a good answer, but he didn't. "I have no idea, Judy. I just know that none of this is worth dying for. Kern isn't worth dying for. We have to move on—both of us. Kern used us. Do you want to let him win this time too? Do you want the press to forever paint you as the girl who was Kern's puppet?" He sensed movement in his peripheral vision, but didn't tear his attention away from Judy.

Judy's eyes narrowed. "I'm nobody's puppet."

"That's right, you're not. That's why you have to cut the strings. Do what *you* want to do. What *you* feel is right."

She nodded and slowly eased the gun away from her head.

Mark took a deep breath, but before he could let it out in relief, Jim shouted, "Behind you!" He saw Jim rushing the stage, his gun in hand, but he bypassed Judy without a glance and Mark whirled.

There was no time to duck, and barely time to register Kern standing with a gun pointed before something slammed into Mark, as he staggered back, two more impacts sent him flying onto his back.

Pain ignited in his chest, and he couldn't breathe. Dimly, he heard another shot, but the edges of his vision closed in.

His awareness returned by degrees, but he didn't know if he'd been out seconds, minutes or even hours. He blinked, wanting to see what was happening, but the agony in his chest kept him motionless. At least he wasn't dead, and his breathing returned even if every inhalation felt like someone was stabbing him.

He turned his head. One of the agents lay several feet away, his face contorted as he clutched his right thigh. Blood oozed between his fingers. The other agent was nowhere to be seen. Where had Jim gone? Shouts, the clang of the chairs, and feet running across the stage penetrated his brain. He curled onto his side with a groan, but bit back the sound as he took in the scene before him.

Kern stood with his back to Mark, holding Jim in a headlock with a gun digging into his temple. Beyond Kern, Jessie and Dan stood at the edge of the stage, their guns aimed at Kern, but neither would be able to take the shot without the risk of hitting Jim.

"Reverend Jim is a fraud and a murderer! I saw him pull the trigger. He shot Mark Taylor. Then that young sweet girl ended her own life when hope of forgiveness died with Taylor."

Mark stifled a moan of pain as he rose to a sitting position, fighting the darkness that encroached on his vision as he sat and waited for his sight to clear. The lack of blood on his robe, and the fact that the pain was easing reassured him that the vest had done its job even if it did feel like he'd been kicked by a mule. As he put his hand down to move to a standing position, he felt something cold and metallic. The agent's gun. He picked it up, not quite sure what to do with it. Not only had he never fired one, he'd never had reason to point a gun at another human being.

Standing, he blinked, getting his bearings before he straightened as much as his aching ribs allowed. If he could distract Kern, Jessie or Dan might be able to take him out. He aimed the weapon at Kern's back. It crossed his mind to shoot the man, but he didn't trust his aim, and didn't know if the bullet would pass through Kern into Jim.

"Kern." He'd wanted to sound strong and forceful, but

he hadn't been able to take a deep enough breath to add volume so Kern didn't hear him above the sound of his own shouting. His second effort was louder, and Kern pivoted sideways, yanking Jim along with him. A trail of blood welled from a groove along Jim's head. It explained the glassy look in Jim's eyes and how he'd been captured.

"Well look here. It's a bon-a-fide miracle!" Kern eyed Mark, his mouth twisting into a sneer. "You're not dead."

Jessie took a tiny step to her left, indicating to Mark with a subtle gesture that she wanted him to keep talking. Mark shook his head at Kern. "Nope. As you can see, I'm very much alive, so you can release Reverend Jim. He didn't murder me."

"You think I can just let him go and everything will be fine?"

Before Mark could answer, Kern tightened his grip, and Jim's eyes went wide as he clutched at the arm across his throat, his fingers digging into Kern's flesh.

"What do you want, Kern?"

"I want you. More specifically, I want your power. Reveal it to me, and I'll let this old man go."

A couple of dozen audience members still huddled on the floor where they must have dropped when the shooting began. Several lifted their heads, curiosity replacing the fear in their eyes.

"I don't have any power. Don't you think I'd have given it to you the last time we met if I'd had anything to give?"

"At first, I didn't believe you had any powers. I was just using the media hype to inspire my followers."

Mark felt bile rise, and swallowed convulsively. His hands shook, his aim wavering. The whole ordeal had been just a ploy for Kern to look good in front of his pathetic group of followers?

Kern shrugged and continued, "But now, I'm a believer. How else do I explain the dream I had last night? I saw all of this, and I know how it ends. I heard your speech and everything. The only thing different, is you were wearing a blue shirt, instead of that robe. I haven't figured out why that's different, but the rest of it—it's exactly the same."

A chill swept Mark. So Kern had been present in the dream. He wished he could somehow cleanse his mind and wash out any lingering trace of of the evil man.

Jessie was almost behind Kern.

He had to keep him distracted just a moment longer. "You're delusional."

Kern hiked Jim higher as he moved a step closer to Mark. His face twisted in rage. "I'm delusional?" He chuckled. "I'm not delusional, Taylor. What I am is your fiercest believer. Who do you think will spread the word on you when you're dead?"

Mark ignored the fact that Kern seemed to think he was bestowing a great honor upon him. "I'm nothing to believe in, Kern. Save that for God."

Jim appeared to have regained his awareness of what was happening as his right hand inched behind him. Mark hoped it was for another gun, but he tried not to watch, not wanting to signal Kern with his eyes.

"Speaking of God. Are you ready to meet Him?" Kern pulled the gun from Jim's head and pointed it at Mark.

At the same time, Jim spun and ducked, escaping Kern's grip.

Almost simultaneously, four shots sounded. Mark

flinched and closed his eyes, waiting for an impact that never came. He risked a look when something hit the stage with a loud thud.

Kern lay motionless on the stage, his eyes open and unseeing. Mark took a step back and glanced at the gun he held. Had he shot Kern? He bent, releasing the weapon to clatter to the floor. Had he killed a man?

Jim knelt, his weapon still pointing at Kern, but his other hand rubbed his throat. Jessie and Dan rushed the stage.

Dan said something into his shoulder mic, then went to Jim. "Lie down and let me get a look at you."

Jim shrugged him off. "I'm fine." He moved to a sitting position though, despite his protests.

Jessie checked Kern for a pulse, then turned to Mark. "How about you?"

Mark had a hard time tearing his gaze from Kern's body, sickened that it had come to this. "I don't know." He rubbed his chest, even though it did no good through the thick Kevlar. "I'm okay, I guess. I think I've used up my lifetime allotment of miracles though." He gave a strangled laugh.

She nodded and came to him, her arms opening. He pulled her into a hug. Jessie tilted her head, her eyes locked on his as she said, "When the shots came and you went down, I thought you were dead." Her voice shook.

"Me too." Mark gave her a gentle squeeze, then grunted when she returned the favor with a little too much feeling.

She stepped away. "Sorry." With a deep breath, she seemed to regain her composure, her bearing once more that of a detective. "Let's see the damage."

Mark tugged the robe over his head with a grimace. Three slugs remained embedded in the vest, flattened into a mushroom shape. He willed his hand to stop shaking.

"We'll need the vest for evidence."

"Here, you can have it." He ripped open the Velcro straps and shrugged out it.

"Just put it on top of the robe. Then sit down until the paramedics check you over."

"I'm fine." He lifted his t-shirt, examining the ugly bruises, two on the left side of his chest, and one on the lower right. "I think I was just stunned from the impact."

"It's standard protocol, Mark. You could be bleeding internally and not know it. Besides, you were out for several minutes."

The implication slammed into him. "So for several minutes, you thought I was *dead*?"

She shrugged, but avoided making eye contact. It hit him full force why she'd left him. The pain in his chest had nothing to do with the shots he'd taken. He nodded. "I understand."

He knew Jessie caught the meaning behind his words because her eyes flew to his and her lip trembled before she bit it and returned the nod.

Police and paramedics swarmed into the warehouse, some approaching them on the stage, but a few tending to people on the floor.

"What happened while I was out? I kind of remember another shot. What did he," Mark inclined his head towards Kern's body, "mean about some innocent taking her own life?"

Jessie darted a look at a group gathered around someone on the floor of the warehouse, just in front of the stage. "It's Medea, although we don't have a positive ID yet."

Like another mule had tattooed him, Mark staggered. "She killed herself?"

"I don't think so. I think Kern shot her on purpose after he shot you. It was pretty chaotic though, so I can't say for certain. We'll have to watch the tapes to know for certain."

He pushed past her to the edge of the stage. Judy Medea lay crumpled, a paramedic in the act of covering her with a yellow blanket, but he caught a glimpse of her before it settled over her face. His stomach flipped, and it was all he could do to hold onto its contents.

Mark backed away, pointing towards Medea. "Two people are dead, Jessie. And for what? I don't understand." The shaking that had been present since he'd come to, intensified. "It's so damn pointless!"

"You're in shock, Mark. You need to sit."

"I don't want to *sit*. I want to get the hell out of here."

She reached for his arm, but he shrugged her off, and made for the back of the stage. He ignored her calls to come back and heard Jim tell her to let him go. Back in the office, he ran both hands through his hair, bent at the waist as he tried to choke back the anger and sorrow. It didn't help. The pain intensified and he sagged to sit on the edge of the old desk. He was supposed to have stopped this. It was why he had the dreams, but it hadn't worked. Their attempt to manipulate the dream had failed.

Voices approached the office. Why wouldn't anyone just leave him alone? He straightened and grabbed his jacket before pushing out the door and into the alley.

Instead of the solitude he sought, he found police cars, flashing lights and dozens of people. He turned to the front of the building, intending to find a cab or walk to the 'L', steeling himself to pass through the throngs of people and police.

"Mark Taylor!"

As soon as the crowd spotted him, he didn't have a chance to escape unnoticed. The crowd closed in. Police reacted quickly, corralling the people behind a cordon of yellow tape. News vans already parked along the street, their blinding lights focused on the warehouse. It was a madhouse.

"Mr. Taylor, could I speak with you for a minute?"

The voice was familiar and Mark turned, seeking it out. A woman waved him over. He recognized her from somewhere, and he started towards her. When he was close enough, she stuck out her hand. "Hello Mark. I'm Denise Jeffries. We spoke on the phone a few weeks ago."

Mark stopped dead. The reporter. His throat tightened. So many images flashed through his mind. His crucifixion, the crowds pawing at him and Medea lying dead in the warehouse, her brains splashed across the floor.

"You!" Ignoring her hand, he pointed at her. "*You* did this! You wanted your story, and didn't give a damn who got hurt. Well, now you have an even bigger story. Congratulations."

He didn't wait for her to respond, but turned and shoved his hands in his pockets as he stalked past the crowds, glowering at anyone who came near.

A block later, the crowds were gone and the street all but deserted. He headed for the closest 'L' and climbed the steps to the platform. It was empty and he wasn't sure when the next train would come, but it didn't matter. Eventually, one would arrive.

Mark eased down to sit on the bench, holding his ribs. It was as quiet as night time in Chicago ever got. Distantly, sirens wailed, a door slammed and the ever present hum of traffic filled the air. A shudder coursed through him. With nobody around to see, he allowed the sob, stifled for so long, to escape.

* * * * * *

The End

Find <u>DEEDS of MERCY: Book Three in the Mark Tayor Series</u> on Amazon: available in print, ebook and audiobook formats.

U.S: <u>http://amzn.to/zgKfKx</u>

U.K.: <u>http://amzn.to/yZ6Hbo</u>

Acknowledgements

I wouldn't have been able to finish this book without the help of so many people. First and foremost, I would like to thank Jessica Tate. For about four years now, we've been pushing each other to write via our online writing sessions. I'm not sure what I would do without that push.

Without my amazing beta readers, this book would have been a complete mess. What I found interesting was that all of them had different strengths. One was great at noticing missing words--and you'd be surprised how often that happens as my mind thinks faster than my hands can type—another caught various plot point issues. Several zeroed in on my many typos, and one was a comma guru. So, in no special order, I'd like to thank, Vicki Boehnlein, Al Kunz,, Lala Price and Allie Brumley and Dianna Morris.

And last, but not least, a huge thank you to my 'forumily'. You all know who you are. I love that there is a place I can go to get support, feedback, vent, or just get a much needed laugh. You are all awesome!

About the Author

I know a lot of these are written in third person, but that just feels too unnatural for me so I'm going to be a rebel and write this in first person. I'm M.P. McDonald, and I live in a small town in Wisconsin with my family, just a stone's throw from a beautiful lake, and literally spitting distance to a river on the other side. We love the peace and quiet and being able to go down to the beach on a hot summer day for a quick swim. Chicago and Milwaukee are just an hour's drive away in either direction, so we are never far from the excitement of a big city.

As you can tell from my books' settings, I love Chicago. One of my sons used to do commercials and modeling in the 90s, so we spent many an afternoon driving to auditions and look-sees in Chicago. Mark Taylor's studio/loft is based in part on the many cool photography studios we encountered during his years in 'showbiz'. One thing I didn't like was trying to park there, so when possible, we took the train from the northern suburbs, so it was fun incorporating that experience into Deeds of Mercy.

When I'm not writing, I work as a respiratory therapist at a small hospital that is part of a large hospital system in eastern Wisconsin. I enjoy my work and since it's completely different from writing, it keeps things interesting.

I love to hear from readers. No, I mean it. I *love* to hear from readers, even if it's not all good. Without feedback from readers, I might never have undertaken these books. I hadn't planned on writing a series for Mark

Taylor, but readers kept asking, so I was happy to deliver. I have an unrelated book I've put on the back-burner twice now in order to complete the last two books in this series. I'm hoping to finish that one soon

After that, I have ideas for a book that takes place after Deeds of Mercy. I love the dynamic between Mark and Jim and so I know the next book will involve a lot of interaction between the two men. Does that sound like a plan? Let me know!

CONTACT ME

Here are some ways you can reach me, and since I am an internet junkie, I'll probably write back very quickly.

Email: mmcdonald64@gmail.com

Facebook http://on.fb.me/15vkkMV

Twitter: @MarkTaylorBooks

Pinterest: http://pinterist.com/mpmcdonald

Website: www.mpmcdonald.com

Made in United States
North Haven, CT
19 November 2023